Battered

A Whipped and Sipped Mystery

G. P. Gottlieb

*To Rachel — with lots of love
(and a little murder!)*
G. P. Gottlieb

D. X. VAROS

Acknowledgements

Thank you all:

Writing coach SL Wisenberg and writing planners Natania Rosenfeld and Thalia Bruehl; friends and family who had faith in me, read early drafts, and encouraged me to keep at it: Annie Gottlieb, Jean Gottlieb, Faye Jacobs, Melissa Malmed, Starry Schor, Sydney Reiner, Debra Rosenberg, Tami Warshawsky, Arna Yastrow, and Ray Zwerin; my supportive children: Danielle, Rebecca and Gabriel and parents, Helen and Alex Pinsky. Most of all thanks to my loving husband David, who, while I was immersed in this murder mystery, completed his PhD at the University of Chicago.

And many thanks to everyone who tested the recipes included in the book: Betsy Epel, Harry Gottlieb, Martha Gottlieb, Pam Grad, Joy Horwich, Maggie Kast, Linda Kupfer, Suzie Lampert, Gila Lesky, Carol Neel, Emily Pinsky, Efrat Rebish, Sheri Ross, Sally Sachar, Aviva Samet, Helen Singer, and Sandi Wisenberg.

<u>Cast of Characters and ages</u>:

Alene Baron-38 – Owner of Whipped and Sipped
Alene's children: Sierra-age 12, Quinn-age 10, Noah-age 8
Alene's ex-husband: Neal Dunn-43
Alene's father: Cal Baron-65
Alene's ex-mother-in-law: Mitzi Dunn-67
Alene's sister: Lydia Baron-34 (married to Theo King-36)
Alene's best friend/college roommate: Ruthie Blum Rosin-38
     (m Benjie Rosin-40) three children
Alene's next door neighbor: Brianne Flynn-52 (husband
     Dennis died in 2008) two children
Alene's cleaning lady/helper for her dad: Blanca-49
Alene, Brianne and Gary's trainer: Michael Jay-32
Alene's employees at the Whipped and Sipped Café: *Ruthie*
     Rosin, Edith Vanza, Olly Burns, Kacey Vanza,
     Jocelyn DeVale, Rashid Freeman, Manny Reyes,
     LaTonya James, Estella Cabrillo, Sally Sims, Zuleyka
     Martinez

Alene's across the hall neighbor: Gary Vanza-64
Gary's sister: Edith Vanza-60 (also an employee at the café)
Gary's eldest son with 1st wife: Bill Vanza-43
Bill's girlfriend: Tinley Rico-36
Gary's second son with 1st wife: Sandy Vanza-40
Gary's daughter with 2nd wife: Kacey Vanza-22
Gary's 2nd wife: Isobel-56
Gary's 3rd wife: Joan Stone-54
Gary's step-son, Joan's son: Jack Stone-34
Gary and Joan's former boss: Henry Willis 1940-2000

Detective: Officer Frank Shaw-42

Chapter 1

An hour before closing, Alene Baron started chopping carrots for the next day's soup. It was actually Kacey Vanza's job, but Alene didn't trust her with a knife, yet. Maybe, thought Alene, if the entire Whipped and Sipped staff watched out for her, Kacey would stay clean.

At the large counter to Alene's left, Kacey was helping the pastry chef to prepare batches of sweet dough to be refrigerated overnight. Alene was still thrilled to be working side-by-side with her best friend from college, Ruthie, at the very place they'd fantasized about during their study breaks. Whipped and Sipped was a vegetarian café that served excellent food and coffee, and where even the walls were painted in the tasty-sounding colors of Crimson Claret and Crème Brûlée.

Alene was proud that Whipped and Sipped had become a beloved institution in Chicago's Lakeview neighborhood. The big crimson wall was the backdrop for monthly exhibitions of local art. Above the windows on the wall facing the street, large, sparkling geodes were glued to hand-built shelves. When Alene had been the manager, even before she had bought the café from Kacey's father, Gary

1

Vanza, she'd reorganized the tables to create a cozy, home-like setting. A sliding, barn-style door separated Whipped and Sipped from Tipped, the bar next door.

A monthly book group met at the café, to talk over hot drinks and Ruthie's decadent but healthful desserts. The Saturday children's story hour, which Alene had started back when her children were little, was still going strong. She also led a Tuesday morning knitting group – they were currently working on blankets to donate to refugee families, settling in Chicago. Alene had established a connection to a nearby women's shelter, and the manager came by, every other day, to pick up trays of unsold pastries.

When Kacey's father, Gary, had owned the place, he could sit for hours drinking coffee, hosting meetings, and entertaining friends at Whipped and Sipped. However, not long after Alene's divorce settlement, Gary had announced that he was ready to retire. He knew that Alene had always dreamed of owning a café and he told her that he could no longer stand the constant discussions over which fair-trade coffee to buy or which sugar alternatives to offer. He set a price below what the place was worth – in return, he asked that she continue to employ his daughter Kacey and his sister Edith.

Alene would have kept Kacey on even if Gary hadn't asked – Edith, was another story, she was a cranky and depressed woman. However, Alene still thought Whipped and Sipped was practically perfect. It was only ten minutes' walk from the high-rise where she lived with her three children and her father. In addition to repainting and reorganizing the furniture after taking over from Gary, Alene had sewn and installed old fashioned curtains for long summer afternoons when the sun over-flooded the café. She woke up every morning looking forward to going to work.

Now, Alene swept the chopped carrots into a bowl and began on the celery. "I'm going to the grocery store, instead of straight home, after we close," she told Kacey, who was kneading the last section of dough with her bone thin, colorfully tattooed arms. If only Kacey hadn't gotten derailed, she would have just graduated from college. Alene imagined Kacey living in an apartment; maybe saving for a fabulous trip with a serious boyfriend. Instead, she was fighting her addictions and living at home with Gary and his wife.

Alene and Kacey had walked home from work together, every day, since Kacey had recovered from a near-fatal overdose three months before. "Do you want to stop at the grocery store today?" Alene asked. "Otherwise you'll be on your own."

"No problem," Kacey said, sweeping a few stray dark-blonde waves from her face. She adjusted her glasses, turned to the sink to rewash her hands, and went back to kneading. "I'm pretty sure I can manage the ten-minute walk home without getting into trouble."

It was healthy for Kacey to push back with a little sarcasm, Alene thought, giving her a thumbs-up. Then she noticed the tray of leftovers on the counter. "Your new pastries are going to be a huge winner, Nine," she told Ruthie, using her college nickname. "There are only six sweet potato muffins left."

"That, my dear Six," Ruthie responded, with Alene's college nickname, "is because no one wanted the ugly ones."

Just then, Olly Burns pushed through the swing-door into the kitchen carrying dirty dishes and bad news. "Jack Stone's out front," he said in his sing-song voice. "Apparently he wants to work here. With us."

Alene rested her knife on the counter and cringed. She'd once smacked Jack Stone when he'd drunkenly tried to feel her up, about a decade before. He might have been somewhat attractive if he matured and cleaned up, but as far as Alene knew, he'd never been able to overcome his

3

drinking problem. "Gary Vanza asked me to hire Jack, as a favor, to last week," Alene said, "but Jack's probably never held a job longer than a few months."

She paused with her knife in the air, imagining Jack Stone working in her café with his long, greasy hair and torn jeans. Alene glanced briefly at Kacey and said, "I'm a little worried about trying to teach an old dog new tricks."

With a straight face, Kacey said, "It might work if we held a cookie above his head."

Ruthie said, "Really, Six, no one's ever too old to learn good habits." Sometimes Ruthie's faith in people made Alene want to tweak her beautifully braided hair, but Ruthie's optimism had buoyed Alene many times over the years.

She replied, "If he hasn't pulled his life together yet, I doubt he can muster up any enthusiasm to do it now."

Kacey, serious and pale, said, "He was always enthusiastic about selling me my vikes." Alene and Ruthie looked at her with alarm and she cracked a rare smile. "I mean, before I straightened up."

It was too soon for Alene or Ruthie to find any humor in Kacey's addiction. Her pretty face was drawn and pale, she looked brittle, and she seemed to subsist on black coffee. "You're doing great, Kacey," said Alene, "and we're rooting for you." Kacey scurried out of the kitchen. She hated being reminded of her fragility.

Alene said, "Olly, would you please tell Jack that I've already gone home for the day?"

"Come on, Six, that's ridiculous," said Ruthie as she bagged sections of dough. "Don't you move, Olly."

Olly struck a dramatic pose of a person in mid-stride: "Yes, ma'am."

Ruthie turned to Alene. "Go talk to Jack, and then really do go home."

Olly, still frozen in place, spoke like the tin woodsman, out of one side of his mouth. "Should I tell him you'll be out in a minute, Alene?"

Was she ethically bound to hire Gary's stepson just because he'd been so magnanimous in selling her the café below market price? "Don't go anywhere yet, Olly. And please stop performing."

"That'll never happen." Olly stuck his tongue out at Alene. She stuck her tongue back at him. He unfroze and started removing dirty dishes, as he looked through the window of the door into the café. "Jack's still weaving around the tables," he said.

Olly started snapping his fingers. "One of you better tell me what to do about him STAT, or I'm going to go sing to him – hit the road, Jack and don't you come back no more, no more no more no more..." He mimed as if into a microphone, "thank you, I'm here all week."

Just as Olly exited, Kacey pushed through the other swinging door carrying a nearly empty tray from the pastry counter. "I think Jack's making everyone a little nervous," she said.

Alene wanted to hug her and feed her a couple of Ruthie's pastries. "Did he say anything to you?"

Kacey shook her head. "Jack hasn't said more than ten words to me about anything, except money, since his mother married my dad."

Just then Edith Vanza pushed through the door, carrying one part of the coffee machine in each hand. "Why is Jack Stone marching around the café? He's creepy," she huffed, "and I'm the only one left in front. Why is it always up to me to deal with this crap?"

That was so farfetched that nobody answered her. Edith turned on her heels, muttering to herself. Only twelve years older than Alene, she was already a crotchety old woman. When anyone asked how she was, she crabbed about some

5

ailment or other. She dyed her hair herself in an effort to look younger, with little success, and she wore way too many floral prints.

"I can't take the pressure," Alene said to nobody in particular, wrapping the last, misshapen muffin in a napkin and heading into the café. She forced a bright smile. She was truly cheered by the sight of twenty tables, each topped with a small flowering plant in a painted ceramic pot. There were only a handful of customers still there, this late in the day, a few of them regulars. Jack was pacing in front of the windows.

"What's up, Jack? Would you like a snack and a cup of something to drink before you go?" Jack stopped pacing and sat down at a table next to the deep-claret wall, covered with drawings, photos and paintings. "It's on me," she added.

"I already asked for a cup of hot chocolate." She hadn't expected a thank-you. Maybe he'd be nicer looking if he showered, dressed like an adult, and got rid of his messy hair and beard, but how would that improve his personality? Alene followed his gaze to the crimson wall. The Whipped and Sipped staff contributed suggestions for art exhibitions, and the current display was of photographs and painted landscapes. Each picture was marred by the inclusion of cell towers, phone lines, or power plants. There were gloomy scenes of mountain tops destroyed by surface mining and rolling hills disfigured by open pit mining. Jack looked back at Alene. "These are pretty negative. Don't you guys believe in progress?"

She sat down across from him and said, "The staff is in charge of it, so you'd have to ask one of them." Alene glanced around the café. "We're closing soon, so only a few of my employees are still here. All these pieces are for sale. Is this what you wanted to discuss with me, or are you particularly interested in the green flier about our upcoming exhibition on harvesting for sustenance?"

Alene waved at the elderly couple sharing a savory muffin and sipping from large cappuccinos at the next table. They turned to look at the wall as if they hadn't noticed it before, even though they stopped by all the time. She recognized a thirty-something guy who had lately been sitting for hours nursing a single cup of decaf while scrolling through job listings on his cell phone. At another table, two women sat hunched over their phones, lingering over long-emptied cups.

"How many people does it take to run this place?" Jack asked as Edith approached with a steaming cup and placed it in front of him. He gave it a sullen look.

"Didn't anyone ever teach you to say 'thank you'?" Edith asked, as though he were a seven-year-old child.

"I ordered hot chocolate. I don't drink coffee," said Jack.

"Maybe I didn't understand your mumbling," Edith retorted.

Alene said in a low voice, "Edith, please bring a cup of hot chocolate for Jack."

Edith tightened her thin mouth and glared, before bustling away. Alene turned to Jack. "Most of our employees are part-time. Your Aunt Edith manages the drinks section, and I'm sorry she didn't get your order right."

"She's never liked me. And she's not really my aunt. She's just Gary's sister."

Alene had been as surprised as anyone when Gary married Jack's mother, Joan. Jack sounded like an insecure child, and Edith was right, he did mumble. Maybe he was just limited, as some people can be, and she was being too harsh on him. Alene slid the pastry across the table. "This is on the house, Jack. It's the very last sweet potato muffin."

He took a bite and spoke mid-chew. "It's pretty good."

Alene wondered how he'd reached the age of thirty-four still talking with food in his mouth. Jack Stone had never been on her list of favorites. She remembered her sister Lydia, about nine years old, coming home from school humiliated after he'd frightened her into peeing in her pants. Then, at age eleven, Jack and his friends had called her "Lydia the lesbo" after they'd seen her and a girlfriend holding hands and twirling in a circle. Lydia had cried afterwards. Now, Alene tried to act professionally. "What can I do for you today, Jack?"

He chomped up the muffin and began biting his nails. He smelled of cigarette smoke and motor oil, as he shuffled in his seat. It seemed impossible for him to stop squirming. "My step-brother and his girlfriend are helping me look for a job."

Alene had met the girlfriend, a hair stylist at a toney Gold Coast salon. She didn't think much of Jack's stepbrother, Bill, who was absorbed with his thinning hair, watched inordinate amounts of television, and spent hours in the gym. He was good friends with Alene's ex-husband, Neal, and worked for him at his car dealership. Alene thought that Bill was always strutting and peeking at himself in mirrors, and she was surprised that someone so self-centered could hold onto a girlfriend or help his step-brother look for a job. "That seems nice of them."

Jack mumbled. "They think I'd be really good at working here."

Maybe the girlfriend had come up with the idea, but what a quick way to lose customers. On the other hand, she'd made some questionable hires before, and with a lot of oversight, they'd turned out all right. Alene sighed. "So, Bill's still dating Tinley?"

"Um, yeah, they're like, almost married." Jack hesitated and said, "Actually Tinley said I should talk to you first, and then she'll come and help convince you about why you should hire me." He spoke in a monotone, scratching his head and looking at the crimson wall.

Alene gaped at him. "I wonder if working next door at the bar might not be a better fit for you, Jack. I mean, we get a lot of little old ladies and children. Not really your crowd."

"My case manager says I can't work in a bar," Jack responded, "but I could work in a coffee shop. Listen, Alene, I'm smarter and faster than Edith, and I'm not schizoid like Kacey or fruity like that red-headed kid. I could probably learn how to do everything in like, half a day."

"Really, you think so?" Alene stood up, exhausted from the brief conversation. Should she say something about not labeling people? "I'm, um, well, okay, Jack, thanks for letting me know, and I'll be happy to look at your resume, but we're not actually hiring anyone at the moment." Would he think she sounded sincere? "Okay, so look, it's almost closing time and I've got to get moving, but once you forward it to me, I'll let you know if there's anything you can do to improve your resume."

"I don't have a resume," Jack said.

"Oh. So, how about asking Tinley or Bill to help you write one up? That would be a really good first step to finding employment." Alene looked at her watch. "I've got to run, Jack, but thanks for stopping by." She fled back into the kitchen, guilty about having been so abrupt.

Shortly after that, Olly returned to the kitchen, deposited more dishes into the sink, and came over to put an arm around Alene's shoulder. "Jack liked the muffin but didn't think you were very friendly. He said you have no idea what he's capable of." Olly hesitated. "I wonder if he meant that as a threat."

"Maybe he meant Alene doesn't realize that he's capable of holding a job," said Ruthie.

"I don't think so," said Kacey, shaking her head. "Jack's more into threatening."

Battered: A Whipped and Sipped Mystery

Chapter 2

Still a little unsettled by Jack's visit, Alene adjusted her backpack and strolled up Broadway towards the grocery store. The sun warmed the top of her head as she inhaled a heady mix of fragrant flowers and exhaust fumes. How could she hire Jack Stone? Why couldn't he clean floors and fill shelves at the bar next door, when it was closed during the day, or at any other restaurant in the city?

She tried to stop thinking about Jack, focusing instead on the expressions of people passing by. Her mother used to invent names for passers-by and she'd make-up stories about where they were heading. Had Alene spent enough time teaching her children to use their imaginations? There was no rush to get home - at this time of day her father would be watching a baseball game, sprawled in his post-nap, comfy chair. Blanca would have given him a snack and tidied the apartment. Zuleyka Martinez, originally hired as a nanny, but now an employee at the café and a frequent babysitter, would have picked up the children from day camp. Alene's phone vibrated in her pocket.

It was her oldest, Sierra. "Mom, we're done with our chores and there's nothing to do. Can me and Quinn go to the playground?"

"Hi Sierra honey, did you have a good day at camp?" Alene asked.

"No, I got pushed into a door and this is probably the stupidest summer program I've ever done. Also, a lot of my friends are already babysitting for younger kids, Mom, so I could be Quinn's babysitter."

Alene paused. "You can babysit as soon as you learn how to treat your siblings respectfully, Sierra. For today, Noah probably wants to go to the playground too and I'd prefer that Zuleyka walk the three of you over there."

"MOM," Sierra wailed, "She speaks Spanish the whole time and never stops Noah from bothering me and my friends. She's the worst babysitter, ever."

Alene didn't even know where to begin. "I can only hope you didn't just hurt her feelings by saying that when she could hear you, Sierra," said Alene. "You know she's from Panama, and Spanish is her native language. We wanted you to learn it from her. Also, it's your brother's birthday tomorrow and it would be nice if you included him."

"I would, if he wasn't such a brat," said Sierra. "You know that when we go to Dad's, he lets us play outside by ourselves."

Alene stopped so abruptly that a woman walking behind her stepped on the back of her foot. Alene yelped. She'd repeatedly reminded her ex-husband that all three children still required supervision when they were with him, even though he lived in the relatively safe Lincoln Park area. It wasn't just in her nightmares that the city was riddled with crime – there were always stories about guys trying to entice children into vans. Sierra continued, "Dad's going to drop me and Quinn at the playground by his house after he picks us up. It's a better playground than the stupid baby one close to us."

Neal was supposed to have the kids from Friday through Saturday afternoon. Did he really plan to leave them in a playground after dark, by themselves? If she brought it up, he'd mock her for being a worrywart, and do whatever he wanted anyhow. "It's Quinn and me, not me and Quinn," she told Sierra.

"MOM," Sierra whined.

"We'll talk about it when I get home, Sierra. I'm walking into the grocery store right now. Would you please remind Quinn and Noah to do chores and pack their overnight bags?"

"I'm only going to remind them once," said Sierra, "and by the way, I've asked you four times to buy me some cantaloupe."

Alene decided not to respond to that. "Please help Zuleyka start the pasta for dinner."

Sierra exhaled dramatically. "Why, can't she boil water by herself?"

"You can help her choose the pasta, Sweetie," Alene replied, "and help her find the big pot."

Sierra, who'd been kind and sweet as a child, clicked off without saying goodbye. Alene wished she'd ended their conversation with "I love you." Ruthie Rosin always ended conversations with her children that way, but her twelve-year-old daughter had also recently started to mouth off like a teenager. Would saying "I love you" more often really make a difference?

Alene sniffed five cantaloupes before finding one that smelled sweet. Maybe she'd also handled Jack badly, but how could she be expected to hire such a wastrel? Bill Vanza was a bonehead to think it was a good idea for Jack to work at Whipped and Sipped.

Bill, who acted like he was still the star quarterback he'd been in high school, had been one of Neal's best friends for years. When Alene and Neal were still married, Bill would come over on Fridays after work and stretch out on the couch without removing his shoes. He and Neal would spend an inordinate amount of time in the living room, drinking beer and watching sports. Alene had been wrong to let Neal buy that enormous flat-screen LED television. Then, after the divorce, he'd splurged on an even bigger screen with higher definition. The kids loved it.

Except for their three children, Alene considered her marriage to Neal a wasted eight years. Their relationship had started out fun and spontaneous, but she shouldn't have assumed he'd mature with age or that having children together would turn them into a loving family. At least the divorce settlement had allowed her to buy the Whipped and Sipped Café from Gary Vanza. Her dad had refused to let her pay rent, after she'd moved back into his four-bedroom condo, where she and her sister Lydia had grown up. Her father loved the daily interactions with his grandchildren, and they mostly loved his jokes, endless patience, and non-judgmental listening. They also enjoyed the spectacular views of Belmont Harbor and the lake, and they'd quickly made friends in their new schools.

In the bakery aisle, Alene picked out Batman candles for Noah's birthday cake. How could her baby be turning eight years old? *It didn't seem so long ago that she'd gone into labor with him. She'd been visiting her father that day, with four-year-old Sierra and two-year-old Quinn. They'd walked over to the playground while her father had his after-lunch nap. She remembered leaning heavily on the stroller; Sierra was old enough to walk but insisted on riding, and Quinn sat on Sierra's lap. They'd stopped at the harbor to look at the boats. There'd been a soft breeze from the lake, but she hadn't appreciated it because she'd felt*

14

bloated, unattractive, and was stabbed by sciatica with each step.

Alene had suddenly noticed people running a few hundred feet ahead towards someone lying in the gravel along the bike path. She'd thought it was probably another maniacal bicyclist who'd fallen or an inattentive walker who'd ambled into the bicycle lane. But as she got closer, Alene recognized her neighbor Brianne Flynn kneeling on the ground next to her husband, Dennis. He was sprawled a little too close to the bike path and Alene worried that someone could run into him. She saw Dennis and Brianne's bicycles flung nearby, on the grass, and bikers zoomed by from both directions, all trying to steer clear of Dennis.

Sierra and Quinn had gone uncharacteristically quiet and stared with interest at the gathering crowd. "Look, Mommy, there's Kacey. Kacey," yelled Sierra, "come and play with us!" Alene had been delighted to see her even before she realized how much of a godsend Kacey would turn out to be.

Alene pushed the stroller as quickly as she could. The little girls thought it was a game and called out, "Faster, Mommy!"

"What happened," both Kacey and Alene asked as soon as they got to where Dennis was lying. As the sirens got closer, Alene locked the stroller in place.

"We decided to go out for a ride," said Brianne, who was slouched in the grass, her voice anguished. "We were about to get off the path when some idiot barreled into Dennis. Everyone saw him fall but nobody noticed the other guy ride away as if nothing happened."

"I would have pulled him off his bike and bashed in his skull if I'd seen him," said Kacey.

Alene gave her a look and Kacey, remembering the children, quickly said, "I mean, shame on that man for

15

pushing Dennis down. He should be punished." Alene smiled gratefully until they all heard Dennis moan.

"Oh my, he looks hurt, and - bloody," said Alene, swaying unsteadily. She whimpered as a gush of warm water trickled down her legs. Luckily, the girls were facing away and couldn't see her plop gracelessly to the ground. What an idiot for thinking she could run in her condition.

"Alene, are you all right?" Kacey asked.

"I might be in labor," said Alene. She paused as a wave of pain ripped through her body. "Yup. Baby coming," she tried to smile. "Kacey, can you please... call Neal?" She exhaled as the pain faded. "I'm sorry, Brianne. Give my love to Dennis. I hope he didn't break anything."

Kacey promised to take the girls home, and the next thing Alene knew, she was screaming with another huge contraction, lying in the back of a police car heading south to the hospital.

The next day, as she was nursing baby Noah, Brianne, still in the clothes she'd been wearing on the bike path, stopped by Alene's room.

Brianne stood in the doorway and said, "He's gone."

Alene pulled her concentration away from the baby and, asked, "What do you mean?"

"Dennis had a heart attack. He died in the ambulance on the way to the hospital," said Brianne, barely above a whisper. "I think that biker ran into him on purpose."

Alene started crying. "The police will figure it out, Brianne," she said. "They're not going to let the lake path be overrun by hit-and-run bikers."

But nobody came forward, nobody saw anything, and nobody was ever caught. Eight years later, Brianne was still angry at the police for dropping the investigation. She hadn't been consoled when the city of Chicago finally expanded the bike path and the number of collisions between bikers and pedestrians decreased.

16

Now in the grocery store, filling her cart with a baguettes, salad ingredients and vegetables, Alene remembered going into labor with Noah. A kind police officer had accompanied her into the hospital and sat with her through the birth, since Neal had only appeared after the baby had been measured, cleaned up, and returned to her.

Was Noah's birth always going to be connected in her memory to Dennis's death? Standing in the checkout line, Alene wiped away the tears that sprang up every time she remembered that day. But Noah had been a healthy, happy baby, and now he was a happy, spunky, science-loving child about to celebrate his eighth birthday at the Shedd Aquarium. He'd invited seven friends to celebrate the following afternoon, and Alene was relieved that only five of them were coming. She'd also invited her sister and brother-in-law, and Ruthie Rosin and her family for dinner and birthday cake after Noah's party.

She had to get Neal to be a more responsible parent. As she strode home with the groceries and birthday candles in her backpack, Alene called her sister, who'd been Alene's divorce attorney and who would know how to make sure Neal kept the children safe. After the fourth ring, Lydia answered in a clipped voice. "Hi, what's up?"

"Neal is doing his 'let's-aggravate-Alene-by-putting the-kids-at-risk routine, do you have a minute?"

"I'm still at work." Lydia sounded rushed as usual.

Alene said, "It's not an emergency or anything, but can you call Neal and tell him he can't let the girls play outside by themselves? He told them he'd drop them off at the playground after dark tonight."

"That's a call you can make, Alene. I'm trying to get out of here early today. Theo and I have reservations at Alinea. It's our fifth anniversary, remember?" She sang the last words.

"Right, congratulations! That was super thoughtful of Theo – I've read about how hard it is to get into that place. You have to make reservations, like, six months in advance."

"Ha," Lydia replied, "you think he was the one who planned dinner?"

Alene said, "I bet he's going to give you a really magnificent gift." No doubt extravagant as usual, she thought, like diamond earrings that would look striking with Lydia's long dark hair. He'd given Lydia a diamond necklace for her birthday, and a diamond bracelet for their last anniversary. Also a lawyer, Theo King was a decent guy, but he repeated everything two or three times, had a phony-sounding laugh that reminded her of a horse's whinny, and talked incessantly about his mother, who had recently moved to an assisted-living facility in Florida. His generosity was oppressive - he always spent way more than necessary on gifts. When he and Lydia came to dinner, they'd present Alene with a crystal vase filled with roses or an extremely expensive wine when all she was serving was pot roast with mashed potatoes. For Lydia's sake, she always tried to overflow with gratitude.

"Whatever he gives me, I'll love it, and I'll wear it when we come over tomorrow night," Lydia said. "Theo's picked out an enormous Lego something-or-other for Noah's birthday and I ordered a fabulous Batman ice cream cake with three flavors and sprinkles."

"He's going to love everything," said Alene, suspecting that the Lego set was going to be much too complicated for Noah. "You can skip the call to Neal, I'll take care of it. As usual, I've been reminiscing all afternoon about the day Noah was born. Do you remember?"

Lydia was busy shuffling papers on her end. "Wasn't there some drama when you went into labor? Something about Dennis Flynn?"

"I'll never forget that," said Alene. "He was pushed off his bike and then he had a heart attack in the ambulance on the way to the hospital. Brianne took over the bar and made a go of it, but she's been alone since he died."

"I'd love to talk, Alene, but I'm really rushed." Lydia said brusquely.

Alene knew that if she really had to go, she'd just hang up. "Brianne was the one who had spilled the beans about Neal, while she was still in mourning for Dennis."

It had been warm for September, the sun was shining, and the city was still garlanded with sidewalk gardens and tubs of lush fall annuals. Alene had met Brianne for lunch at a cute place on Clark, just a mile south of Whipped and Sipped. They were both off on Sundays.

Alene pulled herself back to the present. "Lydia, you won't believe who came in asking for a job today." There was no response since Lydia had already ended the call. Alene put her cell back in her pocket and kept walking.

The weather had been like this that day when she met had Brianne for lunch – hot and humid. Three-month-old Noah was nestled against her chest, papoose-style. A basket of warm whole-grain rolls and three salads had been placed on the table.

Brianne had been heartbroken after Dennis died and was angry that the coroner listed the cause of his death as a heart attack. She was a fine-boned, still beautiful woman with the posture of a former dancer, but Alene noticed her ashen skin and the bags under her eyes. Before he died, she and Dennis had been planning a trip, to celebrate their twenty-fifth wedding anniversary.

Alene wished she'd been more helpful to Brianne back then. Brianne said she was fine, but she'd just become a widow at forty-eight. She had a twenty-year-old son and a fourteen-year-old daughter who still required parenting. How did she have room to worry about Alene?

"It's about Joan and Gary Vanza," Brianne had said.

In addition to being her boss at the café, before she bought it, Gary had always been a wonderful neighbor. He was friendly and generous and he'd often dropped by for a game of chess with Alene's father, to check if anything needed fixing, or just to say hello. However, twice in the previous month while Alene was visiting her dad, Gary's wife, Joan Stone, had gotten into the elevator and let the doors close, even though Alene was just a few yards away with her three children.

Alene wasn't all that interested in hearing what Brianne had to say about Gary Vanza and his wife, with her dyed-orange hair and surgically-enhanced chest, especially while her own breasts were so sore from nursing the baby. She'd tried to make a joke of it. "Let me guess – Joan has passports under different names and nationalities, and is actually a Russian spy?"

Brianne gave a hint of a smile. "No. Gary found another stash of money. This time she hid it in a kitchen drawer. He told me he was looking for a zester to grate orange peel."

Alene wondered what he'd used the orange peel for. "Maybe Joan is a pick-pocket. There, I just solved the case."

Brianne insisted, "Thirty. Thousand. Dollars. And Gary told me that it wasn't the first time he's found such a huge amount." It seemed that Gary was telling Brianne the things he used to be able to tell Dennis.

Alene sipped her tea. "Maybe Joan doesn't use banks. She's a dingbat, but so what? Why are you telling me this?"

"Gary asked her where she got it and she yelled at him for snooping."

"So?" Alene rolled her eyes while sampling a pastry from the platter in front of her. "I'd yell at Neal if he started messing up drawers."

"Joan said she won it gambling in one of the casinos," said Brianne.

Alene felt a combination of jealousy and revulsion. "I never win anything. Was it at the casino in Rosemont, off the tollway? I once had lunch at the seafood restaurant there."

Brianne shook her head. "I don't really know where she goes, just that she gambles every Friday night."

"I'll add gambling to the list of things I don't like about her." Alene took a sip of water over the baby's head. "It's kind of unfair that she won so much, though, if that's really what happened."

"Joan doesn't go to the casinos by herself." Brianne held her head up with her hands and looked miserable.

"That's nice." Alene said with her mouth full.

Brianne took a deep breath, to steel her nerves, and then she continued in almost a whisper. "I am so sorry, Honey, Neal goes with her."

Alene nearly choked on her salad. "What do you mean, 'Neal goes with her'"?

"Neal and Joan are together on Friday nights. They've been seeing each other," said Brianne.

That's impossible," said Alene. "He's in a Friday night bowling league."

Alene remembered how her entire body had gone numb at that point; but, how could she make a fuss in front of Brianne, who'd just lost her husband? It took Alene weeks to fully accept that Neal really was having an affair with Joan Stone. How could she have known? Joan was forty-six years old, mean, and she looked like a scowling red-headed Barbie.

At thirty-five, Neal hadn't yet turned doughy and he still sported only one chin under his always closely-cut beard. Alene thought he looked like a handsome character in a gangster film. He'd worn his hair long back then. It hadn't started thinning forcing him to have it cut short except for a swath at the top of his large forehead. Noah had inherited Neal's strong features – his smile, his full lower lip and eyes closed to slits when he smiled. But Noah's smiles were genuine. Noah had also inherited Neal's olive-skinned coloring, while the two girls had Alene's pale, pinkish skin and wide-eyed smile.

For a long time after learning that Neal and Joan were having an affair, Alene had tried to save her marriage. Therapy helped her work through her feelings and Ruthie encouraged her to keep working on the relationship. However, both Brianne and her sister, Lydia, agreed that Neal wasn't worth saving. They both thought he must have had previous affairs.

Alene never said anything, and always wondered if Gary ever knew about Joan and Neal. Alene's marriage had fallen apart, but eight years later, Joan and Gary were still married and living across the hall. Poor Kacey, Gary's daughter from his second marriage, lived with them. That was another story. Alene walked into the lobby, shook herself out of her reverie, and pressed the elevator button. She still hadn't called Neal about letting the children play outside after dark.

Chapter 3

An hour after Alene got home with the groceries, Neal burst into the apartment closely followed by his old pal, Bill Vanza. Bill slowed down and posed, Alene was sure, so she could admire him. She purposefully turned away. At least Neal wasn't late to pick up the kids (as usual). The two men sprawled on the couch with their shoes on, but Alene didn't think it was worth an argument. Sierra, Quinn and Noah, who were packed and ready to go, plopped down next to their father while Bill fiddled with the remote and zeroed in on a car chase. Alene gritted her teeth. Her father shuffled back to his chair, leaning on his walker, and saw the remote in Bill's hand. He looked up at the television and snorted.

"What the-? What's wrong with you, William Vanza? Who changes stations - on someone else's TV - in the middle of a Cubs game?" Cal huffed indignantly. He had recently been struggling with myasthenia gravis, a muscular disease that made him weak and short of breath. "You know why men are like parking spaces? Because the good ones are taken - and the rest are disabled!" He waited for someone to chuckle, but everyone just continued staring at the television.

"Alene, will you please - take the remote and get my game back on?" Cal grimaced before glancing at Bill and asking slowly, "What are you doing here - anyway, William? Why don't you go visit - your father - for a change? Last time I looked – the Vanzas are right across the hall."

"Dad," said Alene, aware that her children were listening to every word, "maybe Neal gave Bill a lift home from work, especially so he could stop by and visit his father."

"Is that so?" Cal snorted, furrowing his bushy white eyebrows and carefully settling into his chair. Alene was ready to kick everyone out the door to shield her dad from getting overexcited. He was only seventy-two, but the disease made him seem older.

"Because - Gary told me," Cal frowned at Bill, "the only time he gets to see you - is when you want something from him. - You should be ashamed." Alene knew that M.G. also caused her father's speech to slur and was irritated by Bill's mocking grin.

"Come on kids, get drinks and go to the bathroom. It's time to leave," said Alene. "Bill, my children need to concentrate on getting out the door right now, so we'll see you later." Did he have any redeeming qualities? Maybe he gave something to beggars without a disapproving stare. Maybe he occasionally held open a door to let an elderly person pass through.

Bill chortled. "I'm heading across the hall in a few, Alene, so don't get all excited about me sticking around."

Gary Vanza and his second wife had bought the condo across the hall from the Barons when Alene was a teenager. Sometimes back then, when Gary's sons from his first marriage were visiting, Alene would get a glimpse of two lumpy, spoiled boys. Sandy talked to himself, kept his eyes on the floor, and was constantly moving his fingers as though playing some invisible instrument. Bill was always rushing ahead through the building's doors, admiring himself in the glass and never acknowledging Alene or her sister.

Bill and Alene's ex-husband had been friends since they met at a private high school for privileged but mediocre children. Their fathers had worked together at an electronics' manufacturer west of the city. After the company went bankrupt in the early nineties, Bill's father bought the Whipped and Sipped Café. Neal's father bought a car dealership and hired both Neal and Bill. Neal later inherited the business from his father, and the two still worked together twenty years later. Alene scowled at them. They both reeked of cigarette smoke. After all the research proving the dangers of secondhand smoke, Alene was appalled that Neal continued to put her children at risk.

"Also," Bill continued in a sarcastic tone, "I got a ride home with Neal, just so I could stop in and say hello to my father." Bill turned to Neal and rubbed his thumb and fingers together.

How could a forty-three-year-old man have so little self-respect that he would joke about asking his father for money? Alene was embarrassed for Bill, until Neal slapped him on the back and said, "I bet I can get more out of my mother than you get out of your father." She cringed as twelve-year-old Sierra gave Neal a look.

What could Alene say to soften such an obnoxious statement? She looked at Neal and tried to remember when she'd thought he was fun, spontaneous, and personable. She'd once loved his dark-brown eyes and swarthy complexion. He used to scratch her back with his gruff facial hair that required twice-a-day shaving. Now he just looked sinister.

She improvised, "I'm sure your father will help if you need money, Bill, because fathers love their children and will always be there to help them, right Neal?"

Bill and Neal sniggered, and Bill said, "Yup, because my father wants me to be happy."

Cal looked briefly at both Bill and Neal and then turned back to the game without saying anything. Alene dug her nails into her arm.

Neal said, "And nothing makes a person happier than money in the bank."

"Yup," said Bill again, "but unfortunately my dad's tightwad wife controls the purse-strings."

Alene was sickened. Gary's tightwad wife was the same woman who'd once had an affair with Neal. "Maybe you two grown men could concentrate on earning your own salaries and stop worrying about how much money you can finagle from your fathers."

Bill and Neal rolled their eyes like bored adolescents. Cal had dozed off again.

Neal said, "The kids had a great time last week playing at the park, so I'm planning to drop them off there again." He spoke while looking to Bill for approval. The two of them high-fived as if they'd accomplished something.

"See, Mom," said Sierra, "I told you Dad lets us play by ourselves at the playground."

Alene left the room without saying a word, took her phone into her bedroom and called Neal's mother. Mitzi Dunn was often on Alene's side. Within moments, Neal's cell rang, and Alene smiled to hear him accept his mother's invitation for dinner and a swim in her pool that night. Bathing suits added to their suitcases, the children kissed Alene and their grandfather goodbye. Alene felt relieved when the door finally closed.

Neal often made Alene want to scream. How could she stop him from turning the children into the kind of irresponsible, unpleasant person he'd become? She cleaned the vegetables, sautéed onions, and blended zucchini and parsley with canned tomatoes and fresh herbs until the mixture looked and tasted as smooth as plain tomato sauce. During the months after she and the children had moved back to her father's place, Alene had felt like an idiot. As someone who considered herself especially astute about these things, she had not noticed all the signs that revealed Neal was not the man she'd thought she'd married

It felt good to slam the knife down as she chopped the salad into tiny pieces that her father could easily swallow. Until her sister, Lydia, demanded all the paperwork, she didn't even realize that Neal had frittered away their cash savings, probably during his gambling nights with Joan. How ironic, she thought, that Neal lost so much while Joan left piles of money sitting around their condo. During the divorce, Lydia had delved into Neal's finances and found that his father had undervalued the dealership by several million dollars. She explained to Alene that it was a common but illegal ploy.

Lydia had then confronted Neal with a decade of dishonest tax returns. She gave him two choices – pay a lump-sum amount to Alene, or Lydia would feed him to the Internal Revenue Service.

"Do you think you're the first person to try to get away with this, Neal?" Lydia had reenacted the conversation for Alene. "How do you think the IRS will feel about ten million dollars of inventory that went unreported?"

Neal had argued, "It was my father who set the value for the place. No one can prove I did anything shady. In case you forgot, my father just so happens to be dead, so good luck finding out anything else."

Alene had received her lump sum in the divorce agreement, which also gave her full custody of the children. That was 2008, just before the world financial markets began crashing. Alene was able to buy the café from Gary. Neal got the townhouse in Lincoln Park with its huge television and all the furnishings, retained ownership of his business and, in an uncharacteristic but much-welcomed move, offered to continue taking care of the children's health insurance. Alene grudgingly acknowledged to herself that Neal had always been good about taking care of the children's health – driving them to their check-ups and making sure then got their teeth cleaned twice a year.

Alene helped her father to the kitchen table and served him roasted spaghetti squash smothered in the tomato sauce she'd blended, with smoked mozzarella melted on top. In a separate small bowl, she'd scooped a serving of chopped salad tossed in a fresh lemon and oil vinaigrette. "I'm having a pinot noir with my dinner, Dad. Do you want a glass or would you prefer a beer?"

"Nothing for me, thanks," said Cal in his gravelly voice. "You know it slows me down - even more." He took a few bites. "Delicious - if I close my eyes, I'm sitting - on a moonlit evening - and your mother is smiling at me. We'd share - a glass of wine, and - she'd still get a little tipsy - from just a few sips."

Alene said, "I'm like Mom; sometimes I start giggling after half a glass."

Cal said, "Benjamin Franklin wrote: in wine there is wisdom.... in beer there is freedom....in water there is bacteria."

Alene laughed as Cal put his hand on her arm. "Why did William Vanza - come over here tonight? Can't Neal face you by himself?" Cal paused to breathe. "Mitzi knows she raised a fool. He's a disappointment - but I remind her that he helped make our grandchildren."

Alene wiped her eyes with the back of her hand. "I'm not crying, Dad. I'm just so tired of everything. Sometimes I can't wait until the children are grown and I don't have to talk to him, although, of course, one day I hope they'll get married." More tears fell; her mother wouldn't be there for her wedding or the wedding of her future children.

Cal patted her hand, saying, "Now cut that out. You're doing a great job - running a business and taking care of me - in addition to everything else. If only your mother could have been here - to see your kids." Then his eyes teared up as well. "I thought you said the wine would make you giggle."

After dinner, Alene helped Cal back to his room, did the dishes, and confirmed that everything was ready for Noah's birthday dinner, following his party at the Shedd, the next day. Only nine o'clock on a Friday night and Alene was already in her nightgown. She was worn-out, but it sure would have been nice to be going out to hear music or to catch a movie with someone. After her husband had died, Mitzi Dunn always said, "I got nobody to do nothin' with," and Cal started inviting her to join him now and then. It was nice for them both. Alene brushed her teeth, worrying momentarily that Neal wouldn't remind Noah to brush his.

She was grateful to Mitzi for having the children over. Maybe they'd play in the big swimming pool in Mitzi's building, and Lydia would file some kind of injunction to prevent Neal following through on the playground threat the following week. How could a father put his own children at risk? He'd turned out to be a nincompoop in many ways. It wasn't the first time Alene considered that if the Vanzas hadn't moved across the hall from her family, she might never have met Neal Dunn.

Maybe Bill Vanza's girlfriend would join Bill and Neal at Mitzi Dunn's, so the kids wouldn't have to spend the whole evening listening to the inane conversation of two immature men. Maybe the children would have fun with Mitzi and pay no attention to Neal and his sidekick. Alene drifted off to sleep thinking about texting Neal to remind him to get Noah to his birthday party at the aquarium no later than three.

The next morning, Alene sprang out of bed, threw on jeans, a tank top and a light sweater, and walked briskly over to the café. She saw only a few cars pass by, and not one single other person. It had rained in the night, but the day would be warm once the sun burned off the haze. Ruthie always took Saturdays off, so it was usually Alene who removed the trays of prepared dough from the refrigerators, heated up the ovens, and worked with the staff to prepare for a busy day. Edith was already waiting at the back door that morning, as Alene approached, wearing wrinkled khakis with one of her pink floral sweaters. Gnarled toes poked out of stretched sandals. Thankfully health regs required she change into shoes when actually working.

"Nice of you to show up, Alene," said Edith, "or I'd be standing out here all morning."

"It's two minutes after six, Edith." Alene responded dryly, unlocking the door and pressing in the code to release the alarm. When she'd had the key, Edith had twice neglected to turn off the alarm and Alene had paid both times for the false alarms. It would be a long time before she'd give Edith another key. "Sorry if I made you nervous, Edith, but we have a full hour until we open and we're right on schedule." She put on her apron and surveyed the kitchen.

"As if my brother wasn't the previous owner and I haven't worked here for nearly twenty years," Edith griped.

"Let's try to have a nice day, Edith, okay?"

Edith sighed loudly and bustled out of the kitchen to her station at the drinks counter, as the rest of the crew trickled in. On weekends, everyone started at six and they opened at seven-thirty.

Ruthie Rosin's days off were never as much fun for Alene as the days when they both worked. She missed bantering the way they'd done since college, and she missed how Ruthie found something positive to say about nearly everyone. Olly, LaTonya, Rashid, Manny and Kacey got to work preparing fruits and vegetables, helping Alene with the baking, cleaning and preparing the trays for new batches, and placing the cooled pastries in the glass dessert counter.

Kacey looked tired but didn't have the glassy-eyed, wiped-out look she used to have after a night of partying. How many weeks had she been clean this time? She'd been coming in on time and had followed all the rules, but she didn't really seem to care much about anything she was doing. If only she were passionate about woodworking, like her father was, or dancing, or biking, or anything. Maybe fighting her addictions, starting to date again, and working for Alene was enough.

"You know, I've wanted to do exactly what I'm doing for nearly as long as I can remember," Alene said as they filled muffin trays. "Did I ever tell you that not long after Ruthie and I were assigned as roommates, we started dreaming about running a café together? We already knew that she was going to be the pastry chef and I was going to be the business person. I sure wish you felt good enough about yourself to start dreaming about the future, Kacey."

Kacey avoided eye contact by concentrating on the muffin batter. Alene worried that she'd overdone the pep talk and tried again. "You know I adore you and just want you to be happy, right?"

Kacey said, "But not everyone has a Ruthie."

She couldn't argue with that. From the start, Ruthie and Alene had had almost everything in common. They loved reading detective fiction, enjoyed solving complicated puzzles to put themselves to sleep, and talked or thought about recipes and food for hours. They got up early and ran together almost daily, rain or shine. They joined clubs that focused on feeding the poor and supporting sustainable eating and both were both clean freaks, so their dorm room sparkled that first year. Ruthie was patient, spiritual, and trusting, whereas Alene was impatient, areligious, and suspicious. They both felt they'd won the roommate lottery.

They were both born in August of 1976 – Alene on the sixth and Ruthie on the ninth. With the dark humor they shared, they jokingly called each other Six and Nine, the same dates that atomic bombs were dropped on Hiroshima and Nagasaki. For over thirty years Alene had continued to argue that dropping those bombs had caused the U.S. to lose its moral authority and Ruthie had continued to argue that dropping the bombs had saved lives and ended the war. Alene figured they'd argue about it forever.

At college, they listened to country music, disdained make-up, wore t-shirts with serious messages about the world, and attended lectures about the environment. They both tried out but didn't get into a choir and played intermural volleyball on Wednesday nights. They figured out ways to ace their classes. When they weren't inventing mnemonics to help them remember material for exams, they discussed the kind of café that they would run together after they graduated – one just like Whipped and Sipped – and they would live near each other.

If Saturday weren't so busy, Alene would have taken it as her day off, same as Ruthie, except not for religious reasons. But one of them absolutely needed to be there to coordinate everything, and it had become apparent that Alene needed to hire an assistant manager.

Kacey turned away to put two more muffin trays in the oven and added, "I love this place too, you know."

If only Kacey were ready for more responsibility, but after all this time Alene still had to remind her to punch down the yeast dough after it had doubled in size. An assistant manager would also have to know something about every aspect of the cafe. Alene opened the back door for Olly, who headed to the front still wearing earbuds and moving to a beat only he could hear. He certainly knew everything about the café, but was he serious enough?

Alene prided herself on her attentiveness to people. The staff liked to test her skill at figuring out what a customer wanted before the customer themselves knew. Alene would explain that she watched the movement of a customer's eyes across the display case, before she placed, for example, a wholegrain blueberry muffin on the counter.

The customer would exclaim in awe, "How did you do that? That was exactly what I was going to have!"

Sometimes Alene knew from the moment they walked in the door, perhaps from their body language, perhaps from the way they were dressed. Sometimes she knew because so many of the regulars ordered the same gluten-free peanut-butter cookie with the same latte every time they came in.

Even when she was in high school, Alene could always find the one piece of paper that her sister had wasted an entire morning looking for. She'd locate the missing earring that had fallen onto a tray and ended up in the trash or the misplaced dough that turned up behind a pile of plates. She could make friends with the gawkiest social misfits and was friendly to all customers. She remembered the names of people after just seeing them two or three times.

But no matter how clever, perceptive, or psychically gifted she was, Alene couldn't get through to Gary's sister, Edith. Surprisingly adept at creating every kind of coffee and whipping up delicious smoothies, Edith couldn't banter or make small talk, and didn't fit in with the casual joking and camaraderie of the rest of the staff.

Edith seemed to have hobbled through life without ever finding a profession or a relationship. She had worked in one dead-end job after another well into her thirties, and she seemed to always generate negativity from the moment she appeared. Jocelyn DeVale, one of Alene's twenty-something employees, called her Eeyore behind her back. Whenever she casually asked, "How you doing, Edith?" or, "What's happening?" Edith would say, "What's happening is that my ankle is killing me and I have arthritis in my neck."

Alene had listened to Edith grousing about and speaking impatiently to the other Whipped and Sipped employees, for over twenty years. Edith managed to be polite to Ruthie, Alene noticed, but that was because Ruthie was an angel.

Edith was completely different from her brother. Gary was a dignified gentleman, who dressed as though he worked in a bank and listened thoughtfully before venturing an opinion. He could be intimidating if angered, but the only time Alene had ever heard him yell was when his son Bill taunted his other son, Sandy. Alene often overheard Gary discussing investments, in meetings with a parade of folks he'd bring to the café. He claimed to be much happier now that Alene owned the place and was taking care of the details of the business.

Gary was financially comfortable, in spite of supporting two ex-wives, and felt obliged to help his sister. When she turned forty, he bought her a condo, set up a trust to pay for her utilities and fees, and purchased the Whipped and Sipped Café so that she could have a permanent job. He couldn't let her run the place because she was too cranky even back then, but she did have a way with smoothies.

If only she didn't fight every change Alene wanted to make. "Why would a café need to host art exhibitions and a knitting group?" She'd grumble during a staff meeting, or "Why can't we just offer the same food other cafés offer?" Alene thought Edith's scowl was the only unfriendly feature of the café.

Edith was also unhappy that Ruthie refused to use animal products in her baking. Other people in the café used them, but she wouldn't. She'd replaced butter with apple sauce and created nut milks and whipped coconut creams.

To replace eggs, Ruthie used chia seeds for baking and created innovative combinations of tofu and vegetables. She made her own vinegars, mustards and other condiments for breakfast and lunch foods, and began inventing cakes filled with beans and vegetables. She even made a kind of apple butter that was a passable substitute for honey in some of her muffins and cakes. Whipped and Sipped had become known for its healthful vegan offerings.

"I love working here, but I don't know if I'd ever want to own a café," said Kacey.

Alene shook herself back to the present and directed Kacey to sprinkle almonds and demerara sugar on the bottom of each pan before she poured in the batter for her citrus-poppy-seed cakes. "You're really good at this, Kacey, but if you don't love working with food, you have to look for the thing that you love to do. Maybe you'll work with other people who are recovering from addictions."

Kacey looked away. Alene tried not to read anything into it. She said, "After this batch goes into the oven, will you frost the carrot muffins and whip up a batch of Ruthie's non-cream-cheese frosting?"

"Ok, and I'll check if the next batch of muffins is ready to come out of the oven," said Kacey. "I really do love working with you in the kitchen, Alene." Her smile lifted Alene's spirits.

There were always at least three kinds of muffins available at Whipped and Sipped. People gazing into the glass dessert case would look up to see tray after tray of muffins lined up on the slanted shelves that Gary had designed and built. They permitted Alene to set the not-completely cooled trays in a place where the customers could see them without their steaming up the glass display. Not as fancy as placing them on a doily in a glass case, but time-saving.

Almost ready to open the cafe, Alene ran into the restroom, brushed her hair and put on some lip gloss. Suddenly she heard the sound of glass breaking and Edith screaming as though she'd been stabbed. Everyone in the kitchen ran out to the café. The first customers of the day were Bill Vanza and his cute girlfriend, Tinley Rico. Bill had collided with Edith, apparently causing her to drop a bowl of fruit that had skidded in every direction across the floor. Kacey was standing by the kitchen door, ghost-pale and with her mouth wide open.

It didn't look as if Alene was going to get the calm Saturday she'd hoped for. Seven-thirty-five and she had to coordinate a clean-up, calm down Edith, and offer free coffee and pastries to Bill and Tinley. Bill paid no attention to his Aunt Edith and demanded free French toast with his coffee. Tinley helped Edith stand up and offered to take her home even though she and Bill had ridden bicycles to the café.

After everything had calmed down, and the café was running smoothly, Alene sipped her latte and went through the scenario in her mind. Had Bill intentionally caused the little run-in with his aunt? Who does something like that on purpose? She couldn't help wondering; had the police checked his whereabouts on that day Dennis had been knocked down?

Chapter 4

Alene got to the Shedd by two-thirty on Saturday afternoon, twenty-five minutes before the party was set to start. Noah's five friends soon showed up and were immediately immersed in the comic books Alene had cleverly thought to bring in her backpack. After a while, they began using rolled up comic books as swords, and Alene had to make sure they didn't get too rambunctious. She stewed in advance that Neal would give her trouble about the cost of the birthday party. He'd argue and procrastinate about paying his half of the expensive tickets. Exactly one minute before three o'clock he appeared at the side entrance with Sierra, Quinn and Noah.

Once they were inside the Aquarium, Neal took over, as usual. Noah beamed with delight at his father's seeming boundless knowledge of fish and frogs, while Alene rolled her eyes at how Neal suddenly morphed into best-dad-ever. He cracked jokes and churned out a constant stream of trivial facts, such as "goldfish actually have teeth," and "sharks are the only fish with eyelids!"

"Look it up on your phone, if you don't believe me, Alene," he said with a cocky grin. She laughed out loud, grudgingly remembering that he could be entertaining. She took up a position in the rear to make sure nobody got lost in the Saturday throng. She had to keep an eye on Quinn, who, instead of helping herd the little boys, kept lagging behind to get a better look at the colorful poisonous frogs or the spooky lampreys sucking on the glass with their myriad rows of tiny teeth. Sierra, who was always happiest being in charge, helped corral Noah's friends, who were fascinated by the weird fish and entertained each other with fart noises and silly faces.

Finally, as the party ended, Sierra and Quinn quarreled and sulked, Alene sank gratefully onto a bench to wait while the parents picked up their boys, and Neal slunk off to whatever fabulous car he was currently borrowing from his dealership. Then Alene took the children home to rest before dinner. Noah played happily with Neal's gift, a brand-new iPad, while Sierra polished her nails, after having done Quinn's nails a sparkling blue color.

When the girls started arguing about which show to watch, their grandfather, who'd been reading in his chair, tried to distract them by telling an old joke. "Knock, knock," he said, waiting for a response. Finally, Noah looked up and asked, "Who's there?"

"Goliath," said Cal.

"You've told this one before," said Sierra.

"I'll do it, Grandpa," said Quinn, blowing on her nails. "Goliath, who?"

Cal grinned. "Go-lie-eth down. Thou looketh tired," he said.

Suddenly they heard a shriek just outside the apartment, followed by what sounded like Joan Stone yelling through the closed door across the hall. From what Alene could hear, Joan was upset that Bill and his girlfriend had failed to remove their shoes from the hallway. Alene sided with Joan about the shoes; she hated it when the kids left them scattered outside the door, but did it merit hysteria?

Before anyone could stop her, Sierra jumped up and flung open the door to get a better view of the neighbors. Bill nearly hurtled across the hallway, past Sierra and into the Barons' apartment, followed by Tinley, who slammed the door behind them. They convulsed with laughter and waved at everyone in the room. "I love your nails, girls," said Tinley. "Blue is a very happening color right now."

"Thanks," said Quinn, still blowing on her fingers to speed the drying time. "But the last time we saw you, your hair was white and now it's purple with a pink streak and one side is different from the other!"

"Maybe when you're older you can come down to my shop and I'll give you and Sierra asymmetrical cuts, too," Tinley said. "We can shave one side and let the other grow long. How does that sound?"

Quinn shook her head. "Then I wouldn't be able to have braids."

"I like your earrings," Sierra said, staring at the sparkling assortment climbing up the side of Tinley's right ear. "Mom, can I get another piercing on my right ear for my birthday?"

"No." Alene looked at Tinley's left calf, uncovered and completely covered in tattoos of colorful birds and butterflies. "And don't even think of asking for a tattoo."

Tinley laughed. "Are you guys having a fun summer?"

Quinn answered, "Sierra and me go to Park District Camp and Noah goes to a summer program at his school where they do science projects all day."

"That sounds great!" Tinley said it as if she meant it. "I wish I could have gone to summer camp. I always wanted to go somewhere in the mountains."

Sierra mumbled, "My Mom said I can go to one of those camps next year, when I'm thirteen." She looked at Alene as though accusing her of something.

Alene was looking at Tinley, who'd changed into a short, tight black skirt and a silky blouse. It was not what she'd been wearing earlier that morning, when Bill had collided with Edith. Alene wondered if the removal of shoes had really been the reason for Joan's screaming a few minutes before. Tinley's youth and beauty probably horrified Joan, who still dressed liked a teenager and probably thought she looked like one. Gary seemed to like how she looked, so it really didn't matter what anyone else thought. Alene considered telling Bill and Tinley that it was a bad time for a visit but then Cal closed the book and said, "Come on in and sit down."

"I'm reading about anti-gravity and it's really hard to put this book down," he said as they approached his chair. Nobody even cracked a smile – they probably didn't know it was a joke. "Nice to see you, young lady, I know you've been keeping company with William Vanza here." Cal paused to breathe. "But we haven't had a chance to chat yet, have we?"

Bill seemed like he was about to object, but Tinley answered, "I'd be delighted, that is, if we're not interrupting anything."

Alene opened her mouth to mention that she expected dinner guests in less than an hour, but Cal, clicking off the television, said, "Not at all!"

Sierra looked like she was about to protest, but then she rose to leave abruptly. Alene whispered, "Could you please get your stuff off the coffee table before you go, Sweetie?"

"It's clean already, Mom. There's like nothing there," Sierra said, sounding more adolescent than just an hour before. "And, I don't want to ruin my nails."

"Just take your color wheel and your book, please," said Alene.

Sierra made an exasperated face. "Quinn was looking at the paint colors and it's her book." She turned to tell Tinley, "We're getting our bedroom painted and Quinn wants purple, but I want green." Quinn cleared the table and followed Sierra out of the living room, with Noah trailing behind.

Alene's father looked appreciatively at Tinley and said, "I'm Cal Baron, by the way. We moved here when Alene was born, and she moved back with her children after her divorce. So, sit down and tell me about yourself. What's your name again, Honey?"

"It's Tinley, like in Tinley Park," she said, still standing.

"Oh, I know Tinley Park. I had a couple-three customers there when I was a financial advisor. Nice little suburb. Is that where you're from?"

"No," she replied, still standing as Bill sat down on the couch. "I'm from all over the place. We moved a lot."

"Well, that sounds exotic," said Cal, leaning forward in his chair. "As Mark Twain said, 'travel is fatal to prejudice, bigotry, and narrow-mindedness.' What do you do for a living, Tinley?"

"I'm a hair stylist, Mr. Baron."

"Call me Cal," he said. "What a nice, practical profession. I bet you cut Bill's hair, so he doesn't have to pay." He patted the couch again and watched as Tinley sat herself next to Bill. "Did you hurt yourself, Honey? Looks like you've got yourself a limp – kind of like me without my walker. You just have to be careful, they keep saying."

Bill said, "Her ex-husband ran over her foot with his car."

"No need to broadcast my problems, Billy," she said, turning to face Cal. "It's really nothing and I hardly feel it anymore."

"That's terrible," Cal said with a concerned frown. "What kind of person does that? I'm glad he's your ex

41

because someone like that doesn't deserve you. The question is what do you see in young William here?" Alene marveled at her father's ability to ask the question innocently, as if he didn't agree with her that Bill was one of Neal's most insufferable and rude friends.

Tinley smiled. "Well, first off, he's the best-looking guy I've ever dated." She punched him lightly on the arm. "And he's strong. Did you know he can bench three fifty?"

Cal smiled and nodded. "You know, Mark Twain also said that it's not the size of the dog in the fight – it's the size of the fight in the dog. You understand what I'm saying? I was pretty darn strong in my day before I got this damn muscle disease. It's nice that Bill can lift weights, but how does he treat you?"

"Like a princess," Bill interrupted. "I definitely treat her like a princess. She's the hottest girl I've ever dated."

Cal said, "Well so far we've established that you're both good-looking. Luckily that'll never change, and you'll always be able to enjoy looking at each other, if nothing else." Bill continued to beam but Tinley blushed.

Alene could not understand what Tinley saw in Bill, aside from his broad shoulders and buff muscles. Once, years ago before Noah was born, the girls were asleep in the next room, and Alene had shushed Neal and Bill. Bill had chortled, "Are you always on your period, Alene, or what?" Then, after he once called Ruthie "Jewthie", Alene told him that if he ever said it again, she'd kick him out of the house. He'd apologized that time, and Alene had been on the verge of thinking that he was redeemable, but he'd messed up repeatedly.

The only thing Alene liked about Bill was his patience with Sandy, his younger brother, who was thirty-eight and lived in a group home on Belmont. Once, at Whipped and Sipped, after Neal had made fun of him, Sandy had curled up into a ball on the floor of the café and put his thumb in his mouth. Neal snickered until Bill pushed him into the empty wall that Alene later repurposed as an art display.

Sandy was responsible for watering the plants inside and outside of his group home and he took his job very seriously. He didn't know how to hold a conversation, but he enjoyed sharing facts about greenery. He also liked to repeat old clichés, song titles, or quotes he heard on television. Whenever she saw him, Alene would ask about his plants. He'd tell her about a brown leaf that he'd removed from a dieffenbachia, or a succulent that had withered, concluding his story with one of his stock phrases, such as, "That's the ticket," or "There's gold in them thar hills." It wasn't that different from Cal's endless jokes, but it was way more irritating.

Sandy was difficult to be around. Alene always tried to teach her children that the function of manners was to make other people feel comfortable. She had trouble explaining how a grown man such as Sandy was still biting his nails, picking his teeth, and pulling out hairs from his head and ears. Alene had an even harder time explaining why the Vanza family treated each other so disrespectfully. Now, when Sierra and Quinn came back to the living room, Alene hoped Bill wouldn't say anything horrible.

Cal had nodded off, which still worried Alene, even though she'd learned that daytime drowsiness was not uncommon in people who suffered from myasthenia gravis. They hadn't figured out a cure yet, but Cal's disease was pretty much under control. As she set the table, there was more shouting from across the hall, and Bill giggled because now they could all hear Joan shrieking at her son, Jack. Tinley smacked Bill on the arm and he stopped.

Alene needed them to leave the apartment, but Cal had woken up again and had started talking about the time when Alene first moved back home after her divorce and how happy she'd been to have Bill's father as a neighbor again.

43

"Did you know that Alene and her sister Lydia used to babysit for Kacey, when Gary first moved into the building?" He asked. "You were already finished with college by then, Bill, so we didn't see much of you."

After that, Cal brought up a run-in Alene had had with Gary's wife. "So, last week, Alene pulled into the underground parking with the children and five bags of groceries. Alberto, you guys know the son of Albert in reception, who works summers in the building. He starts helping her unload. Then Joan walks in all in a tizzy because her car isn't waiting for her. I mean they're good guys down there but sometimes you have to wait a minute until they bring you your car. Anyway, Joan starts hectoring poor Alberto even though he's busy helping Alene."

"Come on, Dad let's not tell stories about people who aren't here, okay? Everyone has a bad day now and then," said Alene, conscious of Sierra carefully listening to every word.

Bill said, "That wasn't even Joan at her worst."

"I shouldn't have said anything," said Cal, "but as Benjamin Franklin famously said: We are all born ignorant, but one must work hard to remain stupid."

"What does that mean?" Quinn asked.

Alene gave her father a warning look, and he responded with a shrug. "I mean that it's not smart to always look for negative things to say. For example, Alene tells me that Joan and Gary's apartment is always sparkling clean."

Alene gave Cal a nod, but Sierra said, "That doesn't make any sense, Grandpa."

Just then someone pounded on the door and Alene jumped up to answer it, glad to end the conversation. Jack stood in the hallway, grubby as usual, and smelling of cigarettes. Maybe Bill was cutting back since he didn't smell nearly as bad as Jack did.

"Hi, Jack," said Alene. "How can I help you?"

44

Jack couldn't even look at Alene directly. He pointed at Bill and Tinley, saying, "Gary wants to talk to you guys." Then he stood uncomfortably, shuffling from side to side.

Tinley stood and marched to the door pulling Bill behind her.

"I like your father, Alene," Tinley said. "He always says exactly what he thinks. Hey, Billy, let's take Jack out for dinner tonight." She wrapped her arm through Jack's and smiled at him. "What do you say, Jack? Are you free?"

Bill shook his head and tossed up his arms in exaggerated exasperation. "See what I mean about what a sweetheart she is? I've avoided the little shit since his mother married my dad and now Tinley invites him to go out with us like every weekend. It's basically worth it because my dad pays."

Alene looked to see if Jack was hurt by the insensitive comments, but he just showed Bill his middle finger. As far as Alene could tell, Jack was not affected by criticism. Maybe that was a positive trait. She ushered them all out the door.

The minute the door closed, Alene decanted a cabernet and rushed to set out the three vegetable dips with crudités and crackers. She flashed to a memory of the building's annual New Year's party when she'd made those same dips. *Before his wedding to Joan, Gary had designed and supervised the building of built-in benches along the walls of the community room. Joan and Gary had paid to have the room redone in time for their wedding reception. One of the city's high-end restaurants had served an outstanding dinner.*

Olly from the café bartended the annual winter party in the community room that year, and while serving eggnog to Alene and Cal, he had whispered that Joan thought he was hitting on her. "As if I were first of all a straight, old guy and second of all a guy who couldn't see or hear," he'd said, chuckling.

"*Maybe she's just trying to be friendly,*" said Cal. "*Mark Twain wrote that kindness is the language which the deaf can hear and the blind can see.*"

"*Let's just say she's drunk way more than a spoonful of sugar,*" said Olly, bouncing away to serve someone else. Alene had gone to the pot-luck buffet and filled plates with pita chips and the three dips she'd brought (creamy citrus cannellini dip, kale and parsley dip, and roasted red pepper and mushroom dip). She carried the plates over to where her father sat and took the seat next to him just as Joan strode past and with a swipe of her arm swept Alene's plate onto her lap. The first thing Alene noticed was that her children were watching, so she just wiped the food from her slacks without making a fuss. As Gary led Joan out the door, Olly helped Alene clean up and said, "*Don't you let that trash dirty your party shoes, Miss A.*" Joan hadn't attended any more parties in the community room.

Now, right on time for Noah's birthday dinner, Ruthie, her husband Benjie, and their three children showed up hot and thirsty. The Rosin children immediately disappeared into the back bedrooms with Sierra, Quinn and Noah.

Alene's sister Lydia and her husband Theo arrived carrying the Batman ice cream cake and the extraordinary Lego set that Noah might be able to finish before leaving for college. Lydia was indeed wearing stunning diamond earrings that Alene made sure to praise loudly enough for Theo to hear. She asked the couple about their anniversary dinner the night before and was treated to a lengthy, detailed account of every spectacular course, its ingredients and its paired wines.

The children appeared again in time for dinner. After much praise for Noah on the food he'd helped prepare, accolades for the magnificent cake, and shouts of glee for the presents, Noah and Ruthie's son played in Noah's room while Alene's and Ruthie's girls played Rummikub at Cal's bridge table. The adults chatted, until Theo announced several times that he had to get up early to run a marathon. Everyone left by nine o'clock, and Alene was happy to clean up and be in bed, by ten.

The following morning, Alene luxuriated in bed, glad it was finally her day off. The crowd would be sparse until later in the morning. Ruthie was probably already experimenting with new pastries or savory bites. Finally, Alene got up and threw in a few loads of laundry, went for a run, emptied the bins at the garbage chute and took the recycling down to the building's basement. Then she showered and got dressed.

She was drinking her second cup of coffee and enjoying the Sunday comics when her dad shuffled into the kitchen, and one by one, the three children joined them. At about ten, she sent Kacey a text inviting her to join them for a walk to the zoo or to join her later for a drive to the airport to pick up Brianne Flynn.

Brianne was returning from a visit to her daughter in D.C., who'd been Kacey's best friend through childhood, and who'd recently graduated from college. Alene thought again that it a shame Kacey had spent so much time in rehab, during the years she might have been enjoying university life. Kacey usually lived with Gary and Joan across the hall, except for short periods either at a rehab facility or with her mother, the cranky health-nut who had been Gary's second wife. Kacey could be thoughtful and helpful when she wasn't fighting her addictions, but it was a constant struggle. In Alene's view, Gary and Joan's condo did not provide a healthy atmosphere for someone who needed the kind of extra care and attention that Kacey did.

Once, when Kacey was still a kid and Alene was babysitting during one of her weekend visits, Kacey mentioned in that offhand way teenagers have that Gary and Joan had separate bedrooms. She was trying to explain why there was so much laundry and probably didn't realize what she was telling Alene. Poor Gary – Joan was his third wife, but apparently third was not the charm. After all, she'd had an affair with the husband of at least one neighbor.

Instead of responding to Alene's text, Kacey appeared in the kitchen moments later and said, "I can't spend that much time in the sun, but I can go to the airport with you."

"Perfect," said Alene. "Meet me here at two."

Both of Brianne's children had gone to college in Washington D.C. and had taken jobs there. Brianne was always blue in the weeks leading up to the anniversary of the day her husband had died, so she'd gone to visit her children that week. Just before Brianne's trip, Alene had accompanied her to the police station to ask, yet again, about any accidental bicycle collisions in Chicago which might finally provide a connection to the one that had killed Dennis. Eight years had passed, but Brianne wouldn't stop trying.

Alene took the kids to do errands and to the zoo, where she bought them popcorn, as promised. There was a lot of griping about heat and fatigue on the mile-long walk home. She blended a gazpacho and served it with homemade rolls for lunch, before letting the kids lie in her bed watching a movie while Cal enjoyed yet another Cubs game in the living room.

At two o'clock, Kacey and Alene went down together to get Alene's car. On the drive to the airport, they discussed hiring Jack at the cafe. Kacey said, "At least he has thick skin, so nothing you say will hurt his feelings. Not even when you're upset and barking at everyone and I have to close my eyes and cover my ears."

"Oh my, does that happen a lot?" Alene asked with a worried glance at Kacey as they sailed south on Lake Shore Drive.

"Just sometimes when you're stressed," said Kacey, looking down at her hands.

Alene thought she tried to be patient with everyone, but especially with Kacey. "I'm sorry if I upset you," she said.

"Well, you don't usually snap at me, but..."

Alene interrupted her. "You mean I snap at other people and that upsets you?"

"Sometimes," said Kacey, her voice barely above a whisper.

"Like when, for example?"

Kacey thought for a moment. "Like when you shout at Edith, and then it's almost like I can hardly breathe."

Alene tried to count her breaths as a slowdown at the exit made her more agitated than necessary. She thought she always handled Edith calmly. She said, "I don't actually shout, do I?"

Kacey sank further into her seat and stared straight ahead. "It's more like you're sarcastic and impatient."

"Oh," said Alene, suddenly feeling like she had no business running a cafe. "I'm sorry if I do that."

Kacey said, "Well, it's not necessarily your fault, when she chooses that moment to complain about her feet or something. It makes me crazy too."

"Oh," said Alene again, wondering if she lashed out at anyone besides Edith.

Kacey continued, still looking straight ahead. "But, I was just trying to say that you could yell at Jack to jump up and down, clean platters, scrub toilets, or whatever you want, and it won't bother him. It would bother me, but he won't care. That's what I mean."

"So, that's a good thing?" Alene asked.

"Exactly," said Kacey. "I didn't mean to make you feel bad, Alene. You're really a great boss and you're one of the most important people in my life. I appreciate having you as a friend. Jack just seems oblivious to other people's feelings...."

Alene felt somewhat boosted by Kacey's affirmation. "Your dad asked me to hire him."

A few moments passed before Kacey said, "Maybe you can set up some guidelines before he starts so he won't make you nuts. I can handle him, most of the time." She turned on the radio and Alene understood that the conversation was over. When they stopped to pick up Brianne, Kacey got into the back seat. The ride home was slower because traffic towards the city had increased in the hour since they left home. Alene and Brianne chatted, but Kacey responded to their occasional questions with one-syllable answers only.

As they were nearing their building, Kacey asked to be dropped in front, where Olly was going to meet her, as they planned to walk over to the movie theater on Clark. Alene and Brianne exchanged a smile, happy that Kacey was going to do something fun with a friend.

After Kacey got out of the car, Alene pulled around to the garage entrance and rode up the elevator with Brianne, reminding her as they ascended to come over for pizza and salad at about five-thirty. Each of the women approached her own door and let herself in. Alene had just dumped her purse on the front hall table and was about to greet her father, before checking on the kids, when she heard Brianne scream like a wounded animal.

Chapter 5

Alene ran back into the hallway and jiggled Brianne's door handle.

"Brianne?" she shouted.

She grabbed the keys from her pocket, unlocked the door and rushed up the hallway past the kitchen to where Brianne stood in the back of the dining room. Her first impression was that the room was a mess. The shelves were nearly empty. The Rosenthal vases that had belonged to Brianne's mother were lined up like soldiers on the coffee table. The gems and books that Brianne's husband Dennis had collected were bunched in piles on the floor. And a large man wearing fleece pants and a sweatshirt was lying face down on the dining room rug. Alene sucked in her breath.

"It's Gary Vanza," said Brianne, skirting the piles to reach him. She checked for a pulse. "He's dead."

Alene stared. "But I just saw him this morning heading to the garbage chute." She realized how little sense that made once she'd said it and stood glued to the floor focused on the small blue towel in Gary's hand. They were always taking those towels from the trainer's gym by mistake. Alene had a stack of them at home. Blood was seeping out from his right side and spreading onto the yellow rug that Brianne hated and kept saying she was going to replace. Alene saw that Gary was completely still, no longer breathing.

Grabbing her cell from her back pocket, Alene asked, "Where's Kacey? Do you think she and Olly are already at the theater by now?" She took a breath.

"What if they were attacked, too?" Brianne asked with her hand over her mouth. "Or what if..."

Alene pulled Brianne into the tidy kitchen and sank onto a chair as she punched 911 on her cell. Leaning forward, Alene's mind raced. She glanced at the empty shelves. Had someone been searching for something specific? Was anything missing? It could have been a robber, but didn't they usually just run in and out, after grabbing jewelry, cameras and laptops? Had Gary interrupted a robbery in Brianne's apartment? Alene had to clear her throat a few times before any sound would come out. The 911 operator made her repeat the address and apartment number.

Alene texted Gary's son, Bill: "*Come to Brianne's ASAP.*" She added a note for him to contact his brother Sandy, who was too worried about electromagnetic radiation to own a wireless phone.

Brianne poured glasses of water for them both and slumped into the chair next to Alene. "Oh my God, poor Kacey," she moaned into her hands. "Losing her father is going to totally derail that poor girl." She pulled out her cell phone and texted Olly to bring Kacey back ASAP. She showed Alene the message.

"Now we've got to tell Joan," said Alene, jumping up from her seat to knock on the door directly across from hers. She ran back into the kitchen reporting that nobody had answered. "It doesn't seem appropriate to text her, so maybe I'll just leave a message instead." After a moment of wavering, she called Joan's cell and said, "There's been an accident and you should come over to Brianne's as soon as possible." She wondered if Joan would take the time to listen. She assumed their dislike of one another was reciprocal. Maybe she should have added the word, "please."

Brianne looked up at Alene and said, "What about Gary's sister? He's been taking care of Edith for most of her life. Now that poor woman won't have anyone."

When she'd bought the café, Alene had promised Gary that she would keep his sister on. Edith already brooded about everything, so how would she react now that she had something serious to think about? "She'll still have Bill, Sandy and Kacey," said Alene, looking through her list of employee numbers, "although she doesn't have a stellar relationship with any of Gary's kids."

Brianne said, "I think she cares about Kacey – that's why she harps on her all the time."

"I'm sure it makes Kacey feel loved," said Alene as she dialed and waited for Edith to answer. Brianne gave her a disapproving look. Both Ruthie and Brianne thought that Edith was hard-working and loyal and that Alene needed to be more forgiving. But just the day before, Edith had said, "My shoes are ratty because my wealthy brother and sister-in-law are planning to take a cruise."

Why was it Gary's job to buy her shoes? Olly enjoyed the sparring. He'd retorted, "I've been on my own without a single rich brother since I was sixteen, Edith."

Edith had groused, "My brother's going to be sorry one day." Waiting for Edith to answer her phone, Alene wondered if today was that day. Could Edith do such a thing?

Alene was about to end the call and write a text message when Edith answered with her usual brusqueness. "Yes, what is it?"

She could have said hello, thought Alene. Unless she'd just murdered her brother and was feigning innocence. Gary was certainly a lot bigger than Edith, but she was cunning and quicker. Maybe they'd gone together to Brianne's to borrow a book or look at the old gem collection. Edith could have been holding a chef's knife, maybe waiting until Gary was facing the other way. She could have sneaked up and attacked him from behind. Maybe she counted on inheriting his fortune.

And if Edith could kill her own brother, she wouldn't have any problem murdering a disliked boss.

Alene said, "Something's happened at Brianne's and you need to come over as soon as possible, Edith. Do you understand?"

"Well you're speaking English, aren't you?" Edith responded. "Do you always have to talk to me like I'm stupid? I'm in the middle of something. I have a life of my own, as surprising as that sounds."

Edith clicked off before Alene could continue. If Edith had killed Gary, she'd probably pretend everything was fine, and would try to be extra nice to throw everyone off. The fact that she was as bitchy as usual led Alene to think she could be crossed off a list of possible suspects.

Brianne asked, "What if he was trying to stop a robbery? He was always looking out for all of us."

"Yeah, I thought about that too," said Alene. "But we haven't had a robbery in this building for over ten years."

They heard the door open and Kacey appeared at the kitchen door. Olly, just behind her, pulled out chairs at the kitchen table, saying, "I'm delivering Kacey as requested."

Brianne moaned into her hands. Kacey looked confused. "What's the matter," she asked. "The movie starts in twenty minutes."

Alene said, "There's been an accident, Kacey." She swallowed. "It's your dad. We walked in and found him here."

54

Kacey swallowed. "What?" she asked. Her eyes were shiny through her glasses.

"He's been hurt," said Brianne, pointing into the dining room. "He's in there."

Olly was already at Gary's side. Kacey followed him and they stood stock still for several moments before she turned and asked, "What happened?" She leaned forward to pick up a stray geode. Her face was colorless.

Alene stood at the entrance to the kitchen and said, "Don't touch anything, Kacey, honey. The police will want to look for fingerprints. It must have happened sometime today, because I just saw your dad this morning. He held open the door to the garbage chute for me."

"He was always such a gentleman," said Brianne, who'd joined Alene at the opening to the dining room.

Olly wiped his eyes. "I thought he was the best kind of gentleman." He put his arm around Kacey, who stiffened. She opened and closed her mouth but said nothing.

Alene wondered if she'd let herself cry. "I'm so sorry, Kacey," she said.

The doorbell rang and because Brianne didn't move, Alene went to answer. A plain-clothed police officer showed her his badge and introduced himself along with two uniformed policemen, standing behind him. She introduced herself, immediately forgot their names, and led them to the dining room where Kacey, Olly and Brianne were still staring at Gary's body.

"That's our friend and neighbor Gary Vanza on the floor. This is Brianne Flynn," said Alene, feeling more and more miserable, "and this is her apartment. This is Kacey Vanza, who lives across the hallway with Gary and his wife, Joan. This is Olly Burns, Kacey's friend who also works at Whipped and Sipped."

"Kacey is Gary's daughter," added Olly.

"Thank you." The policeman directed the other two towards the dining room and opened an electronic notebook. He looked up said, "I'm Officer Frank Shaw. Please accept condolences from all of us. I know this is difficult, but I'd like to speak to each of you, one at a time."

The doorbell rang again, and one of the two uniformed policemen answered it while Alene, Brianne, Olly and Kacey sat stiffly at the kitchen table. Alene wondered what Gary had been doing in Brianne's apartment. When Dennis was still alive, the two of them used to be back and forth all the time. They had each other's keys, so getting in the door wouldn't have been difficult, but why? Two technicians of some kind passed through the kitchen, each raising a hand in silent greeting as they headed towards Gary.

Returning to the kitchen, Officer Shaw said, "Again, I'm so sorry for your loss. I know this is really painful. Do any of you know of anyone who might have wanted to harm Gary?"

Kacey looked down as Olly rubbed the back of her neck.

Officer Shaw, still standing, continued in a softer, gentle voice. "Would you please tell me a little about your dad, Kacey? It could help us figure out what happened here."

"Kacey works in my cafe here in Lakeview." said Alene, as if that would clarify anything, adding, "It's the Whipped and Sipped Café."

"How long have you worked there?" he asked. Kacey took off her glasses and wiped them. Alene saw her tapping her foot under the table.

Olly tried to answer for Kacey, "She's been there nearly as long as me, nearly eight years. Her dad used to own the place."

"I bought the café from Gary," said Alene, "and Kacey is my assistant." Alene didn't think it was the right time to say anything about Kacey's addictions, or her stints in rehab. The police could find that out. "Gary adored her."

"She was his favorite child," added Olly.

Officer Shaw smiled and repeated, "I'll want to speak to each of you, one at a time." Alene understood that he wanted Kacey to answer for herself and felt a little embarrassed. He added, "So please stay put until I get a chance to get to you."

"I have to run next door to make dinner for my family," said Alene, "but I'll come back as soon as I can." Pizza with Brianne would have to be postponed. On her way out, she was glad to see both Olly and Brianne moving their chairs closer to Kacey's.

The officer bobbed his head. "Please give your contact information to my colleague before you leave." He turned away as the other officer approached her and wrote down her name and number. She got the sense that the first officer disapproved of her leaving. Well, too bad.

In the quiet hallway, Alene decided to knock on Gary and Joan's door. Joan was probably out spending money, as usual. She wasn't the kind of person who stayed home on a nice summer afternoon. On the other hand, what if she'd stayed home in order to murder her husband?

Alene remembered that Gary had been clasping a little blue towel, the one their trainer used in his gym, so she messaged Michael to ask when he'd last seen Gary Vanza. She knocked on the Vanzas' door again, but there was still no answer, so she slipped out her key and let herself in. If Joan was there, she could always say that she was looking for Kacey. Everything seemed to be in order in the front hall, living room, kitchen and dining room. She didn't peek in the bedrooms just in case Joan was napping, or Jack was at home.

Alene hurried back across the hall to her own apartment. The door was unlocked as usual. Since they had a doorman, and nothing ever happened, they'd always felt completely safe in the building. Now she'd need to give the kids keys and retrain them about locking the door. Her father and children were sitting together with all eyes glued on a nature special.

She opened the refrigerator and freezer. She needed a few minutes to pull her thoughts together before telling them about Gary and cooking lemon-leek chicken seemed like a good way to soothe her nerves. She pulled out celery, carrots and leeks, a large package of frozen chicken thighs, and a container of frozen chicken stock. Should she come right out and say that Gary was murdered, or should she build up to it with a story about appreciating our family and friends? She chopped the vegetables and sautéed them in a little olive oil, defrosted the stock in the microwave and added it to the pot along with the chicken. Nothing she said could cushion the blow – she should just be honest without giving too many details. She covered the pot and feeling a little more in control of her emotions, went to tell her father and children about Gary.

Alene took a deep breath and turned off the television. "I have some bad news."

Even her father complained, adding his dismayed voice to the children's sighs. "We were in the middle of a show about sharks, Alene!"

Alene joined them all on the couch. "I'm sorry, everyone, but sometimes really sad things happen. Our good friend Gary Vanza passed away today."

Gary always remembered their birthdays, let them read the comic books he'd saved from when his children were young, popped in with ice cream or showed up with tickets for fun events. He often stopped by to visit Cal and would chat with them all. The kids loved him. Cal considered him to be one of his best friends, although Gary was over a decade younger.

Noah, a sensitive child, looked down at his hands quietly. Sierra and Quinn sat up straight and took turns asking questions. "Why? Did he have a heart attack? Is it something we can catch? Why didn't they call a doctor?"

Alene stretched her neck. "It was too late to save him, but the doctors will figure out what happened." She didn't mention the mess in the dining room, or the possibility that Gary was murdered because of a botched robbery.

"I peeked out the door when I heard some noise, and saw policemen going in," said Noah. "I said hello to Kacey, but she was rushing and didn't even wave."

Alene improvised. "The police need to come when there's a death at home." That sounded less scary than, "When someone is murdered at home."

"I thought someone got hurt, because I saw ambulance guys too," Sierra reported.

"Does that mean Uncle Gary's already an angel?" Quinn asked.

Sierra hissed at her sister. "Don't ask dumb questions."

Alene said, "Please don't start bickering now, girls. Quinnie, we already talked about how angels are something you can't prove, but lots of people like to believe in them. That's a different subject, and all we need to think about right now is how to be extra nice to Kacey. She just lost her father." Alene felt a little guilty about not mentioning anyone else who might be upset about Gary's death, such as his wife and other children. "This will be a difficult time for everyone who loved Gary."

Alene's father spoke softly, shaking his head. "What a shame. He was in the prime of his life. Mark Twain once said that a man who lives fully is prepared to die at any time, and I think it's wonderful that Gary lived fully."

Quinn pouted and said, "I was just asking about the angel. Anyway, I'm going to draw a picture for Kacey right now." She cheered up visibly, pleased with her idea.

"That's a really thoughtful idea, Sweetie." Alene got up and headed to the door.

Sierra muttered, "She's just doing it for attention." Alene flashed a warning look at Sierra.

"When are you coming back?" Noah asked.

"I'll be back for dinner in about forty-five minutes, but right now I need to help Brianne and Kacey," she told them, opening the door. "Quinnie, please set the table and help your sister make the salad. Sierra honey, please remove the chicken from the soup when the timer goes off and add a cup of orzo to the pot. I'll add the lemon and dill when I get back. Noah, please pour water for everyone, and do it slowly so you don't spill. Okay, guys? Ask Grandpa if you have any questions."

"I have a question: why are we having chicken?" Sierra asked.

Quinn added, "Yeah, you said Brianne was coming over for pizza and salad."

"We always need to be ready for plans to change, girls," said Alene as she left.

While she'd been gone, a few more people had arrived. Alene thought one was probably a medical examiner and others were there to transport Gary's body. Officer Shaw and the original team seemed to be finished taking notes, measuring, and photographing. Brianne, Kacey and Olly were still sitting around the kitchen table. As Alene joined them, Officer Shaw approached holding a plastic bag. They all looked up.

"Do any of you recognize this?" He asked, not mentioning where they'd found the gun that was inside the bag. She wondered if he'd waited until she came back to show it to them. They'd probably found it immediately after they'd arrived.

Brianne said, "We keep a registered gun at the bar I run, but I don't have one here."

"It might have been Gary's. He used to talk about protecting his family," said Olly. "He was worried about the

60

government taking away gun rights, and he took his kids for shooting lessons, but Kacey sucked at it."

Kacey said, "I learned about gun safety, though. Sandy refused to even touch it, but I think Bill has a gun permit." Her eyes had sunk into her face.

Alene looked at the officer. "Bill is Gary's eldest son. I texted him, so he might show up. Gary's younger son, Sandy, doesn't believe in cell phones so I'm not sure when he'll find out about his dad."

Shaw acknowledged her and asked the group, "Does anyone else on the sixth floor carry a gun?" He spoke with a note of compassion in his voice instead of business-like precision. Alene thought something about him seemed familiar. Maybe he'd given her a speeding ticket or stopped her once when she'd forgotten to update her city vehicle sticker.

Kacey asked, "Was that used to shoot my dad?"

"Your father wasn't shot, Kacey." For some reason they were all relieved. "But this was in his pocket. It's not registered. Was Mr. Vanza worried about something in particular, or did he always carry a weapon?"

Kacey shrugged. Olly said, "Maybe her stepbrother, Bill, knows. If he wasn't shot, how was Gary killed?"

It seemed as if the police and technicians had been studying the murder scene for a long time. They'd gone over every inch of the dining room with their latex gloves, cataloguing and photographing everything. Now they were standing in the dining room taking notes and talking quietly. Officer Shaw turned to confer with another officer as Brianne, Kacey, Olly and Alene held their collective breath. "It looks as if he was stabbed, but we won't have cause of death for a few days." Shaw answered softly and waited a moment before continuing. "Why was Gary Vanza in this apartment while Brianne Flynn was out of town?"

Brianne answered, "Maybe he was trying to stop a robbery or something. We all have each other's keys. I mean Gary, Kacey, Alene and I have each other's keys."

Shaw nodded at Brianne and turned to Kacey. "Did you notice anything unusual in the last few days, Kacey? Was your dad worried about anything in particular?"

Kacey shook her head, still colorless and sweaty. They were all exhausted. Brianne said, "He was taking drugs to lower his cholesterol."

Alene thought about all the times Gary had shown up at her apartment or at Brianne's. Sometimes he dropped off fresh peaches from the farmer's market, sometimes he was there snaking a clogged sink or re-painting a scratch he'd noticed on the wall. Maybe he'd let himself into Brianne's apartment, knowing that she was due home later in the day, to fix something. Maybe he was browsing the bookshelves, which were filled with Brianne's enormous cookbook collection along with how-to manuals, novels, histories and biographies, science and nature journals, and books about gemstones.

Alene loved browsing those bookshelves too. She said, "Sometimes he would walk around our apartment looking for things that needed tightening or fixing or painting."

Brianne said, "Sometimes I've come home late from the bar and there's Gary drinking a glass of wine in my living room, all by himself. I think sometimes he just needed a little get-away."

The officer smiled. "I don't often see neighbors spending so much time together. You've got something special going on here on the sixth floor. Does anyone know if Gary had any enemies or anyone who wanted to cause him harm?" Shaw asked. Nobody answered. "Is there anything else any of you can tell me, perhaps about this gun?"

Brianne said, "I remember Gary buying a gun after some reckless bike rider knocked my husband down on the bike path across Lake Shore Drive, eight years ago. Dennis and Gary were best friends. My husband died in the ambulance on the way to the hospital." She paused to wipe her eyes with the back of her hand. "They said he had a heart attack. It was a horrible accident."

Olly said, "Gary didn't think it was an accident."

Shaw looked down at his notes and stroked his chin. "I might have been one of the first responders that day. Your husband's name was Dennis Flynn? That sounds familiar. Was your daughter with him that day? I recall a young girl there. Then there was another woman who went into labor and...." He stopped for a moment and looked at Alene.

"Mrs. Alene Dunn," he continued. "I was the one who drove you to the hospital and held your hand while you gave birth to your son."

Alene froze. Had he recognized her from the moment he walked in?

"Mrs. Dunn, you're the only one I still haven't talked to, not including the family members who haven't yet arrived." He looked at the rest of them and said, "We'll try to be out of your way soon, folks. I'm so sorry this has to take so much time. Now, please follow me, Mrs. Dunn."

Alene walked behind him slowly, to the living room. He politely offered her a seat on the couch before sitting opposite her on one of Brianne's swivel chairs that her kids liked to swirl in. He turned it right and left while Alene cringed, remembering that her waters had broken and it had looked as if she'd peed in her pants when he'd taken her to the hospital with his siren on.

He couldn't have known how much being called by her married name upset her. She opened her mouth to say she'd meant to contact the police department to thank him back then after his help during Noah's birth, but it hardly seemed relevant at the moment.

Battered: A Whipped and Sipped Mystery

Chapter 6

She thought she'd introduced herself as Alene Baron. Now it didn't feel right to explain that she was divorced. "Well, um..."

She noticed his muscular neck and wondered if he'd played football. He interrupted, "Small world isn't it?" He gestured for her to sit down on the living room couch and sat across from her in Brianne's comfortable swivel chair. "I know this is exhausting and awful for everyone."

Alene gaped at him. She liked his strong chin and broad forehead. He'd rushed her to the hospital and helped her through Noah's birth. She'd have to try not to snap at him if he called her Mrs. Dunn again.

He swiveled in the chair and said, "I'm sorry I have to grill you like this, but your answers might help us, so let's start with when you last saw Mr. Vanza."

"This morning," she answered. "We both happened to be throwing our garbage down the chute at the same time." Alene focused on his hands, the hands of someone who worked outdoors or with tools.

"Did the two of you talk?"

She gazed into his clear, deep-set gray eyes and tried to remember, "Maybe a little but I don't know what it was about."

"I understand that you and Kacey Vanza drove Brianne Flynn home from the airport today. Can you go over what happened when you got back, Mrs. Dunn?"

Alene clamped her mouth shut. How could she tell him her correct name now that he'd brought up Gary? He must have noticed her unease, and said, "I appreciate your having returned here to Mrs. Flynn's apartment after taking care of your children. Is everything all right?"

It was decent of him to ask. He stopped swiveling and bent his head forward as he spoke, as though he really wanted to hear her answer. "I just prepared dinner," replied Alene, noticing that he didn't wear a wedding ring and that his finger nails were clean and trimmed. "I'll have to go back to settle everyone in."

"I'd be grateful if you could start from the moment you unlocked the door, Mrs. Dunn," said Shaw.

She had to say something.

"Listen, Officer Shaw, I'm divorced, and I actually go by my given name now, Alene Baron. Please just call me Alene." She didn't want to tell him that her husband's affair with Gary's wife had precipitated the divorce.

"Oh. Okay, thank you, Alene." He gave her a quick smile. "I'm sorry to hear that you went through a divorce."

That both surprised and pleased her. Gary's death was making Alene feel lonelier than usual. "Well, I'm sorry I never thanked you for your help during my labor and Noah's birth, Officer Shaw."

"You thanked me a hundred times that day so forget about it – and please call me Frank."

He was the kind of polite guy Alene had hoped to meet someday. She knew she didn't present herself as someone who was interested in dating anymore. In the year after her divorce she'd worn too much eyeliner and heels that were too high, but at least she'd cared about how she looked when her friends dragged her out for an evening. When had she gotten too lazy to do more than tie her hair back in a ponytail and smear some gloss on her lips?

Frank looked like he was checking through the Rolodex of his memories.

"I was on patrol back then and taking you to the hospital was probably the highlight of an otherwise mundane day."

"I guess I forgot about you, once I brought the baby home," she said, thinking to herself, "Oh my, how do I take that back?"

Frank said. "You were probably pretty busy. You look the same, though. I mean except you were pregnant." He reddened.

Except for the wrinkles and the ten extra pounds. "I remember that you stayed until Noah popped out, but I was too busy screaming to pay close attention. Sorry about that, Officer Shaw."

He grinned. "It's Frank. Of course, I stayed with you. Nobody should go through that alone."

She'd always tried to bury some of that day. "My ex-husband didn't show up until I was in recovery. You held my hand during those awful contractions, and you stayed through the birth."

"I've never been gripped so hard in my life." He chuckled. "I have two children of my own."

"Jeez." So, she'd managed to remind him of how she'd been at her absolute worst – blotchy, screaming, and completely crazed.

"Later that summer I got transferred to a different department, and again, I'm sorry I never followed through," he said.

"That was exactly eight years ago." She couldn't help remembering that Dennis had probably suffered that fatal heart attack about the same time she'd been struggling through labor and giving birth to Noah. Maybe Officer Shaw had forgotten the part when she pooped a little during delivery. "I know, because yesterday we celebrated Noah's eighth birthday," Alene told him.

"Congratulations. I hope he had a great day." He went back to swiveling and glanced over to the dining room. "Back to Gary Vanza – you ran into each other at the garbage chute?"

"Yeah, and he looked totally fine." Alene said, noting how he'd brought the conversation back to that. "We wished each other a good morning and asked each other how things were."

"Okay," Shaw nodded. "I understand you all loved him."

"That's true." He was a good friend.

"What about the other families that live on this floor?"

Alene shifted positions, wondering if the casual chatting was a technique for getting information. She certainly did feel calmer – for the first time since they'd found Gary. "Can I just ask you if anything was taken?"

"That's something we need to figure out," said Frank. "But our first order of business is the relationships between your families."

Alene leaned sideways from the couch and partially saw into the kitchen where Brianne, Kacey and Olly were still sitting. "Well, we really are in and out of each other's apartments all the time, so it's not a mystery that Gary was here. Maybe he was just in the wrong place at the wrong time. What if the burglar shocked him into having a heart attack? Remember that hit-and-run biker, who probably caused Dennis Flynn's heart attack? What if it was something like that?"

He leaned closer, and she tried to make leaning back seem as though she was straightening her posture. "The cause of death is unclear, but he was definitely stabbed, Alene."

Alene inhaled sharply, "With what?"

"We'll know more after the autopsy," Frank answered.

Maybe police officers are trained not to give information, she thought. "Okay, but Gary is tall and broad," she said. "Wouldn't stabbing him have been difficult? I mean, someone would have had to know how to stab such a big guy in the exact right place. It's not all that easy."

Frank simultaneously frowned, raised his eyebrows, and nodded. "Let's circle back to the people for now and return to the details later. What can you tell me about your personal relationship with Gary?"

"We've been good friends for years. I was in middle school when he moved in with his second wife, Isobel. My sister Lydia and I babysat for Kacey, their daughter, whom you just met," Alene said. She barreled ahead thinking about all the murder mysteries she'd read, "You know, you can hurt someone with a knife or a tool, but stabbing requires either medical precision or good luck. Gary might have already been close to the ground or sitting down. I don't think anyone would have tried to bring down such a big guy unless it was a sure thing. Also, how do we know it was only one person? What if there were several of them working together? How do we know they didn't kill Gary in the kitchen and drag him into the dining room?"

"There was no blood anywhere else, Alene, and no signs like the scraping of chairs. It looks as if he was stabbed right where he fell. So, did you socialize with Gary and Joan?" He was speaking more quickly. Maybe she'd annoyed him by playing detective.

"We hang out with Gary, all the time," said Alene, putting a slight emphasis on his name. She was unable to stop herself from further theorizing. "Maybe the murderer was tall, then. That could have worked. It could have been someone he knew, as well, because there are no signs of forced entry, right?"

He tilted his head. "You're not going to answer my questions until I answer yours?"

"I told you that we hang out, sometimes," said Alene. "I can assure you that Gary wasn't killed in his own apartment. I just checked, and it looked and smelled as if the cleaning lady had just left."

His eyes narrowed. "You entered the victim's apartment in the middle of a police investigation? Why would you do that? What if it was the cleaning lady who stabbed Gary?"

"Well, I didn't mean that she literally cleaned there today," said Alene. "She doesn't work on Sundays."

Shaw looked at her with a stern expression. "You said you were going next door to make dinner for your children."

"I knocked first," she said.

To avoid his disapproving gaze, Alene looked around the living room at the treasures Brianne and her husband had collected, while he was still alive. She admired the vibrant Murano glass chandelier hanging from the ceiling. Alene always enjoyed Brianne's stories about the little Greek village where she and Dennis had found a treasured vase, or the shop along the Seine where they'd first fallen in love with the painting hanging on the wall above the couch.

Another plain-clothed officer entered the apartment. Frank introduced him as his partner and rose to confer with him, while Alene leaned forward to look into the dining room again. The cobalt-blue ceramic vase, filled with dried hydrangea, was still standing undisturbed. The large conch shell from a trip Dennis's mother took to the west coast of Florida in the early 60's, and a striking three-D printed Fibonacci clock, were on the hardwood floor. She wondered if the police had lifted each piece to test for fingerprints. Now the partner went into the kitchen and Officer Shaw turned back to Alene.

She said, "I'm sorry if peeking in the Vanzas' apartment was wrong, but I'm just trying to help. That answer to your question is that nearly everyone in the building liked Gary. He was a good guy and a wonderful neighbor."

"What made him a good neighbor?" Shaw asked, now seating himself next to Alene on the couch.

She thought for a moment as she sank back against the cushions. "After he designed and built those bookshelves in the café, he built them in Brianne's dining room and at my dad's place. He was helpful with my dad, fixed things for us, and would stop over to say he was doing a grocery run, did we need anything? When the Vanzas first moved in, I used to go over there whenever my sister got on my nerves, or when I just needed a break from home. That was before Gary married Joan."

He paused a moment before asking softly, "What can you tell me about Joan Vanza?" He made it sound like a friendly question, but it was statistically likely that Gary had been stabbed by someone he knew. How likely was it that the person who stabbed him was his wife?

"Joan Stone. She never changed her name." said Alene. "She's one of those people who are addicted to having a perfect body, so she's had work done. Her make-up is always perfectly applied." To be honest, Alene was a little envious about the make-up.

"She was always a little jealous of how much Gary loves Kacey. Gary never seemed to notice that something was off about her." Would he think she was just a gossipy neighbor?

"He used to join my dad and kids and me at Grant Park concerts, because Joan wouldn't go." Alene tried not to say Joan's name with a weightiness that implied distaste. "Even my children loved Gary, because he always had candy for them and never forgot their birthdays. Last week he got Noah a remote-controlled helicopter, which broke, unfortunately, when Noah crashed it into the wall, but Gary said he'd fix it."

"He sounds like a nice guy," said Detective Shaw.

"He and Brianne's late husband Dennis were like brothers." Alene said, wiping her eyes. "They met years ago when they both worked for the same electronics company. That's where Gary met Joan, too, but he was still married to his second wife, then. Joan is his third wife, and in my opinion, she hasn't been much of a wife."

"How so?" he asked. Had he moved closer to her? It was a little disconcerting.

"This may be more than you want to know," she said, feeling like she lost time on earth every time she told this story, "but while Neal and I were still married, he and Joan used to go gambling together every week. I mean they did more than gambling. She's older than Neal but as I mentioned, she works hard to look younger. Maybe they still see each other, but he's no longer my husband, so I don't care."

Shaw got it right away, and said, "It must be tough to live across the hall from her."

Alene grimaced. "You have no idea. Her son, Jack, is kind of a lost soul. He came by the café on Friday and asked me for a job, but he doesn't have a resume or any experience. Gary asked me to hire him, and I – well – the thing is that Jack Stone is his step-son, but I think the only job he has ever had was working for Dennis at the bar next door to the café. He's my sister's age, about thirty-four, but he has almost no work experience. Gary tries really hard to be accepting." Alene realized with a start that she'd just used the present tense to refer to Gary.

Shaw asked, "Are you going to hire him?"

Alene heaved a sigh. "I was going to discuss it with Gary. I couldn't have bought the café without his help, and the only thing he ever asked of me, until this, was to keep his sister and daughter on."

"Gary's sister is -" he checked his notes, "Edith Vanza?"

"Yes. That's another story. She's another one who's not easy to be around. She's a competent employee, but I think she has a serious psychological problem and she refuses to go to a therapist or take medicine. I think there's also something wrong with Jack. He's always coming into the café and sitting there doing nothing. Sometimes he just watches me. He's like a stalker." Why was she blathering? Maybe Frank brought out the worst in her.

He squinted at her and folded his arms across his chest. "You could report him if he's stalking you."

Alene sat up straight and stammered, "I didn't know there was a law against being a pest."

"I'd be happy to help you with it," said the detective. "Stalkers often get more and more aggressive, so you might want to stop him now. It could help later, if his behavior escalates."

She felt bad for telling on Jack. Ruthie would remind her that everyone has limitations, and Alene should just strive to be kind. She continued, "I'm no psychologist, as I said, so I don't know if Jack's dangerous or just pitiful. On the other hand, it is possible that he followed Gary across the hall, stabbed him, and then left the building."

Shaw sat there just waiting for her to continue, as if he had all the time in the world. Alene's stomach grumbled. She scooped some spicy pecans from a crystal bowl that Brianne kept on the distressed-wood coffee table next to the couch – always the hostess. She offered him the bowl and he took a handful.

He chewed and his eyes widened. "These are delicious."

She grinned. "Our pastry chef makes them, and we sell them in little cloth bags at the Whipped and Sipped Café. Ruthie is brilliant and imaginative, and she loves coating healthy things with chocolate or spices. Everything she makes is healthier than the usual pastry or candy. She's my best friend."

"I'll definitely want to meet her and taste some of her goods," he said, leaning towards her and smiling. "Now, let's focus for a moment on Gary's daughter, Kacey. She told me that she works for you at your café." He probably learned the leaning part as a technique, to get information out of people, but it didn't stop her falling for it.

Alene nodded. "I've already told you that she's my assistant." Alene wondered why he was spending so much time with her even though she wasn't one of the main witnesses. She felt herself stiffen – what if she was a suspect?

"I'd say everyone loves Kacey," she continued, "except for Edith Vanza, who doesn't seem to like anyone, and she's always fighting with Kacey. By the way, I left a message for Edith, but she still hasn't shown up."

"What do Kacey and Edith fight about?"

"Oh, it's usually stupid stuff," said Alene, "but sometimes it's about Kacey falling off the wagon. She's twenty-four and really can't afford to live on her own, so she still lives with Gary and Joan most of the time. Edith thinks Gary coddles her and lets her get away with a lot of shit."

"So, Edith is upset when Kacey does things that are unhealthy or unsafe?" Shaw asked. "That sounds typical of any loving family member."

She pondered that with a long sigh. "I think Edith is sort of tragic. She fights a lot with Joan, as well. I always ask Edith for help in the kitchen when Joan comes in, to keep them apart."

"I plan to question both of them." He looked down at his notes and it seemed as if he was about to dismiss her, but then he asked, "What can you tell me about Gary's sons?"

Alene answered, "You've probably heard a lot about them already. Bill, the older son, sells used cars at my ex-husband's dealership and is one of Neal's closest friends. They've done a lot of stupid things together – maybe they just concocted some foolish plan to get more money out of Gary. They're all about the money. I'm not accusing them of murder or anything, I'm just saying they're capable of anything. Anyway, Sandy, the younger son, is autistic and lives in a group home. He doesn't interact well with the world." She wanted to slap herself, so she'd stop talking.

Alene crossed her legs and wondered why Gary's death brought all this stuff to the surface. "It upsets Gary that Joan doesn't like his kids. He and Joan met working at the same electronics company as my ex-father-in-law. Dennis Flynn, Brianne's husband, also worked there for a few years, but he left to run Tipped, you know, the bar next door to my café."

Frank waited for her to continue. Would it be rude to excuse herself to get a glass of water? Maybe he was thirsty, too. What was his partner doing all this time while Frank was with her? "I actually met Neal at a dinner party at the Flynns'," Alene continued, feeling like a glass of wine sounded better than a glass of water. Was her story getting too personal? "I was there to help Brianne. Joan came as the date of the married CEO of the electronics company and made everyone uncomfortable. Gary came with Isobel, and Neal came with his parents."

"So, you were all connected by the electronics company, before you became neighbors," Frank said. She'd started thinking of him as Frank.

"No," said Alene, "Our family had already lived next to the Flynns, for years. It was Dennis who told Gary that the condo across the hall had come on the market and Gary moved in with Isobel, when she was pregnant with Kacey."

"Was everyone at the dinner connected to the electronics company?" asked Frank.

Alene nodded. "Brianne thinks that Joan and Neal's father embezzled money – enough to force that company into bankruptcy."

"Did Brianne give you any evidence that funds were embezzled?" he asked.

Alene answered, "No, she just told me about it." None of it was relevant to Gary's death. If he asked anything else about it, she'd have to tell him to talk to Brianne.

"I'll need to look into this a little further," he said. "So, Gary met Dennis, Joan, and your ex-father-in-law at that company?"

"Yes," said Alene, "Hector-Schaf Electronics, somewhere out by Rockford, but it went bankrupt after all that money disappeared."

"What is your ex-father-in-law's name?"

"He's dead," said Alene.

Frank squinted – it made him look younger. "Sorry, I did hear you say that. I'd like to write it down anyway, if you don't mind."

"Patrick Dunn." Alene tried to mask the rumbling in her stomach.

Frank asked, "Did you and your ex-husband ever discuss what happened at Hector-Schaf Electronics?"

"If he did, I didn't pay much attention. As I said, I didn't know anything about it until my marriage started to fall apart." All that Hector-Schaf stuff was so long ago, she didn't really know why they were still talking about it. "All I can say is that if Joan had been caught stealing from that company back then, she wouldn't have had time to have affairs. Maybe she'd still be in jail," Alene said, kind of wistfully.

Frank squinted and turned his head a bit to the side in what Alene thought was an intimidating way. She breathed in and out. "Also, since I'm telling you what I think, I wouldn't be surprised if Neal was cooking the books in his dealership." That sounded like sour grapes, as it came out of her mouth. Would he think she was just another bitter divorcee?

Frank said, "People figure out all kinds of ways to cheat the system, Alene. Maybe your ex-husband earned some of his money the old-fashioned way, from gambling?"

She could feel her face fall into the hangdog expression Neal used to hate. Her mouth dropped open and she stared, boggle-eyed. "How did you know he gambles?"

He answered softly. "You told me a few minutes ago that he used to go out gambling with Joan Stone. I'm listening carefully to everything you tell me, Alene."

She wasn't used to men doing that. "He mostly loses money gambling, but he's pretty successful at selling cars and service plans. He also inherited money from his father so it's not a mystery that he can afford to waste money on a boat at Montrose Harbor, but can't manage to pay his children's camp fees."

"I share a boat that's docked at Montrose. Not everyone considers it a waste of money."

Alene said, "Oh." Way to stick in and rearrange my foot, she thought.

He looked at her blank-faced.

"I love boats," she said, hoping they could get back to the murder investigation.

Just then the door to the apartment opened and Jack Stone moseyed in. For Alene it was as if the barometric pressure dropped, and the room got dark and stuffy. He lifted his chin as a greeting to everyone. He wore torn jeans, a faded black t-shirt, and sandals that flopped as he walked. A red bandana covered his long hair, redneck style. He came directly to where Alene was sitting and she shot up, ready to push him away if he moved another inch forward. Were those crumbs in his beard?

"I heard Brianne got robbed," he said. "Do the cops know who did it?" Why was he asking her? Wasn't it just typical of him, to act as if he wasn't shaken by Gary's death and that he didn't notice Officer Frank Shaw sitting on the couch right next to her!

Alene clenched her teeth. "What do you mean you *heard* about it, Jack? Do you realize that Gary is dead?"

To his credit, Jack's face fell, and he looked honestly frightened. Gary had always been kind to Jack and had treated him as if he were an actual adult. Who else did that? Maybe Tinley, who was the only person who spoke to Jack as though living with his mother and having no livelihood at age thirty-four was normal. Gary had tried to help Jack. He'd arranged the job at Dennis's bar that had only lasted until Jack was caught selling pot in the restroom.

"I'm disappointed, Jack," Joan had said in front of the entire café as Jack sat with his head bowed, fiddling with his sleeves.

Alene had silently congratulated Joan on finally acting like a mother, until Joan turned to Gary and said, "How is your daughter's drug addiction so much better than my son selling a few joints here and there."

Gary had said, "This isn't a competition, Joan. I'm trying to explain to Jack that he crossed a line by doing something illegal in our friends' establishment. He doesn't seem to understand that if he's ever going to succeed in life, he needs to build a reputation as someone people can count on." He asked Jack, "Do you understand what I'm saying?"

"As if either of your sons have any kind of reputation," Joan had muttered.

Alene thought Jack might have accepted responsibility, if his mother hadn't intervened. Instead of a mature conversation, instead of marching back to the bar and apologizing, he'd gotten away with doing nothing.

Now Jack said, "Well, my phone's broken so I didn't hear about it until now. And maybe you could boss me around if you'd have hired me, Alene, but he's not *your* stepfather. Why do you care so much?" He stepped towards her and she stumbled against Frank, who'd stood up. He gripped Jack's arm and moved him away from Alene, to the other side of the room. Jack tried to pull his arm away, but Frank kept a tight hold on him. She watched them interact but couldn't hear anything. Frank's partner had joined them, but he just stood there doing nothing. When Frank finally let go of his arm, Jack pulled out his wallet and handed it over. Frank rifled through it and then returned it. Jack shoved it back into his pocket before stomping out the door.

Frank crossed the room, back to Alene, with the partner just behind him. She asked, "Why didn't you arrest Jack?" She'd forgotten the partner's name but he didn't say anything so it didn't matter.

"He told me that he was at the Cubs game today," Frank said. "He has a ticket stub and witnesses. I promise I'll get to the bottom of this, Alene. We'll look closely into the names you've given us, but we have a long way to go before we start arresting anyone."

"Okay, but Jack's witnesses are probably other guys like him who wouldn't know if he was waiting in line for a beer or running back here to stab Gary between innings."

"Then, what would he have done with the murder weapon?" Frank asked. The partner smirked as if Frank had gotten one up on her.

"If I'd stabbed someone, I'd hide the weapon by burying it in the garden, if I had one, or I'd hide it under a boulder in the lake somewhere far from here, like maybe on the South Side," said Alene. "I think you need to check both Jack and his mother's alibis. He might have gone to the game and stayed for just two innings. Then, he could have killed Gary and cabbed back to the game before the ninth inning. I mean, anything is possible really. By the way, both Neal, my ex, and Bill Vanza have expressed interest in Gary's supposed wealth."

Frank nodded. "I think you alluded to that."

His cell rang, and he answered it, putting whoever it was on a brief hold. He looked up at Alene and asked if he could get back to her if he needed more information. She mouthed "I'm going home." Maybe she'd mentioned Bill always trying to get money out of Gary, but she hadn't told Frank that all three of them came up with schemes. Gary was a smart guy, though, and had invariably poked holes in just about every idea they'd come up with over the years. What if he'd disappointed one or all of them a few too many times?

Alene was exhausted and looking forward to being at home with her father and children. She opened the front door, ready to slip into the hallway, but Joan Stone was there, standing in front of her. As usual, her hair, eye liner, mascara, blush, and lipstick were all impeccable.

Chapter 7

Joan pushed past Alene, stomping through the apartment towards the dining room. She must have looked at Gary, surrounded by plastic-clad technicians preparing to lift his body onto a gurney, for all of thirty seconds before she strode back to the front hall and shoved Alene against the wall. "What the hell happened to my husband?"

Alene's first thought was that if she pushed her back, Joan, who was fifteen years older and scrawnier, would be on the floor. Before Alene could react, Frank's partner, who'd followed Joan from the dining room, stepped between the two women while Frank introduced the two of them to Joan. She turned away from both detectives and hissed at Alene. "You killed him, and I hope you die the way he died, alone in someone else's apartment. Maybe you'll lie on the floor all day before anyone finds you."

Alene gasped. How did she know Gary had lain on the floor all day? Was Joan's tirade legitimate or was she just being dramatic for Frank's benefit? Why hadn't she come immediately, if she thought Gary had been lying on the floor? Did she hear the news, stop at the grocery store to pick up dinner, have a manicure, and then come home? Or was this her doing? Did she bring her husband over to Brianne's, unsuspecting, so that her own apartment would stay clean? Alene looked up at Shaw and shook her head in disbelief as Brianne, Kacey, and Olly rushed into the living room.

Brianne reached towards Joan, saying, "I'm so sorry. Are you all right?"

"How do you think I am?" Joan muttered, pushing Brianne away. Brianne's eyes sparkled with tears.

Frank put his arm around Joan's shoulders gently, barely touching her. "I know you're upset, Mrs. Vanza. I don't want to distress you during this very difficult time, but we do need to talk. We can walk across the hall to your apartment or," he gestured towards the couch with his other hand.

Alene wanted to pat him on the back and say, "Nicely done, Sir." She wondered if his partner spoke at all – the guy hadn't said a single word, so far.

"I don't want anyone traipsing around my apartment," Joan said, sounding as if she was issuing a warning.

Frank continued, "Then how about we sit right here?"

"I'd like a little time to mourn, if you don't mind," Joan said with note of disdain. "What exactly do you need from me?"

"Well, Mrs. Vanza, why don't you start by telling me about your day," Frank said, unfazed, "Then we'd like to know if there was anyone you knew of who would want to hurt your husband."

"I'm not Mrs. Vanza." Joan nearly spat, sitting herself on the couch while Shaw took the same comfortable swivel chair he'd sat in while speaking to Alene. "My name is Joan Stone. You people should be focused on finding the murderer instead of harassing me."

While his partner just raised an eyebrow, Frank recoiled as if Joan had struck him in the face. He really should ask what people preferred to be called. Maybe he was a little thin-skinned for a cop, but Alene admired his calm response. "Excuse me, Ms. Stone, as I said, I'm sorry for your loss, and I'd like to help find out what happened, but I'm going to need your cooperation. I'm not the enemy."

Joan rubbed her face and frowned in a way that made her resemble one of those over-wrinkly dogs. Alene was relieved when pity washed over her, because she'd been starting to feel uneasily callous toward Joan Stone, whose hands were trembling. Could some of her awful behavior be explained by a kind of neurological dysfunction? Ruthie always said that everyone has limitations.

The doorbell rang again. Alene opened it and Isobel, Gary's second wife and Kacey's mother, whooshed past her into the apartment. She barely acknowledged Joan, instead asking, "Where's my daughter?" She didn't wait for a response, and bellowed, "Helloooooo, Kacey, where are you, Honey?"

Alene wished she had the assertiveness and strength to take hold of Isobel, who was taller and more muscular, spin her around and push her back out the door. Frank would probably be horrified if he knew how violent Alene's thoughts could be. Isobel's voice was loud and nasal, and she thundered on toward the kitchen with Alene right behind. "I came as soon as I heard. Are you all right, Kacey baby?"

Kacey, who was still sitting at the kitchen table staring at her hands, looked up at her mother and just shook her head. "You shouldn't have come here, Mom. You know it'll upset Joan." There was no love lost between Gary's second and third wives – they were both scathingly critical and dismissive of each other.

Isobel stopped and turned back to Alene, who barely managed to avoid crashing into her, "Is it true that Gary's dead? What happened?"

"Yes." Alene answered. Everyone at the table nodded, except for Kacey, who said quietly, "You need to leave now before you start a fight with someone, Mom."

At least once a week, Kacey's mother came over to the Whipped and Sipped Café. Isobel was another difficult woman in Alene's orbit, and as soon as she arrived, she usually started lecturing the servers and the people sitting around her about the evils of coffee. She brought her own food in a container that she plucked from her purse. Edith would come running from behind the smoothie section, and sputter about no outside food being allowed.

Having been alerted, Alene would run out to the café and send Edith into the kitchen with a message for Kacey to come out. Then Alene would politely request that Isobel put away whatever she'd brought. "We sell raw pastries with cashew cream and chocolate pecan crusts and we have brownies made from different kinds of beans sweetened with date or coconut sugar, for goodness sake. We offer every kind of salad under the sun, Isobel. I'm sure you can find something to your liking on our menu."

"I'm sure you think your offerings are healthful," Isobel would respond smugly, her chin jutting forward. "But I concentrate on a mostly raw, macrobiotic diet."

Alene would point out the sign on the door that politely explained their policy of not allowing patrons to bring food into the cafe. Wondering why someone with dyed-red hair, who wore mascara and leather sandals, was so concerned with being natural, she would invite Isobel to order from the raw, the vegan or the smoothie menu. Isobel would pack up what she'd brought, glowering, and grudgingly order a cup of herbal tea.

Meanwhile, Kacey would wash her hands and come out to the café, followed closely by Edith, who felt compelled to further admonish Isobel in a shrill voice. Customers would scramble to leave. Alene thought it was like a bad movie that kept playing television reruns. Isobel kept bringing her own food in and each time, Edith ripped into her after Alene had already handled the situation.

Edith then whined to Gary, who would say, "Edith doesn't have anything else in life, Alene. She loves this place. It's the reason she gets up and gets dressed every morning."

"Are you kidding me, Gary?" Alene would ask, trying not to sound too bitter. "Are you sure she wouldn't be happy doing something else, perhaps working somewhere calmer than in a café?"

Gary would smile knowingly. "She has always enjoyed squabbling, believe me, but she has a heart of gold. She needs a reason to get out of her apartment every day."

Alene was always moved by Gary's pleas but couldn't help wondering if he was incapable of perceiving anything negative about the women in his life. She tried not to involve him, every time Edith bumped up against someone in the café. She remembered the last time she'd had to call Gary about an Edith problem. It was after the Chocolate Chip Blackies' incident. They already had the usual interaction with Isobel, who was waiting for Kacey to finish her shift that day. Kacey, usually worked back in the kitchen and came out into the cafe infrequently. She had just placed a tray into the oven. Alene, sitting at her desk, heard Edith ask snidely if Kacey had remembered to wash her hands beforehand. Kacey replied in a way that was completely out of character. She said, "Get out of my face, Edith." Even Alene had been shocked to hear Kacey speak that way.

Edith sputtered. "Did your mother teach you to speak that way to me? I can't imagine why my brother allows an ungrateful, ill-mannered girl like you to live with him."

Isobel stomped back to the kitchen and yelled, "I've also had just about enough of you, Edith." Alene looked through *the open kitchen doors as a mother about to lift her toddler out of his stroller, in front of the pastry case, quickly changed her mind and swiftly wheeled back out the door.*

Alene tried to calm the situation. "Edith, please take over for Kacey." A tray of pastries in one hand, Alene gripped Isobel with the other, pulled her out of the kitchen and led her back to her table. She sat close to Isobel and gestured for her to take something from the tray, saying, "Kacey has been working with Ruthie on a healthy brownie recipe. They're gluten-free and made with black beans, applesauce and figs, with no processed sugar or any other artificial ingredients. Would you like to try one?"

Isobel sniffed at a brownie and nibbled it like a squirrel before spitting it into her napkin. She whispered, "I don't know why I ever married someone like Gary. He and Edith are both low-lives and I don't want my daughter to turn out like his atrocious sons."

Alene had stifled the urge to say something mean. Isobel had no idea that her voice carried, and Kacey could probably hear every word. Alene said the most innocuous thing she could think of, "I sure do empathize with you about having to deal with an ex-husband."

"Gary is a sick, sick man," Isobel had said. "I think his days are numbered. My one consolation is that he probably won't be around to aggravate me, much longer."

Now, as Alene watched the gurney carrying Gary's body being moved out the door, she remembered what Isobel had said back then. Was she capable of making good on her prophecy? Maybe she'd only meant that he was getting older.

Alene said, "You can meet the investigator who is trying to connect all the pieces, Isobel. He's talking to Joan at the moment, but I'm sure he'll want to speak to you, before you go." She gestured for Isobel to follow her back to the living room.

Before Alene could introduce Isobel, Joan said, "You probably don't have the results for the exact time of death, do you, Officer? Is it possible that Alene murdered Gary before she went to get Brianne from the airport?"

Alene's mouth fell open as she crossed the room, "You're accusing *me*? You think I had something to do with this?" Her throat tightened and she couldn't continue. She forgot about introducing Isobel to Frank Shaw and his partner, whose name she still couldn't remember.

Joan didn't miss a beat. "And here's Gary's second wife. I wonder if she has anything to gain from his death. If Alene didn't kill him, I guess it could have been a fat, middle-aged divorcee who couldn't attract a man if she took off all her clothes and danced naked in the streets." Alene covered her face with both hands. Frank would think they were a pack of silly women flinging accusations against each other like Greek gods hurling lightning bolts.

"At least I'm not anorexic," sputtered Isobel. "And I am not at all fat!" She slammed the door on her way out. Alene momentarily wished she'd thought to stick her foot out.

Joan had a way of sticking in a knife and twisting it, perhaps both figuratively and literally. "Isobel got rid of him years ago," Alene fumed. "You have more motive than anyone else here, with your rolls of hidden money, your affairs with married men, and your gambling. I'm not even mentioning your poorly-raised, entitled son."

Frank looked up at Alene, in surprise, and then nodded to his partner, who escorted Joan out the front door without saying anything. Joan looked smugly satisfied with having accused both Alene and Isobel of the murder and didn't bother to reply before the door closed. Alene needed to get home but felt as if she had to wait until Joan was inside her own condo.

Frank said, "I'm sorry about that," as he scrolled through his phone before looking up at Alene. "Are you okay? It's not uncommon for a widow to break down."

"I'm fine. Sorry for letting her get to me." Alene replied brusquely, a little vexed that he'd neglected to take a stand against Joan's absurd accusations.

"Joan's anger had little to do with you and everything to do with her loss."

Alene felt bad for having taken Joan's chiding personally. She looked at her shoes. In a more business-like tone, Frank said, "Moving on, I'm looking at Kacey Vanza's record and I see that she has experience of both jail and rehab."

Alene knew Kacey had been arrested for possession of illegal drugs and had been hospitalized after overdosing or taking something that caused a psychotic episode. She'd spent time in various rehab facilities around the country. A few stints were at the kind of place wealthy parents can park their troubled children in the hope of a miraculous transformation. The problems hadn't gone away, but after she'd turned twenty-one, the police no longer automatically notified Gary when Kacey was in trouble. Alene remembered one day in the fall, when she had found him crying in the elevator, relieved that Kacey was alive but devastated after a near-fatal overdose. He'd cried, "Where did I go wrong with my daughter?"

Frank continued, "Can you help us regarding Kacey?"

Without thinking, Alene said, "Is there something you don't understand about her rap sheet?" It came out more acerbically than she'd intended. Frank's silent partner smirked again. Was there something wrong with the guy?

"It's pretty clear, thanks," Frank responded gently, before she could modify what she'd said, "but it would be helpful if you could be there when we question her." Shoot, she'd just sounded like a total bitch and her only excuse was that she was tired, hungry, and extremely stressed.

Vowing to be extraordinarily helpful from now on, Alene followed the detectives to where Kacey and Olly were sitting on one of the twin beds in what had been Brianne's daughter's bedroom. Did Frank think Kacey might have met someone during one of her incarcerations who later carried out the botched robbery? Did he think Kacey was guilty of something and want to keep an eye on her? Alene thought that just looking at Kacey's drawn face should have told Frank everything he needed to know about the girl. She hoped he understood that Kacey was sweet-natured and had been much-loved by Gary. That she'd felt like drugs were her only escape from physical and psychological pain? Alene sat down on the second twin bed, wishing she'd done more to help Kacey, such as spending more time with her or giving her more hours at the café. Would Kacey ever be able to handle a full-time job after this?

Kacey and Olly were sitting with their backs against the wall. Olly gestured to Frank to sit next to Alene on the second bed, but he stood in the doorway with his partner hovering behind him.

Kacey gave one-word answers to Frank's questions, and Olly drew out Kacey's response. Alene watched as Frank tried to understand Kacey's life. Olly said that neither of her stepbrothers cared about her or did anything to help her. Bill had always been dismissive and Sandy was just incapable of forming a relationship. He had problems talking to or being in a room with other people unless he wore ear and nose plugs so he wouldn't have to hear or smell anyone. Alene had always wondered about the nose plugs.

Olly explained that, after Gary and Isobel divorced, Isobel had married an orthodontist and moved with Kacey to one of the suburbs. The orthodontist died in a car crash just seven years later, when Kacey was just starting high school. Isobel had sustained only a few scratches, but Kacey had broken limbs and pieces of shattered glass had been embedded in her skin. That was when she had first started taking pills to manage the pain. Isobel and Kacey had moved back to the city and Kacey was able to see her father Gary more often. Olly kept looking at Kacey to make sure he was getting the story right and Kacey kept nodding. However, she'd hated school, Gary had remarried, Joan was not very welcoming, and Jack Stone scared her. Kacey gradually found that she couldn't function without the pain pills.

Olly had two insights: "I've been friends with Kacey for a long time and I know all the players. First, you should know that although Isobel might seem like a tough lady, she was never a match for Joan. Second, Kacey gets along with everyone except two people: Joan Stone and Edith Vanza."

"My father's wife and his sister," Kacey clarified for Frank.

Olly added, "Or as I like to call them, Crazy McJoan and Bitchy McEdith."

Kacey said, "They're not all that supportive."

"I remember last summer when Kacey needed treatment, Joan acted as if she wanted Kacey to die so she wouldn't have to deal with it," said Olly. "I gotta say, sometimes Joan's eyes protrude and her face kind of bristles, like a pig during a storm."

"My dad found a really good program," Kacey said, looking down.

Olly continued her sentence, "Joan said she wasn't worth it."

Frank asked, "That must have stung."

"Alene was standing there when Joan said that, and she smacked Joan with the palm of her hand." Kacey said, acknowledging Alene with a smile.

"I just flicked her lightly," said Alene.

Olly said, "But that certainly stung too."

Frank looked at Alene with a puzzled expression and she shrugged. She hadn't been proud of it, but Joan had deserved the knock. She'd just said that Kacey wasn't worth saving.

Kacey offered, "They let me leave jail with the understanding that I'd do rehab. My dad found a place, and ..."

Olly interrupted, "Gary tried to be all enthusiastic about the program so Kacey would like the sound of it, but Joan couldn't stand how much it was going to cost. She has no problem buying Christian Louboutin shoes, but she wanted Kacey to go to Payless for treatment."

Kacey said, "It was about as much as a year of college." Alene remembered Gary spending time talking to her father about what to do – she hoped Cal had been helpful – he'd always been good at dispensing advice.

"So, then I go, 'I'm sorry, Mrs. Vanza, I didn't mean to upset you. I love Kacey like a sister, and I just want her to be happy'," said Olly. "I enjoy calling her Mrs. Vanza now and then, with just the right amount of respect, to keep her on her toes."

"It makes her nuts," said Kacey. Alene felt a little abashed about all the times she'd also tried to make Joan nuts. There was really no excuse for such juvenile behavior – what could she expect of her own children if she herself acted like a spoiled teenager?

Olly stood on the bed in a Joan-like stance with his chin raised and mouth severe. "So, then Joan goes: 'I am not Mrs. Vanza, you little homo. I object to spending money on a drug addict, because I must save it to spend on my wonderful, ambitious son'." Olly saluted and fell back down to Kacey's side, saying, "I might have altered her exact words, but the general content was intact."

"She didn't say the part about Jack," Alene told Frank, "but nice impression, Olly."

Kacey said, "That was the only time I ever saw Alene hit another person."

"Flick," said Alene. "I flicked her." As if Frank didn't already think she was an awful person. Would he believe her capable of physically sparring with another woman?

Frank asked, "What happened after the – flick?"

"I apologized immediately," said Alene. "I'd never done anything like that before and it wasn't at all something that I'm proud of."

"But I was proud of her," said Olly. "Joan gasped indignantly, spun on her heel and stomped out." Olly grinned. "It was like a scene from a movie."

Officer Shaw interjected, "What was the upshot? Did you get the help you needed, Kacey?"

"My dad sent me to the place for about three months, and I came out clean." Kacey answered. "Then I came home, and I've been clean now for over eight months. My dad paid for the treatments." Her eyes filled up. "I don't know what I'm going to." Olly wrapped her in his arms.

Officer Shaw asked for their cell numbers. "Thanks. I'm so sorry about your father, Kacey. I'll contact you if I have further questions." He left the bedroom and returned to the living room with first his partner and then Alene following. She noticed that his dark brown hair was thinning a little on the crown of his head, but he had the silver edges that she admired in men. He'd mentioned having two children but hadn't said, "me too," when she told him she was divorced. No ring, but not all married men wore rings. She shook away the stab of guilt for dreaming of finding someone who would love her despite all her baggage, the way Gary had loved Joan.

"Frank," Alene said, realizing that was the first time she'd called him by his first name. Both men turned to face her and she stepped in front of the partner. "I just want to reiterate that I'm not the kind of person who physically assaults people. That was definitely the first time I've ever done something like that."

Frank said. "I understand. Anyway, as you said, it was only a flick." Was he silently laughing at her? He turned to tell Brianne, who'd just joined them in the hallway, that the police were going to be leaving the apartment soon.

"Thank you," Brianne answered, "we're grateful you're here."

Alene said, "I'll be grateful to know what caused Gary's death."

Frank looked at her sharply, and his partner followed suit like a trained monkey. Brianne, who was always good at smoothing over uncomfortable moments said, "You've probably already learned that Gary was the kind of guy everyone liked. Just minutes after we'd introduce him to someone, they'd be swapping numbers and talking passionately about wood-working or golf or one of his other interests. He had tons of friends. We could probably get you a list of at least some of the people he knew."

Olly came out to the hallway and handed a small notebook to Frank. "This was Gary's address book," he said. "I found it on the dresser next to his bed."

"Thank you," said Frank, squinting at Olly as though trying to see through him. The partner squinted also. Why didn't Frank admonish Olly for sneaking into the Vanzas' apartment? Exactly when had Olly gone over there? It must have been after they found Gary – otherwise why would he have searched for it?

Frank took the notebook and asked Alene, "Can one of you connect me with the management here, so we can take a look at the security cameras in your lobby and garage?"

Alene was about to respond when Bill Vanza and his girlfriend showed up in the living room. Now that Bill's father was gone, Alene hoped Tinley would make Bill behave. Alene waved at the two of them and said "I'm so sorry for your loss. We're all going to miss his bigheartedness." Gary was dead. Nothing she did could bring him back, but at the very least, she could try to help find out who killed him.

She shuffled home, exhausted by everything. She peeked at the kids in their beds, nibbled a few bites of chicken and finished cleaning the kitchen, glad they'd gone ahead and eaten without her. She checked on her father, who was dozing on his bed with the lights on and his book open. Then she went to her room, changed into pajamas, washed her face half-heartedly, brushed her teeth, and got into bed. *Shoot*, she realized with a start. She'd forgotten to call Ruthie back. She thought about texting an apology, but she was too wiped out. The last thing Alene remembered thinking was that she needed to change her vote in favor of having video cameras in the lobby. She'd been on the committee that opposed it for years.

Chapter 8

Alene woke up groggy. She wiped her eyes with the corner of her pajama top and dragged herself out of bed at five, as usual. Through the front windows, the sky billowed lighter where the sun was about to rise over the lake. She was somewhat revived by her morning glass of apple-cider-vinegar-and-honey spiked water. After that, she pulled on shorts and a t-shirt and headed down to run on the lake path before her children or father got up. Alene was only responsible for opening the café on Saturdays. Most other days, her employees took turns opening, and she worked out or ran before going in. She could usually count on Jocelyn, who'd served in the military and was used to waking up at the crack of dawn.

By the time she started running among the first out on the lake path, the sky had turned a hazy azure. Feeling slow and heavy, she circled around "Chevron," the cobalt windmill sculpture across from the Diversey Harbor and crossed back to the other side of the bridge spanning Lake Shore Drive. She'd decided that instead of taking a long run, she'd stop at Michael Jay's small private gym, where she'd been working out for years. She wanted to feel some burning in her upper body.

"Where's my coffee?" asked Michael. It was their ritual greeting. He also trained several of her neighbors and was known for disliking coffee and everything having to do with it.

"Come by and I'll make you something special." They'd had the same exchange forever. She'd warmed up on the way over so she could plunge directly into squats and lunges using five-pound weights.

Michael raised his eyebrow. "You do know that breathing is required, right?"

Alene exhaled loudly and said, "I can't concentrate after what happened to Gary."

"Brianne texted me last night. She said she wasn't up to coming in this morning," he said, "and she told me the basics. What happened exactly?" Alene summarized the story as she worked her core.

Michael said, "I can't believe a big guy like Gary could have been brought down by a small knife."

Alene paused with a five-pound weight over her head in a triceps exercise that she thought of as the 'coffee-press' position. Had she mentioned that Gary had been stabbed? It was crazy to suspect everyone she knew, but she thought of the blue towel Gary had been clutching. "Are you holding that weight over your head for any particular reason?" Michael asked her.

She put the weights back on the rack slowly. "I think I'm too tired today." She ran out without saying goodbye. How could she be alone in a gym with a possible murderer? Why did she feel the need to blame everyone she knew?

By the time she got back to the building, she'd calmed down. Michael liked Gary and he didn't seem to care about much aside from training and going out with buff, beautiful women. What possible motive could he have? She took the elevator, opened the door to her apartment and walked straight into the kitchen, where Blanca was cutting fruit into tiny pieces for Cal. Blanca was a tall Polish woman with a sunny disposition, sharp features and shiny, cranberry-red hair. She was also a curvaceous, beautiful, divorced woman in her late thirties. What if Gary had started an affair with her and then tried to break it off? Maybe she'd killed him in a broken-hearted rage?

Alene remembered seeing where the knife had entered Gary's body, on the lower right side of his back. Whoever stabbed Gary must have been right-handed, and had to have stabbed him from behind, because he'd never have let someone get to him from the front.

She watched as Blanca piled scrambled eggs into bowls and set Cal's vitamins and medicine next to his water glass, all using her left hand. Blanca was definitely not a suspect. Alene told her what had happened, whispering in her ear even though they were alone in the kitchen. Blanca shook her head and crossed herself, again with her left hand.

Hearing one of the kids' alarm clocks, Alene dashed in and out of the shower, the fastest she'd moved all morning. Ten minutes later, dressed and with her wet hair tied back in a ponytail, she was spreading sunscreen on Noah, who wiggled whenever she tried to kiss his soft little back. She French-braided both girls' hair and confirmed that Quinn was wearing clean socks, but then she started thinking about Gary's murder and forgot to make Sierra wash off her mascara.

While Blanca served breakfast to the children, Alene helped Cal sit down at the table and kissed the top of his head as he began to sip his cocoa and read the first of his three newspapers – the Chicago Tribune, the New York Times, and the Wall Street Journal. After making sure everyone had brushed teeth and washed hands, Alene accompanied the children down in the elevator, waited until the girls were picked up, and then walked Noah to his summer park-district program at a nearby school. Seeing two friends already running around the playground, Noah disappeared with a brief, "Bye, Mom." Alene signed him in and continued walking to the café.

Olly was slouching behind the drinks counter slowly swirling foam on a cappuccino as Louis Armstrong sang a little too loudly on the sound system. Alene guessed that Olly had chosen the music to cheer everyone up. Sally, a tiny young woman with straight strawberry-blond hair, freckles and an all-day smile, was ringing up a box of muffins for a woman wearing a long flowing dress. Zuleyka, the chatty, dark-haired young woman from Panama, who also babysat for Alene's kids, was stocking the dessert case. Alene gritted her teeth to see that Edith Vanza hadn't yet appeared, but then she remembered the reason.

Since Kacey had also taken the day off, Ruthie had asked Grant, a tall kid with a yellow buzz-cut, to help her with the large baking trays. Ruthie hugged her as Alene made herself an espresso with whipped almond milk, cocoa and cinnamon.

"Poor Gary," said Ruthie, "I can't imagine how awful this has been for everyone."

"Sorry I didn't call you back, Nine," said Alene, releasing the tightness in her neck and shoulders. They sat and munched on day-old spinach-mushroom quiches as Alene brought Ruthie up to date. "Do you need my help with starting doughs?"

"Thanks, Six," said Ruthie. "They'll go faster if we're both working on them."

They worked silently for about an hour until Olly came into the kitchen. "Jack Stone is here again," he said, without even a hint of his usual sparkle. Maybe he could tell how she felt. Any other day he'd have started singing, "Hit the Road, Jack."

She just didn't have it in her to be friendly. "Please give him a complimentary hot chocolate and make sure to express condolences about Gary, okay?" She added, "They didn't get along, but Gary was his stepfather. If he's finished his resume, ask him to leave it for me."

"I used my X-ray vision to check if he was carrying anything, but he's clean," Olly said.

Alene waved Olly away and went back to work, lulled by the tactile enjoyment of kneading dough, blending batters and preparing trays. She and Ruthie fell back into their comfortable routine of many years. During a moment when Grant was washing the utensils and bowls, Alene leaned over to Ruthie and said, "I'm really lonely sometimes, you know, Nine? Why haven't I found someone yet?"

Ruthie threw a pebble sized piece of dough at her. "You've been kvetching for nearly eight years, Six, but you've refused to do any of the online dating apps. I could tell you a dozen stories about women who met wonderful partners using one of those applications."

Alene waved her arm. "I want it to happen naturally, like meeting at a party or at the beach or something – or maybe to be fixed up by a real person."

"Okay, Six, and that's why you're still alone." Ruthie pursed her lips.

Alene said, "I'd go out with one of your husband's friends, because then I'd know for sure that the guy isn't a serial killer."

"Brianne tried to set you up with someone last year and you refused," said Ruthie.

"I was sunburned that month," said Alene. Ruthie just smiled knowingly.

Alene said, "Okay, maybe you're right, but how is it possible that Joan Stone can find love and I'm still alone after eight years? It's not fair. And it's not fair that my husband turned out to be such a jerk."

"So, you think life is supposed to be fair, do you? You got three beautiful children out of that marriage so you cannot legitimately say it was a mistake," said Ruthie, as she poured batter into muffin pans. They'd had this conversation many times.

"Yeah, but what advice can I give them when they grow up and start searching for partners? I sucked at it," Alene said, and smacked rye bread dough onto the marble counter.

Grant had returned to the counter with the cleaned appliances. "Both of my parents have been married and divorced several times," he said. "I'm never getting married."

"Don't say 'never,' Grant," said Ruthie, kneading the dough with her arms and elbows. "You don't know when you'll be smitten by someone who's compatible in every way, and you find yourselves discussing every little thing that might possibly occur in your lifetime. You meet his or her family. You talk about where you want to live and how you want to live, and what role money plays in your life. You spend hours discussing what kind of faith and value system you are going to impart to your children, because those issues will come up down the road."

"Amen and hallelujah," said Alene.

"Says the least religious person in the world," said Olly.

Ruthie set the fully-kneaded dough aside, rested for half a minute and started another. Grant asked, "Can I just come to you if I ever fall in love, and you can remind me about all that?"

"You damn well better come to me," said Ruthie. "As for your children, Alene, I would make sure they understand that marriage is a partnership that requires more time, effort and work than any job anyone will ever do."

"All wise-sounding, Ruthie, but imagine that Sierra falls in love with some yahoo. I disapprove of him, of course. Then she'll ask me why I think I'm good at judging people

100

and I'll have to admit that I suck at it," said Alene. "Pass over one of those trays for me to decorate."

"We've got to finish making the colored frostings first," said Ruthie. "You can always just tell your children that you're unlucky." True that, thought Alene, except I'm only unlucky some of the time.

The rest of Monday was uneventful. That night following dinner, Alene had a petty argument with Sierra about sewing a button on a dress. She played a game of Boggle with the other two and then watched an episode of SpongeBob with Noah and Quinn. Once the children were in bed, Alene worked in her room on the café's accounts. She felt bad that she'd gone on about feeling lonely when she should have been thinking about Gary Vanza.

Tuesday morning, after a slightly better night of sleep, she woke early and ran a couple of miles, this time at her usual speed and farther. Again, she stopped on the way home at Michael's gym. Maybe thinking of him as a suspect was kooky but she still needed to rule him out. She greeted him and started stretching, wondering how best to bring it up. They often talked about their weekends, so she ended up blurting out, "Hey Michael, do anything special over the weekend?"

"It was so long ago, I've already forgotten," he replied, admiring his biceps in one of the surrounding mirrors. "But I can see, in your smoky detective eyes, that you really want to know where I was when Gary was killed."

Alene stopped trying to balance on one leg. "He was holding one of your blue towels when we found him."

Michael shook his head. "Let that be a lesson to everyone who takes my towels home."

"Too early for jokes, Michael," Alene said, thinking there was no way Michael would have joked about towels if he'd murdered Gary. "I do also want to know how much you drank and if you met any cute girls on Saturday night. I need details so I can live vicariously."

Michael practically sparkled in his response. "Saturday night I was at a fancy dinner. I looked smashing in my tux and ate only salad but drank like a fish. On Sunday morning, I drove up to the Dunes with a young lady who resembles Wonder Woman. We spent the day frolicking there, and then I cooked an amazing steak dinner that included baked sweet potatoes and asparagus. Dessert was, well, do you need any of the salacious details?"

"Thanks, that'll do." Alene smiled at him. How could she have thought he was capable of murder? What motive could Michael have possibly had? She finished her workout, ran home, showered, dressed, got the children out the door, and walked Noah to camp. At the café, she was working at her desk when Olly rushed in and announced breathlessly that "the very attractive Detective Frank Shaw" was asking to see her. Although she knew he was there to discuss Gary's murder, Alene couldn't help feeling a little nervous, so she fixed her ponytail and reapplied her lip gloss.

Olly seemed a little more himself than the day before, and sang: "Luck let a gentleman see, just how nice a dame you can be..."

Alene just made a disapproving face and said, "I'll be right out. Please take his order."

Frank and his partner were sitting at a corner table near the window. Was his name Lee or Leif? Frank flashed a quick smile and that moment of thinking that a man was happy to see her was enough to improve her mood. He said, "Thank you for making time to see us, Alene. Can you sit for a minute?"

She glanced at her watch out of habit, but really, what did she have to do except keep the place running? "Sure," she said, trying to sound casual. "Did Olly already take your order?" Before he could answer, Olly appeared with a black coffee for Frank, a tea for the partner, and Alene's favorite, an espresso with whipped almond milk, cocoa and cinnamon. They thanked Olly, and Frank picked up his mug with both hands while Alene took a dainty sip. The partner was scrolling through his phone.

Frank looked at the shelves behind her, which were filled with more of the gemstones and minerals that Dennis Flynn had collected over the years. They were of varying shapes and colors, from the size of a deck of cards to one as big as a boot. Alene said, "I love the deep blue lapis lazuli on the far left, but look at that Mexican fire opal here, and the exquisite aquamarine." She pointed in their direction. "You probably saw the best part of the collection at Brianne's condo. These ones here are solidly glued down so they can't be easily grabbed." She showed him by pulling over the chair, standing up on it and trying to lift one.

"They're something," said Shaw. The partner glanced briefly away from his cellphone while she was standing on the chair.

The silence was anxiety-provoking. Sitting back down, she saw Frank shift his gaze to the gallery wall. "We change the artwork every month," she said, because the worst thing would be silence. "They're usually exhibitions by locals and we try to make sure each show is unique."

He raised his cup and with his other hand gave her thumbs up. "Nice, aren't they, Lee?"

So, his name was Lee. He registered Frank's comment with a barely perceptible nod. "Our coffee roasters are a brother and sister team," said Alene. "Ruthie and I went to school with the sister. They fly to all the highest elevations where the best coffee beans grow, Guatemala or Peru, where they personally choose the most superb organic, free-trade beans. Nobody else in Chicago sells this brand and I won't even share the name of the company." She knew she was running on, so she stopped yammering and sipped her drink.

"This coffee is great," Frank said. "It's pretty early but the place is hopping. How many employees do you have here during a typical day?" He'd turned away from the gem collection to face her.

She counted on her fingers. "Today we have Ruthie, our baking goddess, Zuleyka, the gorgeous brunette who also babysits my kids, Grant, the string bean with yellow hair you can see through the kitchen window, Sally, who looks like a young Meryl Streep, and me. Usually Edith would be behind the drinks counter and Kacey would be helping Ruthie with the baking. I like to have six to eight of us here, depending on the time, throughout the day." Why did she always blab uncontrollably when Frank was around?

"Can you give us a list with contact information for all your employees?" asked Frank.

"Of course," said Alene, thinking for a moment. Hadn't she already given it to him? "They all knew Gary. I told you that he was the former owner, right, and he still comes in, I mean he used to come in all the time? Just to clarify, no matter what Joan told you, I had nothing to do with Gary's murder. I can account for the whole day and I had witnesses. I went running, came home and showered, did some cleaning, and made sandwiches. The kids and I walked over to the zoo to see the new baby camel, 'Alexander Camelton.' We stopped to buy new markers and some groceries on the way home. Then after they showered, my children climbed into my bed to watch *The Wizard of Oz* even though it was a lovely day, but they'd gotten enough sun, so I wanted them to stay inside. Then at two, Kacey and I left for the airport to pick up Brianne." She took a deep breath.

Frank seemed amused. "I never thought you had anything to do with it, and I would never question a mother who lets her children watch a movie on a summer afternoon."

"Thanks," said Alene. "I also have a question though; can you tell me what Gary ate on Sunday?"

"Why do you ask?"

"Well, he told me he was taking Kacey out for brunch," said Alene. "They didn't come to Whipped and Sipped, so where did they go?"

Frank asked, "When did Gary tell you he was taking Kacey out for brunch?"

Alene thought for a minute. "It must have been we were throwing our trash down the chute."

He scrolled back through his notes. "You said you just greeted each other."

"Oh, sorry, he also said he was planning to hit balls at the driving range. That didn't happen, did it?"

"Why not?" asked Shaw.

Alene sat up straighter. "He would have been sunburnt. I know he was dead when we found him, but I looked at his face. He had fair skin that burned easily, and even when he wore a hat, he was always bright red after a day of golf or even after just an hour of hitting balls." She didn't realize she knew all that until she articulated it.

He seemed appreciative. "That's very observant." Lee acknowledged her with a frown that she chose to interpret as his way of being impressed.

"If they weren't at the café, they probably didn't eat the kind of healthy food we serve, and if Gary had a sweet roll or a muffin of some kind, there would be evidence."

Frank squinted. "What evidence would we find from a sweet roll or a muffin, aside from the usual flour and sugar?"

Alene checked his expression to make sure he wasn't making fun of her. Was she being ridiculous? "Our baked goods are not filled with as much fat and sugar as others, and we use healthy ingredients such as seeds. Sometimes,

Ruthie will substitute applesauce for oil. What if someone like Joan gave him a muffin laced with poison that caused him to faint? Then she could have easily stabbed him."

"Wouldn't the poison be enough without the stabbing?" Frank asked. Did he wink at her?

True, and they hadn't found any traces of poison. "Maybe she wanted it to look like a robbery," said Alene, "or maybe she just got so angry when she saw him on the ground that she stabbed him gratuitously."

"In my experience," said Frank, "stabbing is rarely a gratuitous event, but if the goal was to murder her husband, why at Brianne's condo?"

Lee asked, "Why not just poison and stab him in the bushes near the lake path?"

So, he was physically capable of speaking, Alene thought. His comment reminded her of what had happened to Dennis Flynn eight years before. They never did find the person who'd caused his fatal heart attack. What if Joan Stone was responsible for both murders? She wouldn't get away with it a second time. Alene scrunched her face. "Maybe she wanted to steal something from Brianne and kill Gary at the same time."

"You've all told me how you're in and out of each other's apartments," said Frank. "What if someone actually wanted to kill Brianne, but found Gary in the apartment instead?"

"Oh." Alene closed her eyes and concentrated. Then she looked up and blurted, "Or what if Joan wanted Gary dead so she could inherit everything? Wasn't it suspicious that she came home so late on Sunday even though I contacted her much earlier? Maybe she'd actually been home all afternoon and knew that her husband was at Brianne's. Maybe she didn't want a mess in her own apartment."

"You sound convinced that Joan killed her husband," said Frank. Lee nodded in agreement.

"No, I'm still considering other possibilities. Maybe, even though he's no longer a suspect, Jack and Joan planned this together so they could get Gary's insurance. Or maybe they thought Gary took some of the money that Joan embezzled from Hector-Schaf Electronics, you know, that company where they used to work. We still haven't ruled out Bill Vanza or my ex-husband."

"We?" he asked.

"Well, the police," she replied.

"Lee checked Hector-Schaf out, by the way," said Frank. "They did go belly up in '99, and we're still looking into the details." Lee was back to sitting there without speaking.

Alene imagined how satisfying it would feel to solve Gary's murder. "Did you find out exactly what happened to them?" she asked.

"Not yet," said Frank. "So, tell me more about the café. What's a typical day for you?"

"Where do I begin?" Alene thought for a moment. "Aside from researching healthy food trends, studying businesses that supply to the restaurant industry, and working with the suppliers to make sure their organic standards align with ours? Aside from ordering and stocking everything we need to run the café? Aside from dealing with employees and supplies and coordinating events?"

Frank smiled. "Tell me about Ruthie Rosin."

"She's my best friend," said Alene. "She is the best pastry chef in the world - always trying new flavor combinations and creating spectacular desserts, mostly without any animal products whatsoever. That might not sound difficult; but, remember that eggs are from hens and butter is from a cow, and she doesn't use either. Honey is produced by the work of living creatures. Honey sounds simple and wholesome, but worker bees suck the nectar from the stomachs of the honey bees, so it involves a kind of spitting-up between bees, if you think about it."

"I can't believe you just made honey sound absolutely revolting." He sipped from his cup. "So that's done – no more honey for me." Lee scowled in agreement. "What's Edith's position in the cafe?"

"She's supposed to be running the smoothie and juice section under that gorgeous rainbow mural painted by Olly." She pointed, "Look at the cornucopia of fruits and vegetables; it subliminally makes people long for a smoothie. Olly's also talented with woodworking, and he helped Gary build all the shelves and the display cases. Gary did the bulk of the work, because Olly needed to focus on the mural. Anyway, we all work well together, except for Edith."

His forehead crinkled. "It's a lively mural. What's wrong with Edith?"

"She sees a cloud through the window and announces rain, she constantly goes on about her physical ailments, and she makes a fuss about every little change we make, from offering vegan food to altering the recipe for a smoothie. She even has something to say when I move the tables around a bit."

Frank blinked and Lee curled his upper lip. Alene wondered if she sounded as disgruntled as Edith. She added, "Also, she's not friendly with my other employees and she talks to customers in a clipped way, as if they're wasting her time. I really wish I could convince her to act like a nicer person, whether or not she becomes one."

"Why don't you fire her, then?" Frank asked. "You can demand standards of behavior, can't you? You can fire people who don't meet those standards."

Alene had been speaking quietly, not wanting any of her regulars to hear. To her left was the woman with the gap between her teeth and to her right was the woman who helped facilitate Alene's experimental coupons-for-the-homeless program. Alene leaned closer to Frank. "Gary sold me this place for below what it was worth with the stipulation that Edith and Kacey continued working here. Then about a month ago, he asked me to hire Jack even though he knows that Jack is problematic. Now he's gone and I'm going to have to hire Jack but can't fire Edith. She doesn't have anyone to advocate for her."

"She seems much older than everyone else on the staff, so it's not surprising that she's not friends with any of your other employees." Frank said.

"You're probably right, but I think she should still be on your list of suspects."

Lee asked, "What would be her motive for harming her own brother?"

"I don't know, but you should just check into what he ate," said Alene. Apparently, Lee spoke, but only to ask questions.

"I'll do that when I look at the autopsy report." Frank tapped Alene's arm and she hoped her shrug was friendly enough.

"You're really passionate about this place, aren't you?" Frank asked.

"I love it. There's no other place like it. Whipped and Sipped has made the Chicago Tribune's list of Most Interesting Coffee Shops, Best Vegan Desserts, and Best Healthy Breakfast for seven years. We've won awards from national magazines. We've been invited to cater just about every vegetarian event in the city. Even though we're not completely vegan, we serve only vegetarian fare."

"Very impressive," Shaw acknowledged.

Alene beamed. "Also, we do something I wish other restaurants would copy. Our customers can buy dollar coupons to give to homeless folks, and anyone who comes in with that coupon gets a cup of healthy soup and a cookie. Also, we donate trays of day-old baked goods to a local homeless shelter."

Alene dashed into the kitchen and returned with two slices of a Chocolate Applesauce Cake that was too misshapen to make it into the display case. "It's even better with a cold glass of almond milk." Was she yapping like an overexcited puppy?

Lee just nodded his approval, while Frank tasted his slice and said, "I like it. And it's healthy, right?"

She made a face. "It's better than the usual slice of cake because it's packed with fruit and won't slowly chip away at your body like most commercially produced food. It's one of the things I love about this place." Alene looked up and stopped talking.

Jack Stone was stomping in with a determined look on his scraggly face. Alene was glad to have police officers sitting there. She imagined Jack and Joan following Gary across the hall to the Flynns'. Joan could have approached from behind with a knife in her hand, while Jack distracted him. She might have spent all day cleaning up the blood, like Lady Macbeth. That would explain why the kitchen was so pristine on a Sunday afternoon.

Jack came a little too close to Alene, his overgrown hair and beard giving him a wild and somewhat deranged appearance. She said, "Is there something you need from me, Jack, because I'm in a meeting at the moment." She gestured towards Frank and Lee.

"I just want to remind you about the job. Gary promised that you'd hire me," said Jack. He reached out and grabbed her arm. "I really want to work here, Alene. Please tell me what I have to do."

He was just pitiful; thirty-four years old and he still didn't know how to get a job. Alene shook her arm free and tried to be patient. "Remember Friday, when I asked you for a resume, Jack?" All she could do was delay the inevitable. It wouldn't be right if she didn't honor one of Gary's last wishes. "How's the resume going?"

Frank beckoned him closer with his hand. Jack stood his ground and looked suspiciously at both detectives. "What do you want from me?" Jack asked. "It's not against the law to try and get a job."

"No one said it was against the law, Jack." Frank lowered his hand. "I'd hoped you would come closer so I could tell you very quietly that most women don't like to be grabbed."

"I wasn't grabbing her. I was just trying to remind her about the job," Jack mumbled. Alene wondered why his manners were so lacking. Had Joan been too self-absorbed to focus now and again on teaching her son how to be a person?

"I suggest trying to get her attention in a polite way," said Frank. "Ask her nicely if she'll help you with your resume. Really, don't be so defensive. I'm just trying to help you here, Jack."

"Will you please help me, Alene?" Jack asked.

Now she'd have to be polite as well. "Could you start by writing a list of everything you've done? Everyone needs a resume to get a job, and it'll help you in the future as well. You can find a template online or you can go down the street to the library and get help with it."

"Okay." Jack sounded smaller than usual. Was he dangerous or just pitiful? "I can ask at the library. Maybe Tinley will help me. She's been really nice. Is it okay if I take my cocoa to go?"

"That'd be fine," said Alene. "You'll have to shave your beard or wear a beard-net, and you'll need a haircut, Jack. My employees can have long hair, but it has to be clean and neat."

Alene raised her hand to get Olly, who ran over immediately. "How may I be of service, Madam?" He loved speaking as though they were on the set of Downton Abbey. He lifted his non-existent hat, "Sirs?"

"Olly, please give Jack a cup of hot chocolate to go. If he writes a resume, gets his hair cut, wears clean clothing, showers daily, and stops scaring me in the elevator, he might join our team." Olly gaped at Alene until she tapped him lightly on the arm. "Now please, Olly."

Jack's smile seemed uncharacteristically genuine, but he kept looking nervously at Frank and Lee. The minute Olly returned with his drink, Jack took the cup and left the café. Maybe he needed to be treated like an adult before he could find a way into adulthood. Worst case scenario, he'd screw up and she'd fire him. That'd be hard. In the nearly eight years she'd owned the café, she'd never actually fired anyone.

After Jack left, Frank said, "That was nice of you. It's not easy to deal with someone like him."

"No, it isn't, but at least I've come to the conclusion that he couldn't have killed Gary."

"Why not?" asked Lee, eyeing her sideways.

"He moves too slowly."

"We've already ruled him out anyway," said Lee.

Frank said, "I like your cafe. It looks as if quite a bustling business." Alene recognized several regulars among the customers – an older couple quietly drinking tea, tables of two or three having business meetings with words like "protocol" and "database" bandied about, nannies with small children enjoying healthy snacks, and one large table taken up by a man in yellow spectacles whose fingers flew across his laptop.

"Just a normal Tuesday morning," she said. "Those people who are using it as an office need to order something every two hours if they want to keep getting Wi-Fi. It's not fair for them to take an entire table for a whole morning." Alene started to feel uncomfortable about how much she enjoyed chatting with Frank. She realized she knew hardly anything about him. "Excuse me for a second," she said, reaching for her cell to send a quick text to Ruthie.

Within moments, Ruthie appeared with a cup for herself and a full pot of coffee to refresh their cups. She wore an 'I'd rather be baking' apron over skinny jeans and a t-shirt and looked more like a college student than a mother of three. She set the pot on the table and joined them. "Hello Detectives," she said, reaching out her hand to shake, "I'm Ruthie Rosin. Has Alene been helpful or is she just going on about how much she loves Whipped and Sipped?"

"Call me Frank, and this is my partner, Lee Batista. We've been looking forward to meeting you, Ruthie. I understand you are the creative genius behind the operation. Alene was actually just sharing some café secrets."

Ruthie looked pointedly at Alene before saying, "Was she telling you about our food or about our fascinating history?"

Alene said, "Brianne Flynn's grandfather started in this location about fifty years ago, but they served meat and potatoes, kind of Irish-themed. Gary bought the café from them in the nineties."

Ruthie noticed empty trays in the dessert case and said, "Excuse me, I'm needed." She stood and turned to Alene. "We're missing both Edith and Kacey. Are you okay?"

"Not a problem, we've got Sally to cover Edith and Jocelyn is taking over for Kacey," Alene assured her. "Do you think Edith stayed home because Gary was her brother or because she murdered him?"

Ruthie looked horrified. "We don't really know that, do we? My God, Six, who are you going to blame next? The nice detectives here? You could wait until they have some facts to go on."

Somewhat chastised for the moment, Alene said, "We don't even know if and when there will be a funeral."

"Excuse us, ladies." Frank and Lee rose from their chairs. "I will leave you to your speculations about who did it, but I will share one tip – for funeral details you can check the obits in the Tribune. Right now, we're going to get back to work to check whether the autopsy is finished. Thanks for the coffee, and we'll be in touch if I have any further questions."

Alene watched him stride out the door, followed by his partner and his shadow.

Chapter 9

They arrived at the funeral home thirty minutes before the service was set to begin. Alene wondered if the ugly paisley wallpaper and somber colors were meant to plunge mourners even deeper into depression. Her father chose an aisle seat at the back, so Sierra, Quinn and Alene had to squeeze past him to reach their seats, after Alene had leaned Cal's walker against the wall. She placed her purse and sweater on the two seats to her left to save places for her sister and brother-in-law. Gloriadine, the elderly neighbor, who lived next door to the Vanzas and across from Brianne, settled in the row ahead and greeted them while her son parked her walker next to Cal's. Another woman with a walker passed by, next to a stooped over, bald man sporting a much-worn suit, followed by a middle-aged lady with a mop of glowing orange hair that was nowhere near as cool as Tinley's. Sierra and Quinn gawked at her before looking slowly around the hushed room. This was their first funeral. Alene had described the required etiquette and hoped they wouldn't ask where Gary's body was.

She'd sent Noah to camp, but thought Sierra and Quinn were old enough to be respectful and attentive. She'd prepared them with polite things to say to Gary's children and to Joan, but it turned out to be unnecessary. A sign stated that the family would not be greeting visitors before the service.

"We'll be able to speak to Kacey and her family later," Alene whispered to her girls. The room filled up. Alene watched as a few older people paraded by the front row to talk to Gary's children, Bill, Sandy and Kacey, in spite of the sign.

Gary's children sat all the way to the left, and Alene could see Sandy leaning into the aisle, as far as he could from Bill. Alene would have liked to have sat next to Kacey, but it would have been too much of a fuss to move her father and the girls. Where were Joan Stone and Jack? If they were waiting in a separate room for grieving family members, why weren't Gary's children also in that room instead of sitting with everyone else?

Why wasn't Edith Vanza in the private room for the family? She was sitting behind Sandy in the second row, next to a heavyset couple Alene thought might be cousins, whom she'd met once years before. Edith was hunched over, clutching a pack of tissues, and crying her eyes out. The cousins whispered to each other and seemed to be paying no attention to Edith, who looked like a wretched old woman with dyed blonde hair. Alene felt a spasm of guilt for not being more patient with her.

Quinn and Sierra pointed and giggled when they saw Sandy Vanza picking his nose. Alene had to hush them. "You need to be on your best behavior, both of you," she whispered. "We don't laugh at people, and we don't giggle at a funeral."

Bill turned to look around the room and waved at Alene and the girls. Kacey turned and Alene could see that her eyes and nose were puffy and red. Ruthie and Benjie Rosin slowed down as they passed, and Alene beckoned them over to suggest that they sit next to Kacey. As they headed down the aisle, Olly Burns whipped around them and scooted into the seat next to Kacey, so the Rosins just settled into two free seats on the side.

Alene was relieved that Olly had come to support Kacey. She wondered if Tinley was missing because Joan had told her not to come or because Tinley, knowing that Bill couldn't keep his hands off her no matter where they were, hadn't wanted to upset a grieving widow. Either way, it was sensitive of her not to be there. The funeral home filled up with people, some of whom Alene recognized as Gary's college friends, fishing buddies, and golf pals. Alene looked around slowly. It was just so wrong that Gary was dead.

As the room filled up, Sierra and Quinn twisted in their seats in order to watch everyone. Neal approached from the center aisle and sat in the seat to her left that Alene had saved for her sister. "What are you doing here, Neal?" She asked. He'd apparently forgotten his affair with Joan. "These two seats are for Lydia and Theo."

"Gary worked with my father," said Neal, "and my mother wanted me to come in her place. She's feeling under the weather today." The girls leaned across Alene to greet their father with high-fives.

Of course, Mitzi knew nothing about the Neal/Joan episode. Alene said, "I'll call her later. But could you please sit somewhere else? These two seats are for my sister and her husband." Just as Lydia appeared, Neal rolled his eyes and started to say that people don't save seats at funerals. She stared him down, and he retreated to the seat directly behind Sierra and Quinn.

Once Lydia was settled, Alene leaned close to whisper thanks. Lydia whispered back. "Where's the body?"

Alene had known that someone was bound to ask. "Joan had him cremated."

"Then why are they calling it a funeral?" Lydia tapped her foot irritably. "It's a memorial."

Alene didn't even know how to answer. She scanned the room. Joan and Jack still hadn't appeared. She'd never asked about it, but what if he'd never known his father? What if he never had a chance at a normal life because his single mother had been too busy controlling her food intake and having affairs? Do mothers really have the power to destroy their children like that? Was bringing her girls to Gary's funeral potentially scarring? What if she taught them everything right, but their father turned it all around? Alene tried to calm herself.

At least she didn't have to worry about the murderer breaking into her apartment. She'd had the locks changed on Wednesday. The only people she'd told were Quinn and Sierra, her dad, Brianne, and Blanca, all of whom needed to have copies of the new keys. She didn't need to make one for Gary, and she sure didn't want Joan coming in anytime.

For the past week, Alene had been answering her children's' questions about what happens when people die. She looked approvingly at Sierra and Quinn sitting with hands in their laps. Then Neal started bantering with them and she had to hush them all. Neal made a gloomy face and a snide remark too low for her to hear but enough to produce a twitter from the children. Again, Alene didn't know how to respond.

She turned towards her sister. "Is Theo okay?"

"He's fine, why?" Lydia responded too loudly.

Alene fought the urge to shush her. "You asked me to save two seats."

"He's really busy at work," said Lydia, as if that was enough of an explanation. She turned with an exasperated sigh, as though Alene had interrupted her in some unforgivable way. Alene, who felt as if her own hair had frizzed from the heat and humidity, wondered if she was destined to elicit an irritable response in everyone that day.

Just moments before ten, Joan slipped into her seat in the front row a few seats away from Kacey, with her son Jack close behind her. Joan sat like a perfectly coifed, stiff board in her elegant black sheath-dress while Jack, nominally cleaned up but uncomfortable-looking in his suit, kept fidgeting. The minister began speaking. Alene glanced at the program to see what kind of minister he was even though she didn't know the difference. Gary hadn't been religious, either, so Alene wondered where Joan had dug one up.

The minister began by talking about Gary and Edith's early days on the West Side and continued on to Gary's high school, college, and work life, including his years at Hector-Schaf Electronics. That's where he met the woman who was now his grieving widow, Joan Stone. Lydia leaned over and whispered, "Was that before or after she destroyed the company by stealing all its money?" Alene looked up and blinked. She'd been studying the picture of Gary in the brochure> His thinning, silver hair glistened in the sunlight, and his eyes squinted slightly through the round tortoiseshell glasses he always wore.

Alene tried to focus on the minister, who said that after leaving Hector-Schaf, Gary had bought the Whipped and Sipped Café to run with his sister's help. He hadn't enjoyed the constant stress of running a cafe and had later sold it to his manager. After selling the café, Gary could focus more on the things he loved, such as woodworking, fishing, and golf. Alene wasn't surprised that her name wasn't mentioned – she guessed that Joan had passed along Gary's information. The minister didn't speak much about Gary's children, except to say that they'd admired and respected him. He also neglected to mention Gary's unlucky marriage record, only mentioning that Joan had been his third wife. No one else spoke.

Everyone waited until the Vanzas left before moving toward the doors, except for Neal, who jumped up and loudly claimed he had to get back to work. Alene saw Edith heading towards Joan, who turned away and scuttled out without speaking a word. Jack followed like a duck behind her. Alene tried to see guilt in their faces but all she saw was Joan looking bloodshot and wretched. She felt a twinge of pity, wondering if maybe Joan had actually loved Gary.

Ruthie and Benjie Rosin drove Cal and the elderly neighbor home, while Alene Uber-ed with the girls to camp. While changing from her dress into shorts and a t-shirt, in the back seat, Quinn suddenly asked "What happens if you or Daddy dies?"

Alene didn't miss a beat. "I'll always be there no matter what happens to Daddy and vice versa. I promise you won't be alone."

Sierra chimed in. "Yeah, but what if you both die?" Alene went down the list of possible guardians, starting with Ruthie and Benjie, going on to Brianne, their grandfather Cal and grandmother Mitzi.

Sierra asked, "Why aren't Aunt Lydia and Uncle Theo on the list?"

Oops, she thought. No way were those two ever going to get a chance to screw up Alene's kids. "Everyone will want to help," she answered, "but nothing is going to happen to us and I plan to get you settled in your dorm rooms when the time comes for you to go to college." After they both got out and slammed the car door, Alene let herself cry a few tears. Her mother had gotten her settled in her dorm, but then her cancer had returned, and she'd missed everything else in Alene's life. She'd have been disappointed about the divorce, but she'd have been Alene's staunchest ally.

That night, Brianne invited the sixth-floor neighbors for dinner, including Joan, who didn't answer her phone or respond to Brianne's text. Elderly neighbor Gloriadine declined, explaining that the funeral had exhausted her for the day. Alene vowed to have Kacey join them instead of sitting alone in her room but she wasn't sure how she was going to manage it. Brianne was planning to order in, but Ruthie dropped off a tray of frozen sweet potato-black bean empanadas with fresh garlic bread, a big salad, and a jar of her homemade, garlicky salad dressing.

Alene decided to send Sierra to get Kacey, who wasn't responding to texts. It was a chance, but Sierra could be very persuasive. Quinn and Noah were reading comic books on the couch in front of Brianne's coffee table while Alene and her father joined Brianne at her round kitchen table. Sierra rushed back into the kitchen looking flushed. "Joan just screamed at me," she said in a hushed tone. "It was unbelievably scary."

Brianne gulped and Cal covered his mouth in surprise. "What did she say?" Alene asked. How dare she scream at a child?

Sierra reported the story as if it had been a big adventure. "She opened the door and said, 'Get away from me, you little shit. I've had just about enough from all of you.'"

"Oh, my goodness," said Cal, "kindness really doesn't come naturally to that woman."

Brianne shook her head. "She's in mourning. We should be patient with her – but who talks that way to a little girl?"

"I'm nearly twelve-and-a-half. I'm not exactly a little girl," said Sierra with a sigh.

"Did you get to see Kacey?" Alene asked.

Sierra said, "After Joan yelled at me and slammed the door, Kacey screamed that the apartment is in her name, it belongs to her, and she gets to decide who comes in and who lives there."

"It's so unlike Kacey to raise her voice," said Brianne.

Cal said, "Some people don't know how to behave after they've suffered a huge loss. As Shakespeare said, 'Everyone can master a grief but he that has it'."

At least he still remembered some of the aphorisms he'd collected over the years, thought Alene. "What did Joan say after Kacey yelled at her?" She asked Sierra.

"Somebody slammed a door and I left. Anyway, I'm hungry." Sierra picked up a plate and asked Alene if she could start.

While spearing a tomato moments later, Alene wondered if Joan had assumed she'd inherit the apartment if Gary died. If she hadn't murdered him, then Alene was ready to feel sorry for her. Alene remembered how people came and went for hours, after Ruthie's father died suddenly of a heart attack in his fifties, leaving Ruthie and her mother little time to wallow alone in their grief. Ruthie and her mother had an entire week of visitors and dinners and camaraderie. After Alene's mother died, they'd all jumped right back into school and work the day after the funeral. Alene would have liked being surrounded by family and friends, sharing stories about her mother, looking at pictures together, and having enough time to mourn.

Alene removed plates from the table and made a pot of coffee. "Maybe I can host a dinner or gathering of some kind," she said. "It'll be good for Kacey to be surrounded by people who knew and loved Gary. I bet it'll be helpful for her to hear stories and relive happy memories."

"Did you want to invite everyone over to the apartment?" Cal asked.

Brianne said, "That could be too many people if you're planning to invite the whole building. Twelve floors with four apartments on each floor...it could be over fifty people even if only half come. Let's just use the community room and make it a pot luck."

"Everyone likes pot luck," said Cal, "Especially when someone brings sweet and sour salami. Alene won't ever make it for me."

"That's because it's really unhealthy, Dad," said Alene. "I'll have to find out if the community room is available for Sunday evening. We don't have to invite the entire building, do we, Brianne?"

Brianne said, "Just the people we like."

"Exactly," Alene said. "Not the grouchy ones." She felt a little bad about being so mean-spirited but couldn't help herself.

The next morning, Alene was relieved to hear that the community room was available. She texted family and friends and invited them for dinner at six. She invited everyone else to stop by after seven.

Kacey agreed to attend. She had come into Whipped and Sipped on Saturday morning even though Alene had told her to take as much time as she needed. "I'd rather be here than anywhere else," Kacey told her. "I've had the whole week off already. What am I supposed to do all day if I'm not working? I need to stay busy."

"No problem, Kacey," said Alene. "I love having you around and you're getting better and better at the job." Alene thought she saw a glimmer of a smile on Kacey's heart-shaped face. If only it happened more often – in that flash of a smile, Kacey went from pale and bland to sparkling and beautiful.

Bill Vanza, who didn't understand why they were doing anything in memory of his father, whom he hadn't liked, said he'd come for the home-cooked dinner. "Tinley is outstanding in the sack, but she sucks as a cook," he said, and snickered into the phone. Alene wondered if Tinley had been standing there when he said it.

Alene couldn't understand how someone like Tinley, who'd already suffered through one terrible marriage, could be serious about Bill Vanza. Maybe dating him and constantly changing her hair color were signs of low self-esteem. Alene told Bill to bring his brother, if Sandy was willing to attend such a gathering. Social situations weren't easy for him in the best of circumstances, so maybe an event in memory of their father would be too difficult.

On Saturday afternoon, Olly went back to Alene's office and announced, "Officer Adorable and his sidekick are in the house."

Alene pulled a brush through her hair and put on lip gloss before heading up front. First thing she noticed were the quadriceps muscles bulging through Frank's slacks. She hated men who stared at women through their clothes and now she was doing the same thing to a man. She shook the thought out of her head and offered the detectives a cup on the house, something they always did for police and firefighters. Frank asked if she had time to talk.

Alene nodded, and telling herself that she would do the same for any officer of the law, plated two slices of orange poppy-seed cake. Lee attacked his piece as if he hadn't eaten in days and then went outside to smoke. Frank's eyes rolled back as took his first bite.

"Mmmmm, this is nirvana," he whispered.

"Thanks." She waited as he polished off the cake. Just to have something to say while it was just the two of them, Alene started talking about the dinner she was planning. "It's in Gary's memory. Jewish people always gather for a week after someone dies, and they sit around and tell stories. I thought it would be nice for Kacey to be surrounded by people who love her."

Frank said, "I know. They call it 'sitting Shiva'."

Alene wondered if any other police officer in Chicago knew about other peoples' customs. She said, "Brianne and

I invited my sister and her husband, my father and Neal's mother, Kacey's mother and at least one of her half-brothers, the Whipped and Sipped staff, and most of the neighbors on our listserv." Alene bit her tongue to avoid saying anything bitchy about Joan. "I left Joan a written invitation, but she didn't reply, so she probably won't show up."

"Sounds like you did the right thing," he said.

Thinking that it wasn't nice to talk about an event to someone who wasn't invited, Alene blurted, "You could join us if you wanted."

Frank took a slow sip and answered, "It's not a bad idea. Murders are much more likely to be committed by acquaintances than by strangers, so I might learn something. I'd very much like to participate - thank you for the invitation." He turned to see his partner frowning and shaking his head. Frank added, "I'll come without my partner, as a friend of the family."

Alene gulped. "Everyone knows you're a cop, Frank."

"I don't wear a uniform. If anyone asks, I'll tell them we go way back. I'll say I helped you give birth." Frank smiled, stood, and thanked Alene for the coffee and cake. As he walked to the door, she wondered if he'd noticed that her cheeks were flushed.

He turned before he got to the door, and asked, "Do you prefer red or white wine?"

"Either one will be great," she responded, wondering if police were allowed to bring alcohol to a dinner.

That night, as she made sure the apartment door was locked, the house phone rang. Quinn picked up with, "Hi, Dad," and answered several questions with one-word answers. Alene shot her the look that meant "be nice when you're speaking to someone on the phone." Quinn passed her the phone, whispering, "I was politely answering Dad's questions." Alene waved her away and was then even shorter than usual with Neal, who'd called to ask again what time he should come for the Sunday dinner.

She hadn't told Frank Shaw that Neal was coming. "Why don't you check your cell, Neal? I already sent you all the information," she said, not giving him a chance to respond before she hung up. Then she was angry at herself for giving Neal another chance to accuse her of being impatient and rude to him. After she'd just told Quinn to be nice!

As she rubbed lotion on her legs before getting into bed, Alene wondered if Neal could have murdered Gary. He was right-handed, selfish, and always angling for ways to get more than his due. Maybe Neal's father, Patrick Dunn, had told him about helping Joan Stone embezzle money from the electronics company. Neal probably suspected that Gary and Joan still had boatloads of money. What if he'd made such a mess of trying to kill Gary that he'd had to clean Joan's kitchen until it sparkled, so that none of his fingerprints remained? But that theory was crazy because Neal had never been that good at cleaning.

He'd told their mutual friends that the divorce was her fault. He thought he'd been perfectly reasonable, but Alene didn't see it that way. Towards the end he could have starred in a television reality show on how NOT to behave towards a spouse. He berated Alene and called her "frizz-head, fatty, and freak," in front of their children. He swore impatiently at Cal and was rude to Lydia and Theo. He lied about his whereabouts. Did that mean he was also capable of murder? And if he was willing to kill someone like Gary, whom he'd liked, how hard would it be for him to slit Alene's throat or stab her if she angered him one time too many?

That night she had trouble sleeping. She remembered how Gary always asked if she needed anything at the grocery or hardware store. He'd changed ceiling lightbulbs, snaked hair out of drains and helped the children with school projects, such building a replica of the Merchandise Mart. Alene zoomed back to a day when she'd been fretting out loud at work about how her refrigerator at home was dying. Gary had been there, and the next day she came home to see a new refrigerator chock-full of milk, cheese, meat, fruit and vegetables. She knew it was from Gary even though he hadn't left a note. Neal bitched on and on about how Gary was just showing off, and Alene couldn't stop herself from saying, "I know, what a jerk to buy us a refrigerator just like that. He didn't even ask. Can you believe the moxie of that man? And all that food - who needs friends like that?" Neal had stomped out like a petulant teen.

What if Neal had joined forces with Bill after they both decided that they deserved some of Joan and Gary's fortune? What if the two of them had got Gary to meet them at Brianne's because Neal no longer had the key to Alene's apartment? Alene's mind reeled and she wondered if she'd become paranoid.

They'd had some happy years together. They'd had weekly date nights even when the girls were little, and had had fun going out to the movies and concerts, or just hanging out with friends. He'd been great at entertaining and had created flavored vodkas that they used to dream of marketing if he ever got bored of the car dealership. They'd bowled together, which he enjoyed, and she liked only because it was a social night out. He'd made her laugh with spot-on imitations of customers and when they danced, he used to make her weak in the knees.

He had his share of flaws, but who had time to dwell on those things during the crazy years of raising babies? Back then, Alene convinced herself that her life was as good as she'd expected it to be; everyone she knew had spats with their husbands or bellyached about water glasses lying around the house, socks strewn on the floor, and not enough sharing of chores.

After Brianne had told her about Neal's casino nights with Joan, back when Noah was three-months old, Alene had felt as if she'd woken up from years of pretending everything was fine. Maybe she could have kept the marriage limping along, but when she confronted Neal, he told her that what he really wanted was an open relationship. She'd glowered at him, and as she left the room he yelled after her. "You've just proved my theory that you don't really care about my happiness."

But it was true that she could never say marrying Neal was a mistake, because she had her three wonderful children. Still awake at eleven, she texted Ruthie, "What if Neal murdered Gary?"

Ruthie, who also had trouble falling asleep, texted back right away, "Stop blaming Neal for everything, Six!"

Alene wrote, "But what if?"

Ruthie texted, "Focus on the positive – he loves his mother."

"But she didn't do a great job raising him," responded Alene.

Ruthie wrote, "Maybe he is who he is in spite of his parents."

Alene asked, "Is he a murderer?" Ruthie must have fallen asleep and didn't respond, but Neal had moved to the top of Alene's list of suspects.

Chapter 10

Home from her run on Sunday morning, Alene roasted vegetables and started putting together dips and eggplant parmesan while listening to her father share tidbits from the New York Times. He especially enjoyed reading articles about science and business peppered with comments. "You know these cranks who think climate change is a hoax? They should visit someplace that's been devastated by storms... And they shouldn't go to the doctor... because maybe their diseases are hoaxes too." Cal wheezed for a few moments after all that talking and slumped in his seat.

"So, people who don't believe in climate change should die?" Alene asked. She brought him a glass of water.

"No," he said, flushed with excitement and pointing at Alene. "They should just avoid contact with all scientists, including doctors. If they don't believe they're sick, I'm sure they'll be just fine."

Alene kept an eye on her father as he got up from the table and pushed the walker slowly to his favorite chair. The house phone rang as Noah sat at the kitchen counter drawing pictures to tape on the community room windows.

Sierra and Quinn continued to argue about whose turn it was to throw in a load of dirty towels, and Alene marveled that no one seemed to have heard the phone, since they usually managed to hear the oven ding when cookies were ready to come out.

It was her sister Lydia, abrupt as usual. "When should we show up?"

"I texted you to meet at five-thirty upstairs in the community room," said Alene, taking the phone into her bedroom and lying down. "You're bringing a pizza, right? Kacey loves spinach-mushroom, and the Rosins are coming, so no meat of any kind, okay?"

"So, rabbit food for everyone," said Lydia. "What are you making?"

"At the moment, a carrot-top dip."

Lydia sighed noisily. "That sounds gross, Alene."

Alene hated talking about food with her sister. Once, they were out celebrating their father's birthday at an expensive restaurant, and Lydia asked if she could just have a "good piece of chicken instead of something so fussed-over that it looks as if you want to photograph it for a magazine." Alene had been embarrassed into tipping the waiter an extra twenty.

"Last time, you scarfed up my entire fennel-parsley dip. And just so you know, except for the pizza, the entire meal is gluten-free, in honor of your imaginary, non-diagnosed disease, Lydia. I'm making my eggplant parmesan and Ruthie is bringing a huge salad of greens and cold roasted vegetables. Brianne is bringing berries and watermelon. Blanca is picking up Mitzi Dunn, who is feeling better and planning to bring several bottles of good red wine."

"I didn't know she wasn't feeling well," said Lydia. "Why did you invite her, anyway? I don't get why you include her in everything. All I can say is just hope she never marries

130

Dad, because your ex-husband would then become your step brother."

Alene still cherished her relationship with Neal's mother even though she and Neal had been divorced for nearly eight years. "Don't be silly, Lydia. She's my children's grandmother, and she's good company for Dad."

"And it doesn't freak you out?"

"They haven't gone anywhere for a few weeks, but Dad likes to occasionally go to a movie or have dinner with someone who isn't you, me, or a grandchild. Mitzi is even lonelier than he is."

"She should get a dog." Lydia bit into something crunchy like celery or an apple and then talked while chewing, which she knew would drive Alene bananas. "Should we also bring white wine? You know red gives me reflux."

Alene wanted to tell Lydia that she shouldn't discuss her food difficulties with anyone except her gastroenterologist. Instead, she said, "I have a Chardonnay chilling."

"I prefer Sauvignon Blanc," said Lydia.

"So, bring it," said Alene. "And Lydia, this dinner is for Kacey to be surrounded by people who love her. You always loved Kacey, and I want your promise that you won't discuss fertility, or your special diet, or your views about addiction. We need to respect that she's in mourning for her father."

"Really, Alene, you act like I have no common sense at all. I know Kacey's suffering but it's not like she was in flawless shape before her father was killed. Wasn't she arrested for trying to buy a drug with someone else's prescription? Didn't she just get out of rehab? I don't even understand how you can employ her - she could just empty the cash register and walk out one day."

"So could I," Alene responded, "but hardly anyone pays with cash these days."

131

"I feel sorry for her, but some people never learn from their mistakes," Lydia said. "She's like Humpty Dumpty – it'll be nearly impossible to put her back together again."

"You know what?" Alene said, after a few yoga ujai breaths to calm herself. "Just plan to be nice to everyone tonight, including Neal. He grew up with Bill, so inviting him is the right thing to do. Also, the kids love when we're all together as a family."

Lydia was silent, and then she said: "What if Neal brings a date?"

Alene felt drained. "He's stupid and mean but not that stupid and mean."

Lydia's voice softened. "Neal doesn't remember that his cheating on you led to the divorce. If, heaven forbid, Theo and I ever split up, I don't think I'd be capable of including him at a dinner party."

Alene knew they were going through a kind of difficult spot in their marriage, partly because of the stress of several failed pregnancies. She said, "It's not a dinner party tonight, Lydia."

"Right. What about Joan? Is she coming?"

Alene scoffed. "Yes, and she specifically asked to sit next to you."

Lydia asked, "Really?"

"Of course not, you twit. I invited her but she didn't get back to me."

After Lydia's usual abrupt good-bye, Alene made another pot of coffee and blended her red pepper-mushroom dip, a big seller at Whipped and Sipped. They'd been making larger batches in their new industrial blender and selling them in cute little glass jars with a ribbon around the lid. They made only thirty jars each day and usually sold out within a few hours. Alene was considering doubling the production.

She was proud of her experiments, and was constantly refining, trying different combinations, and having to change the labels. That morning she decided to throw a bunch of romaine lettuce in with the red peppers. She always measured everything so that she could repeat the recipe. She blended the vegetables with lime zest, salt, pepper, olive oil, a peeled clementine, and parsley.

At five, Alene told the kids it was time to start setting up for the dinner. "Fine," Sierra said, grudgingly looking up from the television, "but we're not your servants."

Alene puffed out air. "I just need you kids to tape up signs, so people know where to go, and then set up the decorations, tables and chairs. Come on, it'll be fun."

Up in the community room, Quinn and Noah did all the work while Sierra gazed out the window at the approaching storm. Alene preheated the oven, set up her speakers and let Sierra choose the soundtrack. When the chores were done, the children started dancing. It was nice to see Sierra behaving like a child instead of a teenager. At least they were occupied until Ruthie arrived with her husband and children.

Lydia and Theo showed up carrying four large pizza boxes instead of one, as Alene had requested. One of the pizzas was dotted with round slices of meat, so Alene pulled it from the pile. "But Theo loves pepperoni," said Lydia, as Alene carried it to the little community room kitchen and hid it on top of the refrigerator.

Alene said, "I don't want Ruthie to have to smell meat all night. You can take it home later." She put the other three boxes into the preheated oven and asked Lydia to keep an eye on the children. Lydia shrugged as she pulled a wine bottle from her bag.

Before Alene could put the fourth pizza away, Lydia's husband Theo opened the box and grabbed a slice, saying, "I don't see why everyone else has to bend over backwards to cater to people who make a personal decision to not eat meat. Why shouldn't they accommodate my choice to eat meat? My mother always says you should accommodate all your guests' tastes. Maybe I'm offended when there isn't any pepperoni pizza." He cackled at what he thought was a witty comment and repeated it. "Maybe I'm offended when there isn't any pepperoni pizza."

Alene just stared at his poufy hair and at the black glasses frames that were way too large for his thin face. Theo never said something once when it could be repeated. His laugh reminded her of a horse's whinny and he constantly shared what he thought were his mother's wise sayings. He also brought Lydia a cup of coffee before she got out of bed every morning and rubbed her feet every night before bed. "Well, now that you've had a piece of it, you won't need to feel offended this evening," said Alene. Theo neighed.

As she was about to walk out the door, Theo added, "We brought a very expensive bottle of Sauvignon Blanc, so let's make sure it's only served to people who appreciate fine wine."

Alene told herself: Be nice! He's good to your sister. "I'll look forward to having a glass of it, then. Would you please open a bottle of the red wine now, Theo, so we're ready?"

He seemed to crave recognition for everything. The Lego set he'd bought for Noah's birthday had probably cost over a hundred dollars. Alene added, "Please save me a glass."

Just as Alene stepped into the hallway, she met some of her employees exiting the elevator. They'd come straight from Whipped and Sipped, which had closed for the day. Jocelyn, Zuleyka and LaTonya carried containers packed with pastries, brownies and cookies while Grant and Olly rolled in the café's enormous wooden tray. It looked like a sixty-inch round table top except for the metal edging. Olly had helped Gary sand it, finish it, and attach the metal edging.

Alene smiled to see the supplies. "Looks like you brought enough dessert for the entire building."

Olly answered without his usual enthusiasm. "Ruthie helped plan it and we baked up a storm today."

"It was slow, so we just kept trying new combinations," said Jocelyn.

Zuleyka added, "We make so tasty vegan cookies and now we make so nice on tray." Alene had hired her as a nanny shortly after Noah's birth, when Zuleyka's previous job was about to end and just before the youngest child started pre-school. She had started to work at the café after Noah had gone to kindergarten, but Alene still needed her help in getting the kids to camp or school and bringing them home afterwards. "You gonna love this flavors."

"I'm intrigued," said Alene as everyone followed her down to her place. "You guys can organize the tray here without children running around. Oh, and my dad is still here. Are you ready to go upstairs now, Dad?"

Cal crossed his arms and leaned back into his swivel chair. "No thanks, Honey. I'll wait for Mitzi, so I have someone to talk to up in the community room."

"Everyone talks to you, Dad," said Alene. "They all love you." She turned away as LaTonya set her camera case on the ground and placed a large piece of thick corrugated cardboard on the kitchen table, saying, "Thanks, Alene. I think we could get quite a lot of catering work if we publicized our special party tray. Nobody else does anything like it." LaTonya was a practical twenty-year-old who always made sure the pastries were centered perfectly on their doilies and the platters were gorgeous.

Alene thought about it for a second. "You know, that's a really good idea."

Olly and Kacey tuned to leave. Olly said, "I don't think they need all of us to put the tray together. I'm going over to Kacey's to wait while she changes out of her work clothes. I want to lie down for a bit." Alene wondered if he was fighting a virus or something – when had Olly ever needed to lie down during the day?

"Jocelyn, Grant and Zuleyka can do it. I'm just taking pictures," said LaTonya.

As soon as the door closed behind Olly and Kacey, Jocelyn pulled Alene aside and whispered, "Can I talk to you for a second?" Jocelyn had a hearty laugh and favored frilly blouses and large colorful necklaces that covered her Adam's apple. She was saving money for gender confirmation surgery and was always happy to take on extra hours. She'd also told Alene that she was the kind of person who didn't need more than four hours of sleep each night and was happy to open the café at five on weekday mornings. Alene was grateful because now she could work out or run in the morning before heading over to the café.

"Sure, what's up?" Alene asked, noticing how Jocelyn's blouse picked up the turquoise in her eyes. She'd already turned out to be an arresting woman.

"Olly doesn't want you to know how depressed he's been all week," Jocelyn whispered, pulling Alene away from the kitchen towards the back of the apartment.

"We've all been depressed this week, Jocy. How could we not be sad about Gary?" said Alene.

As she turned to go, Jocelyn held onto Alene's arm and said, "I'm not sure you understand, Alene. Olly loved Gary."

"We all loved him," said Alene.

Jocelyn shook her head. "No, I mean really, really loved him." Jocelyn and Olly shared an apartment in Andersonville, a few neighborhoods north of Lakeview, and they'd been friends since high school. Jocelyn probably knew Olly better than just about anyone.

Alene's first thought was to feel bad for Olly. Then her mouth dropped open. "Oh."

On one hand, Olly was always falling in love with unattainable men. On the other hand, Gary was nearly forty years older than he was. Was it possible that Olly had murdered Gary? Could happy-go-lucky Olly do something so awful? Dang girl, she scolded herself, your mind went right there. You really need to lay off being the detective!

"Did Gary know?"

Jocelyn tilted her head down and said in a low voice, "Maybe, but he probably thought that Olly would get over it."

Alene moved slowly. Weighed down by her own neurotic thought that Olly could be a suspect, she forgot why she'd wanted to go down to her apartment in the first place. "Don't forget to put up a sign reminding all the neighbors to go up to the community room for dessert later," said Cal from his swivel chair in the living room.

That was it. "Right. Thanks, Dad, see you in a bit," said Alene. She was back in the elevator pressing the button that would take her back up to the community room when Brianne Flynn slipped in carrying a big glass bowl of fruit.

Alene could only nod at Brianne, who said, "I know, I feel the same – just enervated. Thanks for coordinating this dinner, Alene." Alene couldn't answer. Had Gary loved any of his wives, or was he actually a different person to whom she'd thought? Jocelyn hadn't even been sure how Gary felt about Olly, so why did she even tell Alene that Olly loved him?

She told Brianne what Jocelyn had said, and they rode up in the elevator in silence. Ruthie and Benjie had arrived with their three children, Shaily, Eden and Avi, who were already playing with Alene's children. The two twelve-year-old girls whispered by the window while the four younger ones chased each other along the benches that lined the room. Ruthie put her arm around Alene's shoulders and pulled her into a corner. "You look terrible, Six. What can I do to help?"

Alene whispered what she'd just learned about Olly. Ruthie covered her mouth with her hand and they stood together, trying to come to terms with it. "I wonder if Gary was loyal to anyone," said Alene.

Before they had a chance to talk it through, Mitzi Dunn swept into the room and announced, "It is raining cats and dogs out there!"

Mitzi had stopped at the apartment to bring Cal, who hugged Ruthie and said, "You, Ruth Blum Rosin, are a sight for sore eyes. How come you don't come and visit me like in the old days?"

Ruthie laughed. "I'd stop by if I had the time, Cal. We haven't seen you and Mitzi at the café for a few weeks. Why don't you come by more often?"

Lydia approached and kissed Cal on the cheek. Her husband Theo followed and held out his hand as if for a handshake, but Cal hugged him instead. "That's how we do things in this family, Son," said Cal. Theo neighed softly as he and Lydia headed towards the drinks.

Cal turned back to Ruthie and said, "I like your husband. I hope my daughter finds someone like Benjie and gets a second chance." Benjie was doing magic tricks with the four younger children so the noise had decreased and everyone else could hear the Bruno Mars soundtrack that Sierra had chosen.

Lydia hugged Theo and said, "Maybe she'll find someone like my husband."

Ruthie, always the diplomat, said, "We all agree that Alene deserves someone wonderful. It's just too bad she hates dating."

"That's not true," Alene objected, coming suddenly back to the present. She'd tucked away what she just learned about Olly, with plans to think more about it later. "I just hate going out with the kinds of losers and idiots I've met in the past eight years. I'd love to meet someone who's kind, decent and honest like Benjie, and like you, Dad." She gave him a quick kiss on the cheek, and he beamed.

During the year after Alene's mother died, following her battle with breast cancer, Cal had been heartbroken and depressed. He'd left his career of managing investment portfolios and began teaching business and finance at a charter high school on the West Side. He had unending patience for teenagers and felt as if he was doing something more meaningful than choosing investments for already-wealthy customers. He liked the community of teachers and even tried to fix Alene up with someone from his school, several times. She'd never figured out why he thought she would have anything in common with the automotive and welding teacher who only wanted to talk about his muscle car, his ex-wife, and working out.

"Shoot," Alene said, "I really should have invited Michael Jay since he trains so many of us in the building. Gary worked out with him too."

Mitzi hugged Alene and said, "You'll find someone, Sweetheart. Also, you look adorable in that dress. Blue is a marvelous color for you." Alene wondered if Mitzi was at all uncomfortable knowing that Alene was single and alone because of Neal, her son. She took compliments from Mitzi very seriously – Alene's former mother-in-law dressed in the most up-to-date designer fashions, her snowy-white hair was purposely asymmetrical, and her nails were always a flawless, shiny scarlet.

Cal said, "I think my daughters always look beautiful." He turned to Alene. "It's okay that you didn't invite Michael. Every time I do my strength exercises with him, he gives me a lecture about the evils of carbohydrates. He'd only eat the raw vegetables and the salads tonight. Better that he's not here and I can eat without guilt."

"I still feel bad that I forgot," said Alene.

Mitzi hugged her. "You're a sweetie-pie, always worrying about others. I hope you're taking enough care of yourself, Alene, honey."

Mitzi still called nearly every week to ask Alene if she could help with the children. Once a month each child got to spend an afternoon with her doing whatever he or she liked best. In the past month, she'd taken Sierra to dinner and a movie, she'd helped Quinn put together a giant puzzle and gone to a bead store to make bracelets, and she'd accompanied Noah to his favorite place, the Shedd Aquarium.

Alene still loved Neal's mother. Mitzi had kept working despite the life insurance payments she began receiving after her husband died. She loved being a sales associate at the Neiman Marcus store on Michigan Avenue, and laughingly told everyone they'd probably let her work forever because she spent more than she made every month. "Also," she would say with a chuckle, "I know how to get women like me to drop thousands."

Alene hugged both her father and Mitzi. "You're both right. I'm grateful you came. Now we've got to take the food out of the oven."

Brianne appeared and helped Alene and Ruthie set out dinner in the community room's little kitchen. Alene looked at her watch and said, "I asked Olly to bring Kacey up here right at five-thirty. It's quarter to six now – hope she's okay."

"Did we ever get anywhere on time when we were that age?" Ruthie asked. She'd brought a huge wooden bowl and was emptying plastic bags of chopped fresh and cold roasted vegetables into it. She held two big spoons to toss the salad together with her famous dressing. For years she'd kept it a secret, until she had to break it down for the staff to make at

Whipped and Sipped. They needed exact amounts instead of her usual pinch of this, handful of that. The staff gave it the nickname "SDSG – She doesn't stint on garlic."

Everyone nibbled the hors d'oeuvres and played the ever popular "What did Alene put in her dip" game. At Whipped and Sipped she was transparent about otherwise hidden ingredients such as raisins, capers, fennel, or beets, but at home she liked people to guess. Alene looked at her phone and told Ruthie and Brianne, "Olly just texted that he and Kacey are coming soon."

"You can stop worrying now, Six," said Ruthie.

"As if she'll ever stop worrying," said Brianne, sweeping side bangs off her tanned face.

Everyone looked up as Neal emerged from the elevator. He was damp from the rain and dressed in his usual "divorced guy" ensemble. Alene noted the tight shirt that didn't look as good as he thought it did. He reeked of a musky cologne that meant he would be going out later. She longed for a time to come when Neal's annoying little habits of commenting on her hair ("I don't remember it being so frizzy"), scrutinizing the apartment for changes ("I see you finally fixed that flickering light fixture"), hugging her a little too closely, looking everywhere except in her eyes, and licking his fingers while he ate would no longer make her want to throw something at him.

Alene greeted Neal as civilly as she could and then turned to Ruthie. "Have you tried all my dips yet, Nine?"

"They're stellar," Ruthie said, turning to her husband, who wore his standard summer outfit of a polo shirt and shorts. "Honey, did you see that Neal is here?" Alene knew that Benjie would pick up Ruthie's implied meaning, which was that he was needed to deal with Neal. It was one of the things she most admired and envied about Ruthie and Benjie's relationship – their ability to understand each other's veiled messages.

"Hey, Neal," said Benjie with his warm smile, running his fingers through his still thick, dark hair, "Ruthie wants me to trade in my 2006 Honda Pilot, but I love it almost as much as I love my children. Are the new Pilots any good or do you think I should look into a Subaru?" Alene stopped listening, knowing that Neal would be engaged.

Just then Frank Shaw stepped out of the elevator and into the community room. He was wearing khakis and a blue button-down shirt with the sleeves rolled up to the elbows. He held a jacket in one hand and a bottle of Pinot Gris in the other. Alene wiped her suddenly sweaty hands on her leggings. His handshake was warm as she thanked him for coming. She saw Neal raise an eyebrow but pretend not to care. In the years since their divorce, she'd been forced to watch him canoodling with everyone from halter-topped anorexic students to toned, tanned suburban divorcees. He thought nothing of arriving to pick up the children with a bare-midriffed waitress next to him in some little sports car someone traded in, at his dealership. Alene stared at Neal until he blinked, and then turned towards her father feeling a small flash of victory.

"Dad," said Alene, after Frank tossed his jacket onto one of the built-in benches, "This is Frank Shaw, the police detective who has been so helpful all week."

Her father stood a little straighter as if his posture was being evaluated, and said, "Cal Baron."

"Pleased to meet you, sir," said Frank. "I'm not sure if Alene told you that we actually met eight years ago when your grandson was born. I look forward to chatting more, but please excuse us for a moment while I speak to your daughter." Frank steered Alene towards the windows. "I thought I was coming as an old friend of yours who helped deliver your baby."

Alene blushed. "Oops. I forgot. I'm sorry."

"It's all right – they'd all find out anyway that I'm a detective. I'm glad I could come, and hope you'll remember to call me Frank." Alene nodded and mumbled more apologies. Then Benjie Rosin approached, and it turned out he knew Frank through past troubles in one of the buildings Benjie managed. Sierra sidetracked Neal, who was on his way to the refrigerator for a beer, and Alene could see from across the room that she was complaining about one of her siblings. Good, Alene thought, let Neal deal with his adolescent daughter for a change.

Finally, Olly and Kacey showed up. Noah and Avi yelled "surprise" even though both Alene and Ruthie had explained that it wasn't a party. Kacey, looking confused, would probably have left right then had Olly not folded her in a hug.

After that, Kacey's mother, Isobel, arrived looking less healthy than usual, with bags under her eyes and pasty, yellowish skin. She was drenched but wore a nice outfit – a dress of swirling greens and sandals with leather ties. She'd been divorced from Gary for many years, so Alene thought that it was nice that she had showed up.

"Thank you for inviting me, but I realize that I'm not comfortable here," Isobel said.

Alene said, "Probably because you got caught in the rain without a coat."

Isobel gave her a look. "I'll be back in an hour or so to take Kacey home with me. I think she needs a healthier environment."

"Okay." Alene wondered why it felt like Isobel was laying down a gauntlet of some kind. "But you're welcome to stay, Isobel – we've got plenty of food."

"I'm sure I must have mentioned that I follow a strictly macrobiotic diet," Isabel said in a disdainful way. "I would guess that I could eat very little being served this evening, but have fun Kacey, honey, and I'll see you in a bit."

Alene smiled by pressing her lips together and turning up the edges. She watched Isobel step back into the elevator with her head high while Kacey closed her eyes and hung her head.

Olly took Alene aside. She wondered if people were going to be taking her aside all evening. "I'm still having nightmares about finding Gary on the floor," he said. How about you, are you all right?"

"Sort of," Alene admitted, feeling as if Olly would be suspicious if she was to suddenly act cold and withdrawn towards him, since she had learned about his affair with Gary. Had Jocelyn actually said they were having an affair? Alene couldn't remember but tried to act as normal as possible. "This has been hard for all of us."

"I'm glad the cop is here to help. Are they any closer to finding out what happened?" He gestured with his thumb toward Frank.

"I think he's still gathering information," said Alene.

Olly's forehead wrinkled and he pushed aside a stray red ringlet. "About the murder or about you?" he asked.

Alene tightened her lips. She'd have to tell Frank about Olly's relationship with Gary. She didn't feel comfortable asking Olly anything about it, though. "You're doing a great job of taking care of Kacey," she told him. "You're helping her get through the worst crisis of her life."

They both looked at Kacey sitting there pale and withdrawn with her eyes flitting back and forth. She was extraordinarily thin, and Alene wondered if she had the strength to overcome this latest blow. Over the past year or so, Gary had sent her on at least three rehabilitation stints, from which she'd graduated, but after varying amounts of time, she'd always ended up back in trouble. Alene whispered to Olly, "Remember how Kacey used to swoon over Ruthie's pastries when she was younger? I have this crazy feeling that if she would eat just one thing, she'd come around and all would be well."

"Since we're imagining fairy tales, could we get Gary back?" Olly asked. Alene did a double take. Would he speak that way if he'd murdered Gary?

Just then Bill and Tinley entered the community room with Sandy Vanza tagging behind. They must have come from the condo because they were all dry. Alene welcomed Bill and Tinley while Sandy just pushed by as though he had important business to accomplish. He looked as if he might have slept in his wrinkled slacks and white shirt, decorated with a coffee stain shaped like California. Bill was wearing khakis and a dark green polo, and looked as if he'd been smoking pot all day with his red eyes and dazed expression. Tinley far outshone Bill in comportment and looks. Her hair was carrot-colored, and she wore a bright purple romper that showed off her curves and highlighted her cornflower eyes. It occurred to Alene that she was probably not re-dyeing her hair every few days. All the color changes were just different wigs. Of course, a hairdresser must own a lot of different wigs.

Bill strutted into the room as if every eye was on him. Alene hoped that for this one evening, he would avoid bragging about his exploits with women or sharing his poorly-thought-out, simplistic views of politics. Why couldn't he focus on his actual strengths, such as his success at selling used cars or his discipline in body building? Tinley must be the most patient woman in the history of humanity, thought Alene, wishing there were a way to convince her she could do much better than Bill Vanza.

Everyone listened to Tinley describe the violent movie she and Bill had seen that afternoon, while Neal approached the brothers, edged out Sandy, and huddled with Bill as if they were back in high school on the football field. Alene excused herself to attend to the food and noticed Bill with his arm around Tinley and his hand dangling as though he were about to fondle her. Ruthie joined her in the kitchen and jabbed Alene with her elbow. "Disapproval and disgust are written in bold letters on your face."

Alene blushed and lowered her head. "I'm mostly sad for Kacey, but how are Sandy and Bill going to cope? Look at Sandy sitting there by himself, incapable of communicating his basic thoughts."

Gary had once told Alene that he thought Bill and Sandy could be a good influence on Kacey, their half-sister. Alene wasn't sure why Gary thought Sandy was capable of influencing anyone since his conversation mainly consisted of him saying what he liked or didn't like, and snippets of songs or sayings. He liked people who gave him candy and soda, and who didn't ask him questions. Maybe Gary thought that helping Sandy would be character-building for Kacey.

Bill had given Kacey her first beer when she was thirteen and her first hits of pot shortly afterwards. After her terrible car accident at fourteen, he'd passed along pills that were even better than the painkillers she got from the doctors. Alene and Ruthie watched as Tinley smacked Bill's hand away from her boobs, laughing.

"I saw Isobel for half a minute just now, but what about Gary's first wife? What was her name?" Ruthie quietly asked Alene. "Did she show up at the funeral?"

"I never knew Bill and Sandy's mother," said Alene, watching Frank as he chatted with Benjie Rosin. "Gary was married to Isobel when he moved into our building."

Brianne approached, blocking Alene's view of Frank and Benjie. "Come get food before it's gone."

"You've always worried about those of us on the sixth floor," Alene said. "Remember those years when Kacey used to sleepover every weekend? She was like your third child."

Brianne said, "She still is."

146

They'd watched Kacey fall apart during high school. She was still in pain from the car accident that had killed Isobel's second husband. While Brianne's daughter was blossoming into a young woman, applying to colleges and deciding between economics and international studies, Kacey was battling a budding addiction and self-mutilating with piercings, tattoos, and carved collar bones. Back then, she hadn't been consistent about coming into work at Whipped and Sipped. Alene wondered if it would have made a difference had she demanded more of Kacey. Maybe she should have required her to come on time like all the other employees.

When they were nearly finished with dinner, Brianne announced that she was going to light a candle to pass around the table. Whoever held the candle could share a memory of Gary or say something in Gary's memory. Brianne said, "To our friend and neighbor who has helped all of us through our trials and tribulations, rest in peace, Gary. Your light shines on."

Ruthie quoted a psalm and Benjie told a story about Gary teaching him a few wood-working secrets. Sandy refused to speak. Bill said he hoped his father had saved as much money as he'd spent. Alene felt embarrassed for him. Tinley reminisced about how she'd asked Gary for a picture of Bill when he was little. She'd looked through every photograph album, file and drawer but never found it. Tinley concluded with "I hope you can see all your photographs in heaven." Alene thought it was sappy, but sweet. Lydia and Theo both mumbled something about resting in peace. Cal said he was speaking for Mitzi too, and proceeded to tell a story about how Gary helped him after he'd fallen in the lobby. "The two most important days in your life are the day you are born and the day you find out why," wrote Mark Twain, "and Gary realized that he was born to be the best friend, best neighbor, and best father he could be." Cal concluded and everyone applauded.

Then Alene reminisced about times Gary had joined the kids at the annual Lakeview Festival and the free Grant Park Wednesday Evening concerts during the summer. She remembered how he'd once teared up listening to a Bach Suite for Unaccompanied Cello. Alene concluded with hopes that Gary's children would always remember him as a loving father.

Frank said, "There is a Japanese proverb, 'If the character of a man is not known to you, look to his friends' – condolences to all of you on this huge loss." Alene choked up a bit. Frank was really kind of a good guy. Would he ever be interested in someone like her?

Brianne blew out the candle. A summer storm had raged all through dinner, with occasional flashes of lightening followed by loud, rumbling thunder, and then had blown itself out.

Alene stood and said, "I'm still finishing my beer, but does anyone want coffee? The staff is probably bringing up dessert even as I speak."

Frank Shaw joined her in the little kitchen with his unfinished beer. "Look how calm the lake is now."

"Yeah, but I wouldn't want to be in a boat out there after a storm like that," said Alene.

He mentioned the boat docked at Montrose Harbor and said he'd been forced to sell it after his divorce. Alene tried not to turn to look at him again after that revelation. He just kept talking as if he hadn't told her something extremely personal. He'd kept the slip, he said, because he dreamt about buying another boat one day. Alene concentrated on her breathing and forgot about everyone else in the room.

Then Frank noticed that you could watch the sun beginning its descent on the other side of the community room, through the back windows, and they raised their beers in a toast to sunsets.

Battered: A Whipped and Sipped Mystery

Chapter 11

Olly and Jocelyn rushed into the community room and found Alene standing in the kitchen with Frank. "The tray tipped over and has to be reassembled...sorry," Olly said breathlessly while Jocelyn wrung her hands.

"Is everything salvageable?" asked Alene. Frank stood up and politely excused himself from the conversation. She watched him walk over to her father and ex-mother-in-law, Mitzi, and admired his confident stride. She also noticed his butt and felt herself turning red.

Jocelyn said, "They're picking up the cookies and wiping them off. Would you be okay with moving the party down to your apartment? It's too hard to get the tray and three of us holding it into an elevator."

"Sorry," said Alene. "It's an old building."

"If we can serve it at your dining room table, we won't have to risk another cookie Armageddon," said Olly.

Alene said, "But I wasn't prepared for guests."

"We'll clean everything up in ten minutes," Jocelyn said, grinning optimistically, "maybe fifteen at most."

"No other options? We'll need to put a sign on the community room door for all the neighbors. Also, someone will need to help my dad," said Alene. "And Neal's probably going to snoop around and find things to criticize."

Olly asked, "I could wrestle him to the floor if he bothers you."

"No," said Alene, "but thanks for offering." Maybe Olly had loved Gary because he was like a father-figure to him.

Jocelyn said, "Olly can put up the sign, LaTonya will put down her camera to help your father and I'll distract Neal." She did a party-girl dance move to the music of one of the female pop singers on Sierra's playlist. Alene couldn't tell which one it was, but it reminded her that she needed to bring the speakers back to her place.

"I'll need paper and markers," said Olly, mirroring Jocelyn's moves.

"Thanks guys." Alene tried to look deeper into Olly's eyes to see if there was a killer in there. She'd read about smooth, engaging, psychopathic killers. He'd been so depressed and now suddenly he was dancing.

Ruthie saw her expression and immediately ran to her side. Alene told her about the change of venue, and they both started cleaning up. Her husband Benjie herded the children, Brianne took care of the trash, and Mitzi helped Cal get into the elevator and walked him back into the apartment. Everyone else helped clear the community room except for Sandy, Bill, and Neal. Frank entered the elevator just behind Alene. Just as she was about to tell him about Olly being in love with Gary; Neal, Sandy, Bill and Tinley crowded in with them.

In Alene's miraculously straightened apartment, Olly and Jocelyn had started brewing coffee and Zuleyka was setting out the cups, creamer and sugar. The folks Alene had invited from the building listserv would start coming by soon. While coffee was served, she summoned Ruthie's daughter Shaily to go with Sierra and help deliver leftover pizza and salad to a few neighbors.

The two girls stopped first across the hall and returned just moments later. Miss Gloriadine said she was contagious, and they should leave the plate in the hallway. She was too sick even to engage in her favorite pastime of peeking out the peephole when she heard the elevator open. "We saw Joan Stone," reported Sierra. "Did you invite her, Mom?" Alene disliked the expression Sierra used to convey disbelief, with her mouth opened wide and her eyebrows down at the edges.

"Yes, of course I invited her, but I don't think she's planning to join us," Alene replied. Aside from how Joan felt about everyone on the floor, it was possible that she preferred to be alone in her grief. That is, if she was indeed grieving.

Alene then sent the girls to bring a plate to Mehrdad, the Iranian-born CPS teacher and member of the condo board who was recuperating from a car accident. It had taken place just up the street at a badly designed-intersection. Alene gave them the key with instructions to leave the plate just inside the door, so Mehrdad wouldn't need to get up out of bed. After that, they brought a plate to the thirteenth floor for Penny and Melvin Stohl, who'd twisted his ankle during the couple's riverboat cruise in France.

Alene heard the door slam and the sound of the girls giggling. The doorbell rang and she called out to Sierra to answer it, assuming it was one of the neighbors, but then she heard Kacey's mother Isobel announce, to no one in particular, "I think Kacey has had enough entertainment for the evening and I'm taking her home now."

"Hold on, Isobel," Alene called from the kitchen, hustling out to the living room where she could speak in a normal voice. "Neighbors in the building are stopping by soon to pay their respects to Gary's kids, and we haven't even served dessert yet."

Isobel snorted, "The last thing my daughter needs is more sugar to destroy her already fragile balance. Thanks, but no thanks, Alene. Kacey will not be eating your dessert as long as I'm around to protect her."

"But Kacey helped bake it and it's being served in just a bit," Alene said, although Isobel had already stormed out. She dried her hands quickly and hurried towards into the living room just as the door closed behind Kacey and Isobel. She heard them getting into the elevator.

Alene told Ruthie, "She didn't even say good-bye," just as Neal walked by.

With the relish of an ex-husband who enjoys criticizing, he said, "Kacey? Give the girl a break, why don't you? She's in mourning."

Alene squeezed Ruthie's arm, counted to ten, and pretended that Neal was a stain on the wall that would fade with time. She whispered to Ruthie, "I'd hoped he'd leave once we cleared out of the community room and I hoped the Vanza boys would join him."

"Sandy is still here staring out the window, but Bill and Tinley have already left. They're probably visiting friends in the building or something," Ruthie said.

"Or getting high across the hall," Alene added.

Ruthie gave her the look of a disappointed teacher and continued. "You can't change anyone—you can only change your own perceptions and reactions. Let it go."

Olly passed at that moment and heard Ruthie. Then he launched into the first few lines of *that* song from the movie, *Frozen,* while Alene pulled Ruthie towards the door. Alene said, "I'm not going to respond to Neal but I'm going to keep whispering to you because I know it drives him batty."

Ruthie responded with an unsympathetic look. "I'm giving you points for not responding, but you get demerits for engaging at his level. Anything Neal says or does should just go unnoticed, Alene. Aren't you getting this yet?"

Instead of responding, Alene waved at Bill and Tinley, who had come back to the apartment. "We invited several neighbors who wanted to give their condolences to Kacey and now she's not even here," she told Ruthie, just as Jocelyn ran from the guest bathroom carrying a fringed leather bag.

"Isn't this Kacey's purse?" Jocelyn asked. "Did she leave without it? If she comes back will someone tell her I have it?" Jocelyn joined the rest of the staff admiring the enormous dessert tray on the dining room table. LaTonya snapped photos of the tray and the reactions of everyone standing around the table. The she was distracted by the crystal bowl filled with fruit and focused on photographing it from every angle.

"The unveiling isn't as dramatic as I'd wanted," Olly said, sighing. "Luckily, every cookie is guaranteed to be scrumptious. Want me to gather the troops?"

Alene nodded and told Mitzi and Cal to sit in the closest chairs. Lydia and Theo chose seats. Neal sat next to his mother and Bill sat to Neal's left with Tinley to his own left. The remaining three seats were taken by Brianne, Ruthie and Benjie. Alene stood in front of the Whipped and Sipped staff and admired the magnificent cookie platter as Frank stepped into place beside her.

Neal left his seat to go over and whisper something to Sierra. On the way back to his seat he tapped Alene's shoulder and mentioned that the blinds were uneven and that she had several bulbs out. She just glared at him until he passed by. Then she leaned towards Frank and whispered, "Jocelyn told me that Olly was madly in love with Gary even though Gary was straight. Did you know that?"

Frank squinted at her before answering, "No." He pulled out his phone and abruptly excused himself.

Everyone filled a plate and sat at the table except Sandy, who had been discomfited by the move down to the apartment and was still staring out the window. Everyone else approached the gigantic tray and chose a cookie or two. After much study, the children took two or three each and scattered to the back bedrooms.

Everyone munched while LaTonya continued taking pictures. Tinley was first to comment. "I love this chocolate-chocolate chip cookie," she said.

"Mine is coffee-flavored," said Bill, making a face. "I hate coffee."

Tinley smacked him on his shoulder. "Does everyone need to know what you don't like?" Alene wanted to hug her.

Lydia said she loved her cinnamon cookie and wondered if it was gluten-free but nobody responded. She nibbled a few bites before passing it to Theo, who said, "Crunchiest cookie I've ever tasted."

Sandy looked suspiciously at the tray of cookies, then took one and sniffed it before putting it back on the tray. Alene retrieved it and tossed it in the trash.

Cal and Mitzi wanted to taste more flavors, so they shared plates. Neal blurted across the table, "This one is kind of buttery almond. Did you use real butter, Ruthie? I thought you were vegetarian."

Ruthie smiled while Alene imagined an imaginary bubble above her head that said, "Of course there's no butter, you dingbat. Vegans don't use animal products." What Ruthie actually said, in the same voice she used to speak to her eight-year-old son, was, "I'm vegan, and we don't use animal products in anything, Neal. Which cookie did you like best?"

Alene was awed, as usual, by Ruthie. Explaining anything to Neal was usually a complete waste of time, but asking an opinion of someone who likes his own voice best of all? Behind his head, Alene gave Ruthie a phantom high-five, as Neal muttered, "They're both good I guess."

Fourteen neighbors stopped by during dessert. All oohed and aah-ed over the meringues and paid their respects to Gary's sons, Bill and Sandy, and asked where Kacey was. Nobody asked about Joan or Jack Stone. Alene just kept shrugging.

LaTonya packed up her camera and left with the other staff members except for Olly, who sat on the edge of his seat looking very interested in Bill. Alene felt a little miffed; if he'd loved Gary, why was he already assessing Bill as if he were a dessert? Did Bill remind him of Gary? There was a strong resemblance, but Gary had been caring and thoughtful.

When all the neighbors had gone and their plates were clean, Mitzi announced that she'd brought a little something for Brianne to cheer her up since the anniversary of her husband's death had just passed. It was an exquisite silk scarf. Brianne was moved to tears. "This is so lovely, and totally unnecessary, Mitzi," said Brianne, as Mitzi draped it artfully around Brianne's neck.

"I know, I know," said Mitzi, "but I always treat myself to something pretty on the anniversary of my husband's death, and I thought you might enjoy something nice to throw on now and then. I bought myself the same scarf, only yours is in jewel tones that look perfect with your olive complexion."

Sandy Vanza started pacing and muttering that nobody told him to bring a gift. Tinley took him aside, calmed him down, and walked him out the door. Alene wondered if she planned to walk him all the way to his group home near Belmont and Halsted. Bill and Neal stayed on before suddenly disappearing without a word of thanks to her or farewell to the children.

Just as Alene was looking over at Frank, still sitting out on the balcony with Benjie Rosin, the door opened and Kacey Vanza came into the dining room. She seemed in much better spirits than she'd been before her mother pulled her out. Olly shrieked, jumped over to hug her, saying, "I knew you'd come back. How could you have left without your purse, you numbskull?"

The six children ran out of their bedrooms to see what had caused the loud shriek and Alene said, "We all thought you'd gone to your mother's place. I was sorry I missed saying goodbye." Kacey's eyes were bloodshot and her pupils were pinprick-sized, but everyone was delighted that she'd returned. Alene was disappointed, but maybe the stress was too much, and she hoped Kacey had just taken something small and legal to calm her nerves.

Kacey said, "I wouldn't leave without thanking you, Alene. I just went downstairs to get my mother to leave me alone. We fought for a while and then I told her to F off." Kacey cringed a bit and corrected herself in front of the children. "I mean I told my mother that it wouldn't be nice to leave since this event is in memory of my father." Kacey put her purse on the table next to the door.

The girls tittered but Noah and Avi nodded sagely before running back to the bedroom. Olly handed Kacey a fresh cup of coffee and a dessert plate to Kacey, and she thanked him.

"Kacey, you sure have changed since the days when you pretended your cocoa was coffee and you'd parade in front of the mirror wearing lipstick and jewelry with my Dara. Do you remember being that young?" Brianne asked, lovingly nudging a wayward strand of Kacey's corn silk hair back behind her ear. Alene knew she missed having her children nearby.

Kacey said, "Now I brew coffee with one hand tied behind my back." She stroked Brianne's new scarf as Ruthie

158

and Benjie gathered their three children and said their goodbyes.

Alene saw that it was seven-thirty, good time for a Sunday evening dinner to end. Lydia approached to whisper that she and Theo were running back up to the community room to get that pepperoni pizza. Alene said, "Help yourself." She noticed Frank tucking his phone back into his jacket as she and Brianne retreated to the kitchen. She could tell he was getting ready to leave but figured he'd wait until she and Brianne returned to the dining room. "I'm so glad Kacey came back," Alene told Brianne.

Brianne whispered, "I wish she knew how adorable she'd be if she got healthy. She should also get rid of some of those tattoos and piercings."

"If she did that, I'd let her out front to work with customers. Do you remember how many complaints we got? They used to say that the one in her tongue made them lose their appetites." Alene looked out at the dining room and saw Frank talking to her dad. Good, that meant he wasn't about to run out the door.

Just then Bill and Neal sauntered back into the front door. Their eyes were red, they reeked of pot, and they were giggling, as expected. Alene looked at Frank to see if he'd noticed. It's not like he'd arrest them, but how thoughtless could those two be? Tinley was smart to have left with Sandy earlier. Alene had lost patience with Neal by then and was just about to say something sarcastic when he and Bill loudly thanked everyone and left before Alene and Brianne got out of the kitchen.

Olly stayed close to Kacey. Brianne was trying to encourage both Kacey and Olly to volunteer with her at St. Andrew's Hospital, where she'd been a greeter for years.

Kacey jumped up suddenly. "I think I left my phone charger in the community room. I'll just run up the stairs to look. The elevators have been slow all day today." As she left through the front door, Olly went back to the bedroom where they'd all been hanging out and came back moments later triumphantly holding the charger.

"I'll go catch up with Kacey on the stairs." He ran past Alene and out the door. Then, before anyone had a chance to speak, they heard a muffled scream. Alene thought it sounded like it came from the stairwell.

They all jumped up and rushed out. Frank opened the stairwell door. Kacey stood there looking like she might scream again. She was holding a gun. Frank entered the stairwell behind Alene, and said, "Please stay where you are, Kacey, and slowly put down the gun." As Kacey obeyed his instructions, Frank quickly pulled on gloves, picked up the gun and examined it. Alene looked down the stairs, past where Kacey stood, and saw two legs flayed out across the stairs. The rest of Joan Vanza lay on the landing, with her head and shoulders looking like a broken doll.

Frank ran down the stairs, bent over Joan and felt for her pulse. He barked something unintelligible and picked up his phone. Once again he commanded Kacey not to move. Alene turned and noticed that all three children had followed everyone to the stairwell. She gasped and ushered them back into the apartment and into their rooms. It took quite some time to settle them down. They'd seen the gun and they'd seen Joan on the stairs. They had a lot of questions for which Alene lacked answers. She promised them she'd come back as soon as she could, hoping they'd fall asleep quickly.

By the time Alene returned to the hallway, Joan was on a stretcher being carried into the elevator and Frank was interrogating Kacey. Everyone else had left, but a few technicians were taking photos and dusting for prints. They looked as if they were moving much faster than the previous Sunday, but Alene realized they were in a stairwell with nothing except the banister, the walls, and the steps. The banisters must have been touched by so many people she couldn't imagine how dusting for prints would be helpful at all.

Kacey was slumped against the wall, staring into space and her hands were cuffed behind her back. Frank beckoned Alene to where he stood next to the open stairwell door. "Joan was unconscious, but she's alive," he said.

Alene said, "Oh my God." It wasn't something her folks ever said. They raised Alene and her sister without any religion. She'd learned it from Ruthie. "But why are you arresting Kacey? She didn't have anything to do with this."

"She was holding a gun, Alene," Frank said. His pallor looked yellow in the hallway light and he spoke in a clipped, business-like tone. He no longer seemed very alluring to Alene.

"Yes, but she probably heard running on the stairs when she opened the door," Alene said as calmly as possible. "Joan was already lying there, so Kacey screamed, and then she picked up the gun." Alene waited.

Frank continued, "When I bent down to feel her pulse, Alene, I heard Joan said the name, 'Will'."

"Of course," said Alene. "Will, as in William Vanza, as in stupid Bill." Alene felt a wave of exhaustion wash over her. "So, are you finally going to arrest him?"

"Right now, we're going to bring Kacey in."

"Why would you need to take Kacey?" Alene asked. "Joan said Bill attacked her."

"I'm sorry, Alene," said Frank. "I have to follow protocol."

Alene just gaped at him. "Just because Kacey was the first to find Joan doesn't make her guilty." Sometimes Alene ran up the stairs at the end of a workout - maybe that's what Joan had been doing and she'd tripped and fallen. Alene turned away from Frank and saw that Brianne's door was open. She followed the sound of voices inside to find Brianne sitting on the couch. Frank followed her in.

"Kacey was high, Alene," said Frank, very softly. "She needs help."

Alene felt her eyes sting with tears. "You saw her there in my apartment. She didn't have enough time to leave, get Joan, force her into the stairwell, and then push her down the stairs."

Still speaking in a low voice, Frank said, "She was holding a gun, Alene, she wouldn't have needed much time."

Brianne jumped up. "We all saw her run out and she wasn't carrying anything. You were here when she left without a purse and you saw all the neighbors who stopped by tonight."

"Anyone could have taken it," added Olly, who'd been standing quietly behind Alene until then.

Frank asked Olly, "Was Kacey carrying a loaded gun in her purse?"

Olly avoided his gaze. "Well, she's afraid after what happened to Gary. But it's Joan's gun. Kacey told me she borrowed it. That's why I was so worried when she forgot her purse."

Alene was shocked; that meant Kacey had brought her gun into the café even though they had one of those no-gun signs on the door. "Was Joan shot?"

Frank said, "No."

He was friendly when he wasn't being a cop. Now he was terse.

Brianne argued, "Kacey would never hurt anyone."

Alene said, "Frank, she's not the kind of girl who would do something like this, and anyway why does the gun matter when it wasn't even fired?"

"She's an addict and she can use a gun even if she didn't fire one today. Olly, you told me that Gary made her take lessons," said Frank. He stood to interact with two technicians who came to the door. He signed their electronic pad before they left.

"Yeah, but I also told you she sucked at it," said Olly. "And what about fingerprints on the gun aside from Kacey's?"

"We'll check everything," said Frank.

"Will we be able to see her tomorrow?" Olly asked. "What's the charge?"

Frank said firmly, "It depends on what we learn. We're dealing with murder and attempted murder."

Alene interrupted, "You don't know if there's a connection between Gary's murder and what's happened now. Even if Joan ran into Kacey in the stairwell, it's not Kacey's fault that Joan's anorexic and has weak bones."

Olly pleaded, "Couldn't you wait until Joan wakes up and tells you for sure whether Bill pushed her?"

Alene couldn't see a trace of Frank the affable guest. He said, "You know, this is for Kacey's protection as well."

Brianne asked, "How could being in a jail cell be for her protection? She'll get agitated and regress because she'll be around other addicts. Isn't there something you can do, Frank? Isn't there some law that would allow Alene or me to take responsibility for her?"

Frank's face softened and he turned momentarily human. "I'm not sure you're all thinking this through. What if she did enter the stairwell, immediately after Joan fell, as she claims? What if Kacey saw whoever pushed Joan and that person wants to keep her quiet?"

"You never even told us about the autopsy report," Alene protested. He had a point though. It would be horrifying if someone was trying to hurt Kacey.

Frank said, "I'll be happy to discuss it with you tomorrow."

They were silent for a moment, before Olly argued, "You know she didn't kill Gary, right? Kacey would never hurt anyone."

"I promise you she'll be safe," said Frank, not answering Olly's question.

Alene felt frustration bubbling up. She said, "Bill might still be wandering around the building with Neal. They could have done this together." She wondered where Olly had been right before Kacey screamed; and where was Jack Stone all that day?

Before she could say anything else, Frank said, "We have all the information we need for now." He gestured for the remaining officer in the hallway to approach him. Then he looked at Alene and said, "Go get some sleep. I'll be in touch tomorrow."

Alene ran back to her apartment without saying goodbye and slammed the door shut. She was shaking with either fear or anger. Frank hadn't even thanked her for the dinner.

Chapter 12

Alene woke up sweating – she'd dreamt that Neal had pushed her down a flight of stairs. She checked the time on her phone – not even eleven p.m. – had she only slept an hour? After shooting a message to update Ruthie about Joan, Alene sent Edith a separate, carefully-worded text. "Please take as much time as you need as you mourn your brother and help your sister-in-law during her recovery. We're all heartbroken about what happened. Best wishes from Alene and everyone at Whipped & Sipped."

Almost immediately Edith replied: "You shouldn't send texts this late at night."

Really? Why couldn't she just silence her phone if she didn't to get texts? Alene lay wide awake trying not to remember Joan lying at the bottom of the stairs like a cast-off, broken doll.

She'd first met Joan Stone the same night she'd met Neal – just after she graduated from high school. It was at a dinner party next door and Brianne had hired her to help serve and clean up that evening.

Brianne and her husband had invited a few of Dennis's work friends and his boss, who was the CEO of Hector-Schaf Electronics. Gary Vanza was there with his then-wife Isobel, and Neal accompanied his parents, Mitzi and Patrick Dunn. Neal had recently graduated from college and was working at the Honda dealership his father was in the process of buying. He seemed so outrageously old that Alene didn't pay much attention to him.

She remembered hearing Brianne and Dennis arguing in the kitchen, because instead of bringing his wife, CEO Henry Willis had brought his secretary, Joan Stone. Brianne had been outraged and whispered that they should call the dinner off and send everyone home. Dennis said he didn't think it was their job to be the morality police. Brianne kept wringing her hands while everyone ate the first course, Dijon Pistachio Baked Fish served on romaine lettuce, and she'd been unhappy throughout the meal.

Henry Willis was a beefy guy with a receding chin and extremely hairy arms. He wore sickly-sweet aftershave that made Alene feel as if there wasn't enough oxygen in the room. Joan Stone wore her frosted blond hair in the fashion of Rachel, from the television show "Friends." Alene noted how she kept tossing it in a coquettish manner even though she was well into her thirties. Mr. Willis kept smacking his thick lips and exclaiming over the food while fawning over either Joan Stone on one side, or Isobel Vanza on the other. Isobel hardly paid him any attention, but Gary had exhaled crabbily. Alene thought maybe he was worried about making a bad impression on his boss.

Alene remembered a lot about that night. Dennis Flynn sat at the head of the table with Mitzi Dunn to his right. Neal sat next to his mother rolling his eyes at everything Mitzi said and Alene caught him peeking at Joan's cleavage. Neal's father shoveled food into his mouth, paying no attention to Joan Stone even though she sat on

166

his other side. Mr. Willis kept gesturing with his sausage fingers and touching Isobel Vanza, who looked stunning in a shimmery copper-colored dress. It was low cut, but she had a boyish figure, so there wasn't much to see. Isobel told funny stories about working as a nutritionist and training for a marathon. Alene thought she was charming even though her skin looked leathery and over-tanned. It was before she started eating only macrobiotic food and boring everyone about it.

Then, while Alene was collecting plates from the fish course, Mr. Willis whispered something inappropriate enough to elicit a sharp response from Isobel, who looked as if she was about to smack his face. "Do you speak like that to all the women who work for you?" She asked. Alene gave her an approving thumbs-up when no one was looking. Gary turned bright red and bowed his head.

Alene nearly dropped her pile of plates when Joan Stone gave Isobel a thin-lipped death- stare while Mr. Willis pouted and snatched his hairy hand from the back of Isobel's chair. Whenever Alene refilled water glasses or removed plates, she noticed that from then on, he only attended to Joan. Every now and then he would try to participate in the conversation, but Joan would lean up against him and whisper something with her face almost inside his giant ear. He'd turn to her and they'd converse together quietly in an alarmingly intimate way.

It was the first time Alene had ever seen adults acting huggy-kissy in front of her, and she was grateful that her parents never behaved like that. Mr. Willis kept stroking Joan's arm or resting his enormous pink hand somewhere on her flowing black silk dress. Alene couldn't stop staring.

She remembered looking away and locking eyes with Neal, who'd clearly noticed. His mouth twitched and they both burst into laughter. Alene turned and ran into the kitchen, but Neal had to feign a coughing fit. He later *managed to join her in the hallway, where they started talking.*

Now, Alene was unable to sleep. She changed positions several more times and tried to count chocolate-drizzled pastries instead of sheep. She found herself thinking of the food they'd served the night she'd met Neal.

She'd helped Brianne to make vegetarian lasagna with garlic bread and salad with a honey-mustard salad dressing, all of which seemed more glamorous than any food her mother served. For dessert Alene had helped Brianne with a blackberry crisp, served with homemade vanilla ice cream. She hadn't even known it was possible to make homemade ice cream.

Neal went on about how much he liked selling cars and how good he was at it. Alene didn't care because she had no interest in going out with someone who was already working in the world. When he requested her phone number, she told him he could come by Gary's café, where she was working that whole summer before starting college. He came in and ordered a smoothie the very next day, but Alene was busy and didn't spend time with him, so he didn't show up again that summer.

Alene tossed and turned, wondering if Neal knew exactly how his father had helped Joan embezzle money from Hector-Schaf. Did he think that Joan and Gary had taken more than their share, and planned to get back at them? Had he thought he deserved more of it? Maybe he hadn't noticed Brianne and had thought it was Gary on the bike path that day when Dennis was knocked off his bicycle. Maybe that's why Neal hadn't shown up at the hospital until after Noah was born – he was worried that someone had recognized him and was scared to show his face.

Maybe Neal was in cahoots with Bill Vanza even back then, just trying for that big score – but, what would have been their motivation for hurting Dennis? Why would they have killed Gary? Plus, pushing Joan down the stairs made absolutely no sense. Maybe all of it had something to do with the money embezzled from Hector-Schaf. Alene sure hoped Frank was investigating that as well.

Alene had gone to college and forgotten all about Neal Dunn, until a summer day after her third year at Northwestern, when they had bumped into each other at a Wrigleyville bar. Neal bought her a beer and invited her to a Cubs game. That had been her first stout, and she thought it was so yummy she bought a six-pack and shared it with Ruthie, who went on to invent a stout cake. They changed "beer" to "bear" so as not to alarm the customers, and it worked (Cocoa Bear Cake).

Neal told her that his seats were thirty rows up at the first base line, and because – like everyone that year – Alene idolized Sammy Sosa, she'd accepted his invitation. She had a great time and didn't feel at all as if she'd used him for the tickets, but she felt obligated to go on a second date. That was on his friend's boat out on the lake, where the soft breeze felt lovely, at first, after a sweltering day. However, there were way too many people. They were drinking and bragging about themselves and it was too loud on deck to hold a conversation. Alene started to get queasy, and it had not been a successful evening.

She didn't kiss Neal goodnight until the third date. He brought black bread, mixed olives, two kinds of cheese, strawberry jam and a good bottle of merlot and took her to see "As you Like It" at a Shakespeare-in-the-Park production. Alene was impressed at his planning and thought it said something about his personality. Years later she discovered that it had only said something about his mother, who'd organized the entire evening.

That summer they went to Wednesday Grant Park concerts, heard jazz at Andy's and the Green Mill, in-line skated in Lincoln Park, and saw double features of old

169

movies at the Music Box. Neal was usually fun and entertaining back then, always coming up with interesting things to do together. Again, Alene found out years later that Mitzi had been the one to plan most of the activities. What twenty-something guy brings a complete picnic to a Chicago Symphony concert at Ravinia with a comfortable blanket for snuggling under the stars?

Once the semester started, he called a lot, but Alene only saw him occasionally on a Saturday night. She spent most of her free time going home to spend time with her ailing mother. She wanted Lydia to experience a good senior year even though their mother was weakening and in a lot of pain. Cal was worried and exhausted, so having Alene at home on the weekends was a huge help. She would read to her mother or hold her hand and tell her about her dream of running a café with Ruthie. She'd spend hours describing how the place would look, talking about the healthy recipes and unusual pastries, outlining her ideas to bring in live music and offer cooking classes during slow times. Alene drifted off for a bit, thinking about how happy her mother would have been to see that those dreams had come true.

Her mom had died over winter break, in her own bed, holding hands with her daughters while Cal sat holding her always cold feet. She'd asked to be cremated, and they followed all her wishes, including scattering some of her ashes over the Lincoln Park gardens. Vivien Baron had made a list of songs she wanted played, the food she'd wanted served, and had even told Lydia and Alene what she thought would be nice for each of them to wear to her memorial service. Alene thought about all the times she'd checked in with her mother, in her dreams over the years, especially during stressful times like those of the past week.

She'd broken up with Neal before she began her final quarter at Northwestern, wanting to concentrate on finishing school and working at the café whenever possible. Alene often felt as if she was falling apart back then, always thinking about how her mother would have enjoyed hearing about a lecture she'd attended on European political thought, or how much she'd have liked the Ursula LeGuin novel assigned in a sociology class. She'd find herself conversing with her mother in her head, critiquing people and places just as they had always done. Alene didn't even want to participate in the graduation ceremony without her mother there, and her father was too downcast to argue.

Neither Ruthie nor Alene had to undergo a transition to something completely different after graduation – as did most of their peers – since, as planned, they continued working at the Whipped and Sipped Café. Ruthie and Alene loved being there, and Gary gave them freedom to try whatever they wanted. They'd never had time while they were in school to do all the experimenting and innovating they'd dreamed about. Ruthie had already started taking classes in pastry-making and breads. She spent hours testing batch after batch of cookies and pastries while Alene managed the business end of ordering, paying bills, and keeping the books in addition to coming up with ideas to draw in more customers.

Later that summer, Alene ran into Neal at the same bar on Clark Street where they'd met a few years earlier. Her grief therapist, whom she'd seen twice a month since her mother's death, said getting back together with him might have had something to do with Alene still feeling untethered. She suggested that because Neal didn't seem to be very reliable, Alene proceed very cautiously. But by then, Ruthie Blum was in love with Benjie Rosin, and it was fun to both have serious boyfriends. Alene swept aside everyone's reservations and even disregarded the warnings of her own inner voice.

She was starting to feel desperate about getting any deep sleep that night, and flashed to a conversation with their elderly neighbor, Gloriadine Jones. Back when Alene was deciding whether to marry Neal, Gloriadine had given her a cup of chamomile tea and told her that she should pray before making important decisions. Setting out a little tray of homemade cookies, Gloriadine had told her that if she prayed hard enough, God would give her the answer. Alene wondered what her life would have been like, now, if she had tried to pray even though she didn't know how.

Alene finally got up to take something. She only had a few sleeping pills left and treated them like gold. She cut the pill in half and lay back down recalling how Mitzi had needed at least a year to plan the wedding. Alene had spent the year working and taking business classes at DePaul. She and Ruthie took a few road trips and celebrated Ruthie's engagement to Benjie by taking the Zephyr train to California and back. It had been a wonderful adventure.

She snuggled under the covers thinking about how her father would have liked to have paid for the wedding, but – still blue about her mother's death – he wasn't up to arguing with Mitzi and Patrick Dunn. Alene had been ambivalent about the preparations. Her therapist helped her through all the hoopla and said it was totally normal to not care about all the wedding details, but suggested she find just one detail to care about. Alene chose to focus on the cake, but Mitzi even had thoughts about that. Alene had to admit even now that it had been a dazzling wedding even if the groom had turned out to be a jackass, a liar and possibly a murderer.

Mitzi and Patrick Dunn had wanted the wedding to be the most elegant and sophisticated wedding of the century (They constantly retold the story of how they'd gone to England to be in the crowd cheering for the royal wedding of Princess Diana and Prince Charles). For this reason, the wedding took place at the Michigan Avenue Hilton with five hundred guests and a superb menu with way too much food. The dessert tables included every candy Alene adored growing up, a treasure trove of cookies, and her idea for the cake. Ruthie had created a four-foot-tall "cake" constructed of three-inch-square iced cakes on an ascending spiral with a cascade of shiny spun sugar flowers at the top. The smaller cakes were frosted in a metallic-looking icing that shimmered under the ballroom's crystal chandeliers. Had Alene at least been happy that night?

Mitzi had loved it. Poor Mitzi still probably had no idea how horrible her son Neal had become. Always perfectly coifed with freshly-manicured hands, Mitzi sparkled with energy. She wanted everyone in the family to care as much as she did about appearances, and often had something to say about Alene or her girls' choices. "No more dressing Quinn in anything green," she'd tell Alene, "unless you want her to look nauseated."

Just the previous week she'd said, "Sierra, Sweetheart, your big blue eyes in that oval face would look just stunning if you had your hair professionally cut. How about we spend Saturday afternoon at my salon?"

Sierra had come out with a sleek blow-dried style that caused five anguished mornings when she couldn't come close to replicating it at home. Mitzi had solved the problem with another appointment at the salon the following week followed by a shopping trip for a couple of new outfits. Even though Sierra had already been a little too self-absorbed about her looks, Alene was effusive in thanking her ex-mother-in-law.

During the divorce, Mitzi had called to assure Alene that she would always be family and should still be on Alene's emergency list.

Still awake, Alene thought about how different Neal's father had been.

Patrick was skinny with a comb-over and a face that seemed too large for the rest of his body. He was a bit hunched over and greeted everyone by shaking hands and drawing them in for a hug. He adored numbers, cigars, and taking cruises. He liked making friends wherever he went and would tell stories for months after each cruise about everyone he'd met. Mitzi only liked the cruises that offered good entertainment and food. There also had to be entertainment and spa services, or in her view, it wasn't a vacation worth discussing.

Patrick Dunn always seemed to have drunk too much coffee. He never sat still unless he was eating and always bounced his knees or flicked a rubber band against his wrist. Alene thought he used the rubber band to distract himself from feeling any emotion. Once Neal told Alene that his father was conniving and duplicitous and that he prized money more than family. What was that saying about the pot calling the kettle black? According to Neal, whenever his father wasn't at work, he was thinking up schemes or talking about ideas for how to acquire even more than he already had.

Neal used to grumble that his father wouldn't stop talking about money, always complaining about how much things cost and what he thought they were worth. Alene thought it was good that Neal was embarrassed by how his father treated waitresses and cab drivers. "Bring me the check, Honey," Patrick would call across a restaurant, or, "What do you have that I'll like tonight, Sweetheart?"

It was worse if their skin was another color. Patrick would say things like, "I'll have coffee with cream, sort of the same color you are, Honey" or, "Isn't that nice they let you wait tables when all the other Hispanics are bussing. You must be good to have risen to the top." Alene had been pleasantly surprised the first time she witnessed Neal admonish his father for having snapped his fingers to call a waitress over.

Neal had been polite and charming back then - it wasn't until later that he began assessing the spending potential of everyone he met and talking to them as if they were potential customers. Alene hated when he would slip business card to her friends or their husbands, insinuating that he would give them a good deal on a car. She knew that the good deal was always only for him.

This is crazy, thought Alene. She got up and took the other half of the pill. This time she lay back down knowing that she would surely be asleep within the next five minutes. Still her thoughts were of how generous Neal's father had been to them when they got married.

He set Neal up as his partner in the car dealership he'd bought, after leaving Hector-Schaf. Back then, Neal had shared his misgivings with Alene about working for his father. He worried that Patrick might overrule his decisions forever, and he'd never be respected in the company. Neal would set up a competition among the salesmen, and Patrick would cancel it. Neal would plan to offer a special on Honda Pilots, and Patrick would change it to Honda Accords. Neal told Alene that once Patrick put money into something, he just couldn't let go.

Finally, Alene felt her body melting into the bed and her thoughts started to become muddled.

Just a month after the wedding, Mitzi and Patrick had gone on a three-week cruise with Gary and Isobel and were kind enough to invite Cal along. Alene's father had loved it, although he later told Alene that no matter how luxurious it had been and how much they'd all included him, he'd felt terribly alone without her mother there. And then the unthinkable happened.

During the final days of their parents' cruise, Neal and Alene were in the middle of dinner when they received a long-distance call from Mitzi, who was crying too hysterically to be understood. Neal had to ask to speak to someone else, and Gary Vanza had come on the line and explained that Patrick was missing and was presumed drowned. He has last been seen in Hilo, Hawaii. A coast guard rescue team had been sent out to search for him, about three hours after he went missing and a helicopter crew had also arrived a few hours after that, but they couldn't find a single trace. Neal had turned white with fear and was unable to speak. Alene had held his hand and imagined how terrible she would have felt had it been her father who was missing.

They learned after a few days that it was highly unlikely Patrick was still alive. Naturally, Neal sued Royal Duchess, and Mitzi later got a hefty settlement and insurance, which made Neal happy, but didn't pull Mitzi out of her depression. That didn't happen until Sierra was born and she became a grandmother. Meanwhile, Mitzi joined a national group that lobbied for laws to regulate the cruise industry.

One of her finest moments was in 2010, when Congress finally passed the Cruise Vessel Safety and Security Act. To celebrate Mitzi's victory, Whipped and Sipped gave away free cookies in the shape of ships. Remembering those cookies, Alene finally nodded off.

Chapter 13

Monday morning, after just a few hours of drugged sleep, her neck made crunchy sounds as she turned it from side to side. She had just a few hours before she needed to get the children dressed and out the door. As always, she was grateful that Jocelyn had military training, required little sleep, and was happy to open the café five days a week at five in the morning. Someone had to turn on the ovens and take all the prepared trays out of the fridge so they could be freshly baked each morning. Edith Vanza usually helped Jocelyn with opening, but Alene didn't trust her with the keys. First, there were the incidents with the alarm not being turned off, then she lost them one time. There'd been a lot of weeping and they'd had to change the locks.

Alene hauled herself out of bed and brushed her teeth wondering why Frank hadn't arrested Edith as a suspect in the attack on Joan. What about Jack Stone – had anyone seen or heard anything more of him? She stopped herself from delving into it all again. She had to work out, get herself showered and dressed, and take care of her children.

All three were signed up for Chicago Park District summer programs. That week, Quinn and Sierra were heading up to Ravenswood for art classes with Ruthie's girls. Both Noah and Ruthie's son, Avi, were enrolled in a science camp at a nearby school. Ruthie and Alene had organized a complicated driving schedule that required Zuleyka to spend a lot of time in the car.

Alene texted Zuleyka and Blanca to confirm the scheduling for that week before starting to stretch her calf muscles. She was still groggy, so she sat down at the kitchen counter with a pen and notebook and sipped her daily glass of apple cider vinegar mixed with honey, one of the ingredients banned at Whipped and Sipped. Alene honored Ruthie's wishes at the café but at home she ate whatever she wanted, without thinking about the animals that created the products – and she loved honey.

Sipping her drink, Alene went through her list of possible suspects. There was no way her father or Mitzi could ever push Joan down the stairs. Her sister Lydia and Lydia's husband Theo – also not possible.

Wasn't it just too far-fetched to think Olly capable of hurting anyone? He'd been friends with Kacey Vanza for years and had also been arrested a few times for possession or dealing. He'd been Alene's first "chance" hire, one of the kids she'd agree to hire on an interim basis because they had little work experience, no references, or a police record. Olly had become a wonderful employee and always seemed chipper and kind, but could that all have been part of an act? Alene just couldn't buy it.

Edith – bitter and jealous, and maybe she'd always hated her brother. Plus, she owned a gun. She wasn't fast or strong, but she could have managed both Gary's murder and Joan's "accident." Maybe she thought she'd inherit some of Gary's money, especially with Joan gone.

Bill Vanza – he wasn't bright enough to come up with an evil master plan. Neal would have had to be the brains behind anything Bill did, but Joan had said his name just before she passed out. That was a pretty strong piece of evidence. Bill was a crude, unpleasant human being, and as Gary's eldest son he would probably inherit a lot of money, especially with his stepmother out of the way.

What about Neal? He'd been so whiny about child support and constantly talked about needing more money. He always felt as if he deserved more than he had, he was friends with Bill Vanza, and he was a liar. How could she ever explain it to her children if Neal turned out to be guilty?

Maybe he'd lost his touch at selling cars, needed more money than he was earning, and had tried to convince his mother to give him a loan or something. Maybe Mitzi had refused, so Neal had started gambling again to score that big win gamblers dream about. Then he might have suspected that his father was hiding some of the money, allegedly taken from his old company, as had Joan and Gary. Maybe he'd just wanted to scare Gary and had knocked Dennis off his feet, back in 2006, only because Dennis and Gary looked similar from behind. Had Alene been the world's biggest dingbat for having married such a careless, pompous, lying shithead?

She tried to stop thinking about it as she opened the door to Michael's gym at five-thirty on the dot. Michael's eyes popped open. "I'm not at all shocked to see YOU here this early on a Monday morning Ms. Alene, workout machine. Tell me about your sexy weekend."

It was part of Michael Jay's charm that nearly every word out of his mouth was sarcastic. Alene also knew that he was unbelievably disciplined and at work with clients or working out on his own six days a week. Sometimes she was able to spar with him, but she wasn't in the mood for banter just then. "Joan Stone was pushed down the stairs last night.

She's in the hospital, and Kacey Vanza is in police custody even though I'm sure she's innocent. I got maybe five hours of sleep and I just don't have the energy for a run. I thought I could do a light workout instead."

That wiped the smile off his face. "I'm so sorry, Alene. Brianne only texted that Joan was in the hospital," said Michael, now serious. "Are you okay? You need to boost those endorphins. Working out is the best antidote. Let me know if there's anything I can do to help."

He handed Alene one of his little blue towels and she looked at him closely. Both Dennis and Gary had trained with him. He was strong enough to murder someone with his bare hands. "Where were you last night, by the way?"

He smiled. "I thought we'd resolved this, Alene. Are you asking because of your prodigious investigative skills, or has someone hired you as a private eye? Does this mean you suspect me – again?" He rolled his head, as if in agony, and then pointed to the calendar above his desk near the door. "My mother's birthday is celebrated every year on that very date, the twenty-second of June. Didn't I tell you I was going to be at my Aunt Ivy's for a barbeque dinner at which I ate purely protein with no extraneous carbohydrates and merely a sniff of the watermelon and the chocolate cake?"

Alene realized she'd been holding herself tightly. She plopped down on the mat and smiled up at Michael. "Sorry."

"But thanks for your thoroughness in checking up on me, Sherlock," he added.

She lacked the energy to yell at him for not taking her seriously. Michael turned to greet another client who'd just walked in while Alene got on the stair machine. She couldn't manage a second more than twenty minutes and imagined curling up in the dog's bed tucked in the corner but managed to stay vertical.

Michael stopped her on her way out and gave her a hug and then Alene trudged home. She showered and started a pot of oatmeal, trying to concentrate on happy thoughts, such as how nice it would be to date if men weren't so awful. Every time she met someone with potential, he'd turn out to be a jerk, like Frank Shaw. How could he have arrested Kacey when it was so obvious that she wasn't the kind of person who would murder her father and push her stepmother down the stairs? She wondered if she was jumping to conclusions the way she used to do as a teenager. Her mom always had warned her that it was unhealthy and unproductive. Alene got dressed, made a pot of decaf for her father, and woke the children. She stirred hemp, chia, flax seeds and real maple syrup into the oatmeal, packed bag lunches, fought with Noah about wearing a hat to play outside in the sun, and herded them down in the elevator.

She felt stifled and couldn't follow whatever it was that Quinn and Sierra were bickering about. A young couple from the fourth floor crowded in and Alene attempted a friendly smile. Then she waited in front of the building until Zuleyka arrived with Ruthie's kids, made sure all six children were belted in, and watched the big van pull away.

Then Alene walked over to the hospital and stopped at the front desk to ask about Joan Stone. The receptionist's fingers flew across his keyboard and he answered in a deep baritone voice, "I'm sorry, Ms. Stone is not seeing visitors this morning. You might want to try later."

At least she'd tried. Joan wouldn't want to see her anyway but visiting had seemed like the right thing to do. Alene walked back outside through the sliding door and called Isobel Vanza to ask what she'd heard about Kacey.

"I called all the police stations and not a single person would tell me anything," Isobel fumed. "Then, I tried all the city hospitals, but she wasn't listed as a patient anywhere. I don't know where they have her, and just because she's over twenty-one doesn't mean she doesn't need me."

"Do you have a lawyer?" Alene asked, trying to calm herself to counteract Isobel's agitation. "Do you want me to ask my sister, Lydia? She knows people."

"No thank you," Isobel said with what Alene interpreted as a frosty tone. "I'll take care of my daughter."

Alene stopped herself from saying anything snarky, but the bubble above her head said, "If you'd been taking care of your daughter, maybe she wouldn't be addicted to opioids." It was nearly nine in the morning. Poor Kacey had probably spent the night shivering in a scary jail cell. It made Alene so angry that Frank would do something like this. He knew that Kacey was fragile – was he just trying to make sure she ended up back in rehab? Or worse?

Alene cut through the alley, unlocked the back entrance and stepped into Whipped and Sipped's kitchen. The comforting smell of yeast, the enticement of cinnamon and the complexity of chocolate all soothed Alene, who realized she'd been holding her shoulders and neck in awkward stiffness. Ruthie approached with a steaming cup of her favorite espresso topped with whipped almond milk, cocoa and cinnamon powder.

"I talked to Isobel, and she couldn't get any information about Kacey," said Alene.

"That poor girl," said Ruthie. "Let's send her some healthy food as soon as we know where they took her. You're not going to believe this, but Edith came in today."

Alene took a sip of her coffee and nodded, saying, "I texted her last night and told her to take whatever time she needed, but I see her through the kitchen door – looks like she's back making smoothies."

"Yup," said Ruthie, thrusting her hands into a large bowl and pulling out a ball of dough. "You might also notice that you have a visitor sitting in front drinking hot chocolate. He's next to the art wall."

Jack Stone, in baggy shorts and a torn t-shirt, was slouched over his cup. His long hair covered half his face. Alene gave him a cursory smile and raised her hand in a small wave. He jumped up and came so close that she could smell his nicotine breath. He seized her arm. "Aren't you going to offer me condolences, Alene?"

"Your mom is alive, Jack." She gently removed his hand from her arm.

"But someone tried to kill her," he said, more wistful than aggressive, "and my stepfather is dead. I know you think I don't have any feelings, but I do."

Alene softened slightly, and said, "I'm sorry about Gary's death, Jack, and I understand this is a tough time for you."

Jack idly scratched his head, not taking his eyes of Alene. "Sorry doesn't do anything to help me."

She hardened again. "I'm going to proceed as if you were an adult, Jack."

"I'm sorry, I didn't mean that," Jack responded quickly.

"Okay, then let's start over," said Alene. "I tried to visit your mother this morning but she's not seeing visitors. Did you get an update on her condition?"

"I'll go see her later," said Jack, "because I remembered that a long time ago, she told me about an envelope I was supposed to open if anything happened to her. She said that no matter what was going on, I was supposed to drop everything to find the envelope."

"I'm guessing you followed her instructions," said Alene, thinking that it sounded like the plot of a cheap cops-and-robbers flick.

Jack said, "I tried, but I couldn't find it, even though I emptied every drawer and turned everything inside out." He looked sincerely worried.

"That'll be a nice mess for your mother to come home to," said Alene, wondering if he was making the whole thing up just to annoy her.

"I finally found it in the kitchen," said Jack, "and opened it."

Okay, so there was really an envelope. Why did he think she needed to know? "Was it a treasure map?"

Jack said, "I was hoping it would be a fat check, but it was just a letter saying she didn't want to ruin my life by giving me a lot of money but I could have some of it after she died – like a lot of money would be the thing that ruined my life! I hardly even have a life."

Alene gaped at him open-mouthed. She agreed that the way he lived didn't fit her definition of living a life, but to hear him say it was eye-opening. "Why are you telling me this? Your mother is still alive."

"I thought you'd know what money she's talking about and where it is and what I should do next," he said.

"Why would I know anything about it, Jack?" Alene asked. "You probably already know that what you need to do next is clean up the apartment for when your mother comes home."

"I will," said Jack, "but she said something about Whipped and Sipped in her letter."

Alene asked, "Can I see it?"

"I didn't bring it."

"Does your mother have a lawyer?" Alene asked, tired of the conversation. "A lawyer would be able to help you with her estate. Most normal people don't hide their money – they invest it so that it grows." However, Joan wasn't normal. She stole money and gambled.

"I don't know if she has a lawyer," Jack answered, "but I know she worked at a company that went belly up. You can

Google it. I used to listen in on her phone calls so I know she did something shady."

He'd listened in on her phone calls. She left him a letter but no information about her bank accounts or the name of her lawyer. Joan couldn't have done a better job of making sure that her son would never grow up.

"Did you ever ask her about it?" Alene asked.

Jack answered, "No, because she never answered my questions, but she gave me like an allowance. I don't think she wanted me to work."

"That's why you haven't had to work all this time." Alene stated it as a fact. What had Joan been thinking all those years? "Why are you asking me about a job, then? Can't you get by on what she pays you?" Alene still didn't understand why he was even talking to her.

"First of all, I'm thirty-four and it's time for me to do something. Second, she's stopped paying. She told me that someone is trying to take everything she has." Jack took a delicate sip of his cocoa.

"Sounds like the plot of a movie, Jack," Alene said, although everyone on her suspect list knew about the money and could very well be trying to take it.

Jack looked at her with a serious air. "I'm not making this up, Alene. I think my mother hid money, either at Brianne's apartment or here in your cafe. Maybe she had so much that she hid it in both places."

Alene stared at him, hoping she looked calm. "Why would your mother hide money here, and how could she have even done it? Did she come here in the dark of night and dig a cave? Come on. Have you checked under her mattress?"

"I checked everywhere. I thought maybe she slipped envelopes behind your ovens or something. She was probably hoping that if it was ever found, you'd be arrested instead of her," said Jack.

Alene said, "They'd figure out who put it there and she would go to jail too."

"My mother is pretty tough," said Jack. "I know she's not normal."

So true. Alene wondered why she was engaging with Jack. "There aren't any hiding places in a café, Jack, except inside the ovens. There is no room behind or below any of the ovens."

Jack got up and started tapping the floor boards around their table, putting his ear close to the floor to listen for an echo that might indicate a loose board. He must have seen someone do it on television. A few customers glanced at him briefly before turning back to their food, drinks or laptops. Alene said, "Maybe your mother carried it with her at all times, sewn into the linings of her clothes?"

He scoffed. "It was millions of dollars. I know she's a little crazy, but she's also smart."

"Yeah, she seems to have a certain kind of smarts," said Alene, "but I hope you understand this all sounds kind of loony-tunes to me."

"After Gary was killed, last week, I saw that she was frightened," said Jack. "She thought the killer was following her, so maybe she was afraid to expose her hiding places."

Alene was starting to feel disconcerted. Whipped and Sipped was a public place with people sitting at tables surrounding them. Two small girls were eating muffins on their left, while their grandmother – a refined, well-dressed woman, who always ordered chamomile tea – smiled at them as she sipped. A chubby, balding regular, who usually drank at least four cups of coffee, sat glued to his computer screen on their right. Behind him an elderly couple she hadn't seen in weeks quietly shared a piece of carrot cake, nibbling tiny pieces and gazing at the art wall. Alene leaned closer to Jack. "Were you trying to get more from her, when you tried to kill her last night?"

Jack jumped up and grabbed Alene's arm again. Before she even had a chance to yelp, Olly was at her side. "Nobody messes with Alene, you scumbag."

Jack had about fifty pounds on Olly. Alene wondered if Jack still carried the little African finger knife that used to frighten Lydia and her friends back when they were in high school. She had only a second to worry, before Olly pulled Jack away from her and whipped his arm behind his back in a move so smooth and accomplished that Alene gasped. The elderly couple looked up in alarm, but the other nearby customers continued whatever they'd been doing.

"Oliver Burns, is that you or do you have a ninja warrior twin?" Alene asked, rubbing her arm where Jack had squeezed it. She planned to hug Olly after he shoved Jack out the door. But Jack, instead of fighting, went limp, so Olly just pushed him down onto the chair. She still suspected Olly, but only a little bit. Was he only pretending to be a hero?

"I wasn't trying to hurt her. Why'd you have to do that?" Jack asked, slumping. He suddenly seemed like an unloved little boy whose nightmare of a mother controlled him with money and intrigue.

Olly said, "We don't grab people, Jack. Should we call the police or is there a reason I should let you stand up and walk out the door?"

"I just needed Alene to help me with something," said Jack.

Olly smacked him on the shoulder and said, "Go home, Jack."

Could Jack still be a "chance hire"? It had been Ruthie's idea to offer employment on a temporary basis and they'd done it maybe a dozen times in the nearly eight years Alene had owned the cafe. A few were misses, but others had morphed into decent employees with a future. Olly, Grant, Sally and LaTonya had all been successful chance hires.

187

Alene worked with one such employee at a time and brought in the next chance hire only when the current one passed onto actual employment or left the café. All the other employees were charged with helping the chance hires with any and everything. Over the years, Alene had hired kids whose hair hadn't been washed in weeks, kids who didn't have clothes to change into or a warm enough coat for winter in Chicago. She'd hired Dreamers, whose parents had brought them to the country when they were children, and kids who already had police records at age eighteen. Sally and LaTonya had both struggled through high school because their families had been homeless. They now shared an apartment with two other young women. Benjie Rosin had found Grant sneaking into one of his buildings to sleep in the lobby on a freezing winter night and had brought him to the café where with patience and a lot of guidance, he'd become a solid employee.

Kacey hadn't been a chance hire, since she'd started working at Whipped and Sipped while her father had owned the place, but she needed the same kind of guidance. Someone still had to remind her when to punch down the dough, rearrange a pastry tray or refill a canister.

Olly had been their earliest success – he'd lost his way at some point after high school, but now shared an apartment with Jocelyn and was indispensable to Alene. He took care of things without being told and had even been coming up with great suggestions, such as a "puff pastry flight" with four or five little bites of crunch, each one popping with a different savory or sweet flavor. Another one of his ideas that had turned into a neighborhood phenomenon was a "make your own pie" contest for Pi Day on March 14. Customers submitted their ideas for innovative pie fillings and the winner got a private session in the kitchen with Ruthie. The previous year's winner had submitted a recipe for chocolate cashew pie.

Jack Stone as a chance hire? He stood up and left the café with as much dignity as he could muster while Alene rubbed the place where he'd grabbed her arm.

Olly said, "Want me to call that cop?"

"Thanks, but I'll take care of it," said Alene. "Nothing happened."

Back in her office, Alene put her head on her desk. She didn't realize she'd fallen asleep until she opened her eyes in the middle of a dream about pastries. She was shocked to see that it was already two-thirty in the afternoon. Her neck was taut from sleeping at her desk and she felt terribly groggy. Didn't I wake up this morning with this same stiffness in my neck? She wondered. Now, what else was I supposed to do? She asked herself. Who was I supposed to call?

Battered: A Whipped and Sipped Mystery

Chapter 14

Alene slouched into the apartment on Monday afternoon, shuffling her feet in exhaustion. Blanca stepped out of the kitchen to look at her, and said, "You go straight to bed and I make fish for dinner."

Cal Baron looked up from the chess game he was playing against himself and said, "You do seem tired, Sweetheart. Where are the kidzh...?"

She hated when he slurred – it was a sign of his disease. "Hi Dad. All three had playdates after camp and are all getting dropped off after dinner," said Alene.

"Good," said Blanca. "They don't like my baked fish."

"I love your baked fish," said Cal, clearing his throat. "Alene, what did you find out about Joan?"

"They wouldn't tell me anything and she wasn't taking visitors," said Alene. Was her dad's condition getting worse or was she just imagining it?

Cal shrugged, "That's how it is nowadays."

"I'm drained," said Alene, counting with her fingers. "Gary was murdered, someone tried to hurt Joan last night,

Kacey is in jail, and Jack Stone came into the café to bother me again."

"Can't he make hijh own cup of coffee at home?" Cal asked with disapproval. "Where doesh he get money... to buy drinks... if he doesn't have a job?"

Alene answered, "He told me that his mother gives him money every week. Shocker, huh?"

"Nice work if you can get it," said Cal, studying his chess board.

Blanca, wearing her trademark dangling earrings with a blouse and skirt over black hose said, "Even someone gives me five thousand dollars a week, I don't leave you, Cal."

He pointed at her, smiling. "You're my favorite care-giver." She was his only care-giver.

Alene sat and took off her shoes, saying, "Jack told me that his mother wrote a letter he was supposed to open if anything happened to her."

"I have friends who do this," said Blanca with an approving nod.

"Being pushed down the stairs...falls into that category, I think," said Cal.

Alene said, "He had to turn the condo upside down to find it."

"Sounds like something sneaky that Joan would do," said Cal.

"What kind of mother hides something important like that?" Alene asked. "I didn't get to see an actual letter, which calls into question its very existence, but Joan supposedly wrote that she hid some money."

Blanca said, "Everyone hides money, but better is gold."

"You think that Joan Stone... created a treasure hunt for Jack? Highly unlikely," said Cal.

Alene said, "Dad, when I was going through my divorce, Brianne told me she was pretty sure Joan embezzled money from Hector-Schaf. You know, where Brianne's husband

and Gary Vanza worked? That was before he bought the cafe. It's where Gary met Joan and where Patrick Dunn worked before he bought his dealership. Anyway, I think Brianne told me that Neal's dad probably helped Joan embezzle money, but I don't remember the details."

Cal said, "I'd definitely remember something like that, but you've always been that way... about money. The minute I start telling you a story about finances, you stop paying attention."

"I manage to run a business, Dad, so I'm not a lost cause," said Alene, plopping down on the couch and pulling a quilt over herself. "I was going through a difficult divorce when I heard about it."

"What you remember?" Blanca asked as she headed back to the kitchen. "Anything?"

Still trying to get comfortable on the couch, Alene said, "I think Gary told me something about a threatening letter. I don't remember the whole story because I never paid much attention to anything having to do with Joan. I probably thought it was a good idea – maybe the person who wrote the letter told her to stop being a bitch. Anyway, Jack is upset because she only gave him like forty bucks last week."

"Poor thirty-four-year-old kid," said Cal, raising an eyebrow. "You know, Benjamin Franklin said that the secret of getting ahead was getting started."

Alene thought her dad probably quoted Benjamin Franklin more often than anyone else, although he also mentioned Mark Twain a lot. She should check his bookshelves and maybe find him a good biography of one or both. "Do you remember hearing about the company where they all worked, Dad?"

"I certainly do," said Cal. "That was Hector-Schaf Electronics near Rockford."

He closed his eyes and so did Alene, but then he started up again. "It went under after someone funneled money out.

I remember that just months after Neal's father lost his job, the company went bankrupt. Then he bought that Honda dealership on Western. I wondered about it at the time."

Cal rested again for a moment before adding, "I know he was your father-in-law, but how much you want to bet that Patrick Dunn helped embezzle the funds that destroyed the company?"

Cal had always enjoyed relating examples of nefarious financial trickery. Alene kept her eyes closed and let her body relax. "I wouldn't put anything past Neal or his father."

"I just read an article just last week about unsolved financial crimes and guess which company was on the list?" Cal continued, giving Alene one second before thundering, "Hector-Schaf. Can you believe it? Should we call that detective who came to dinner on Sunday?"

Alene opened her eyes. Now she was back to worrying about the situation and wouldn't get a nap. "I already told him that Gary had worked with everyone at Hector-Schaf, Dad," she said. "Anyway, that detective was kind of rude last night."

"He was probably just doing his job, Honey. You should let him know about Joan's treasure hunt letter to Jack."

"I'll do it tomorrow." said Alene. At least she could just lie there.

Blanca had returned with a tray of cut-up vegetables. Alene started to sit up, and Blanca said, "Cal and I talk about Joan and all this terrible thing what happen. You go rest in bed. I do everything."

Alene didn't remember heading to her room, but she slept through dinner. Noah crept into her bed to cuddle for a few minutes, but she was too groggy to respond to what he'd learned at camp about light refraction in water. Next thing Alene knew, it was daybreak, Tuesday morning. She woke up feeling much better but had dreamt about when she'd first started working for Gary Vanza at the café. He'd always been flush with cash in those days.

She stretched on her mat at the base of her bed and started her yoga routine. What if Joan was being blackmailed because of that money she'd helped steal from that company? The blackmailer could have lost patience and pushed Joan down the stairs. The real question was whether Frank would want to hear her speculation about what might have happened. Now that Kacey was in jail, Alene had lost some of her enthusiasm for confiding in him. She showered, opened the refrigerator and pulled out a bowl of overnight oatmeal packed with seeds, nuts, and dried fruit. Blanca deserved another raise.

Sierra entered the kitchen, took one look at the breakfast and whined, "Oatmeal, again?"

Alene looked at her and said evenly, "Guess you'll have to find something else to eat then, Sweetheart."

Sierra's eyes popped open because she'd expected a fight. "Are you okay, Mom?"

So, Sierra was capable of empathy even while going through adolescence. That cheered Alene up a bit. By the time she got everyone out the door, she felt the sun warming the top of her head and could smell something sweet in bloom. After Zuleyka picked up the kids, Alene started walking to the café. On the way, she called Brianne to ask if she'd heard anything about where Kacey was being held.

"No, but Isobel told me she's hiring a lawyer," said Brianne. "Have you spoken to your detective recently?"

"He's not my detective, Brianne."

"Oh, sorry," said Brianne. "I thought you two were kind of drawn to each other like magnets."

"Don't be ridiculous," said Alene as she passed a tiny front garden bursting with color.

Alene told Brianne about Jack grabbing her arm, while watching a bent-over woman trying to keep up with an energetic miniature dog.

"I can't believe Jack still looks and acts like a teenager," Brianne said, "but maybe he's regressed because of his mother. She hasn't woken up yet, and before you ask how I know, Bill's girlfriend stopped by last night. They're staying at Gary's so they can be closer to the hospital while Joan is recuperating. Tinley wanted to borrow some big plastic garbage bags because Jack apparently made a mess in the apartment. Also, Tinley's going to make sure there's food when Joan comes home."

"Did you tell her that Joan doesn't actually require food?" Alene said, quickly adding, "Ooh, that was mean of me." Alene stopped walking, covered her eyes with her hands and shook her head. Would she ever morph into a nicer person – more like Ruthie?

Brianne chuckled. "I know you have a good heart, Alene, no matter what. Anyway, let's talk if either one of us gets news about Kacey."

"Lydia always says the police aren't required to tell us anything." Alene told Brianne.

Brianne said, "Maybe they told Isobel."

"Kacey's over twenty-one. They don't even have to tell Isobel."

"But Kacey still needs taking care of," said Brianne.

Alene said, "The system doesn't care."

They made plans to walk over to the hospital to see Joan later in the afternoon, after work, so Alene decided to wait to tell Brianne about the conversation with her father about Hector-Schaf. She should really ask what Brianne remembered about Joan and the embezzled money. Dennis had been one of the many people who had lost their jobs.

The day flew by. Ruthie suggested three times that she tell Frank about Joan's being blackmailed and about Jack's letter, but Alene still didn't feel like talking to him. She texted Brianne later that afternoon, on her way home from the café, and they stopped into the hospital gift shop together, to buy a bunch of chrysanthemums for the vase Brianne remembered to bring. They left the flowers at the nurses' station, but couldn't get any information about Joan, except that she hadn't yet woken up.

Alene said, "She'll probably make them take away the flowers when she finds out that they're from us."

"Maybe," Brianne agreed, "but bringing them is still the right thing to do."

Tuesday evening, Alene made a healthy version of her mother's tuna a la king, watched a video with the children and played Scrabble with her father until she couldn't keep her eyes open. She woke up Wednesday morning feeling less shattered and ran to North Avenue and back through the zoo, before returning home, stretching, taking care of the kids, and heading to work.

A minute after Alene arrived at the cafe, Ruthie handed her a steaming cup and said, "Be nice to Edith today. She's still suffering a huge loss and she's more delicate than usual." That was Ruthie's mild way of describing Edith's constant prickliness.

"I always try to be nice," Alene said.

"Guess which of your favorite detectives is here drinking black coffee? He's alone today."

Alene let her head fall. "No longer my favorite anything – I'm not even going to go out and greet him."

"Don't you want to tell him about Joan's letter to Jack?" Ruthie looked at Alene meaningfully. "You don't know which piece of information is going to help him figure out what happened."

Alene shrank a little. "I'll go out and tell him, and I'll ask him about Kacey, but I won't sit down and chat."

Ruthie patted Alene's back. Alene pushed through the door and approached Frank unsmiling. "Good morning, Officer Shaw," she said in her most professional voice. "Do you have everything you need? Can I refill your cup?"

He smiled at her, which made her blink, but did not affect her resolve even though his teeth were even and white and his dimples were adorable. "I'm sorry, Alene. I know you're upset about Kacey."

"If you'd let her come home, I wouldn't be so upset," she said, her lip very close to quivering the way it did before she cried.

Frank spoke softly, "I hope you understand that I'm trying to help her."

"You don't have to explain anything to me," said Alene, and proceeded to tell him what had happened on Monday with Jack. "If there's nothing else I can get for you, thank you for coming in and enjoy your breakfast."

"Please sit down, Alene. I need your help. Please? This is a murder investigation," said Frank. He sounded serious. As she grudgingly pulled out a chair, he asked, "When did you say Jack showed you this letter?"

"I didn't say he showed me a letter," said Alene, sitting down far enough from him that she wouldn't mistakenly brush against his leg with hers.

Frank just looked at her without speaking. He placed his coffee on the table and reached out to put his hand over hers. "Do you understand that my goal is to stop anyone else from getting hurt?"

Alene hesitated. "I understand, and that's why I told you about Joan's letter and about Jack grabbing my arm."

Frank said, "Yes, you did. Give me a second, okay?" He picked up his cellphone and directed someone to find Jack Stone before punching in another number. "I've just sent you my direct cell phone number. If anything else happens, and I mean anything at all, I'm begging you to please call me immediately. Okay, Alene?"

Alene wondered what he meant by "anything." She felt her phone vibrate in her pocket. Maybe he saw her as a ditzy witness and all this friendly chatting and placing his hand on hers was just part of his usual method for getting information from women.

"Okay," she said, rising from the chair. "Can I get you anything else?" Had she given him her phone number already?

Frank said, "No, thank you, but Brianne asked me to meet the two of you here this morning, Alene. You were included in the group text."

He must have gotten her number from Brianne. Shoot, she'd forgotten to check her phone since the day before. What else had she missed? She started reading her messages as Brianne walked in. Alene motioned to her with her head, and Brianne came close enough for Alene to whisper. "If we're trying to get Kacey home, Frank Shaw is probably not going to be all that helpful. Also, do you remember anything about Joan being threatened back when everyone worked for that electronics company?"

"Sort of," Brianne whispered back, "but it was a long time ago, and I always chalked it up to Joan's being a drama queen."

Alene said, "I know, because she always suspected everyone of wanting what she had. Also, why haven't we heard about the autopsy yet?"

Frank interrupted, "I'm sitting right across from you, and I'd hoped we wouldn't be keeping secrets from each other at this point in our relationship, ladies."

Alene felt embarrassed, and they both apologized simultaneously. Alene asked, "Is it just the three of us meeting today?"

Brianne answered, "I thought we could help Frank with any questions he might have about Gary and Joan." She turned to Frank. "I hoped you'd tell us what's going on with Kacey."

Frank said, "I stopped by to see Kacey this morning, and she's fine, but she's been using again."

"There's no way," said Alene.

"I'm sorry," said Frank. "I know how disappointed you must be, but after all you told me about her struggles, I would think you'd be grateful that she's getting help. We had fourteen overdoses last week, Alene, and that was just in our precinct."

"I can't believe she's using again." said Alene. Maybe he was just saying it to justify holding Kacey in jail. "How did she even get her hands on anything after cutting off all contact with her previous dealers?"

"Sadly, they always find a way," said Frank.

Brianne squeezed Alene's hand. "We're all so stressed right now," she said. "I can't even imagination how much worse it's been for Kacey. We all need some closure. Do you have results of Gary's autopsy yet?"

"The cause of death was definitely stabbing," said Frank, "and we know that he died at approximately three-fifteen. We've searched your building and have spoken to all the neighbors but haven't found the murder weapon yet. Gary's phone records indicate that he spoke to Kacey at ten-thirty and to Bill at ten-forty. Joan told us that he left the house shortly after eleven, and then she also left for the day."

Alene stared at the space past Frank's ear. She was thinking through what he'd just said, but there were still so many missing pieces and she couldn't make any sense of it. "But where did Joan go? She has hardly any friends, so what did she say she was doing all day."

Frank looked at her sharply then glanced back at his notepad. "She drove up to the northern suburbs and had dinner with a friend. Her credit card shows that she stopped for gas up in Lincolnshire and the friend confirmed it, so I'm not questioning her whereabouts, especially in light of her current situation."

Brianne interjected, "Is she doing any better?"

"We have someone keeping an eye on her just in case someone actually tried to kill her the first time," Frank answered. "We don't want her talking to anyone before she talks to us. Not even her son." Alene understood someone wanting to kill her, but why would anyone want to talk to her?

Brianne asked, "What about Kacey? What did you charge her with? You know that she couldn't have been the one who pushed Joan down the stairs."

Frank answered, "Kacey's going to be okay once she's clean. She'll probably need another stint in rehab, I'm sorry to say, and she isn't ready for visitors. Do you understand that she's not clean right now?"

"I still don't believe it," said Alene again. "Where exactly is she?"

"She's on St. Andrew's rehab floor." said Frank, "where she's not allowed visitors, including her mother."

"How are you legally allowed to keep her locked up," Alene asked, "unless you charge her with something."

Frank responded, "Because we didn't charge her with anything except possession, she was able to choose between jail and a treatment center."

"At least she's getting a break from Isobel," said Alene.

"She's being taken care of," Frank said. "I promise you that."

Alene had to admit that he was treating them respectfully, but he wasn't telling them everything. She asked, "Did you also charge Bill Vanza or Neal Dunn?"

Frank answered, "We're talking to them both, but we don't have any reason to charge them at the moment. Things could change of course."

Just then Edith Vanza pushed open the door from the kitchen and approached the table. "I don't understand why I wasn't invited to this meeting," she said. "Gary is my brother, and Joan is my sister-in-law. Alene and Brianne aren't related to either of them."

Alene got out of her seat. Maybe if Frank had picked up Bill and Neal, he'd have found drugs in their systems too, and they'd be in a restricted facility instead of Kacey. "You're absolutely right, Edith. Why don't you sit down and talk to Frank while I go back to the kitchen?" Walking away, she smiled to herself for the first time that day.

Later, Brianne told Alene, "I think you hurt his feelings."

"I doubt it," said Alene. "I didn't feel like talking to him anymore. Did we ever tell him about all the renovations Gary did here and in in your bar?" Alene pointed around the café, as a few of the regulars waved or nodded in greeting.

"Remember how Gary worked nonstop to get those shelves finished?" Brianne asked. "He used to work when the bar was closed during the day, and then he'd go over to Whipped and Sipped after it was closed, and he'd be there for several hours. I know Olly was a huge help to him, but much of the time, Gary worked by himself with no assistant at all."

"He had an amazing work ethic. Sad that he wasn't able to pass that along to Jack Stone," said Alene. "I just realized that we should have asked Frank about Olly, as well."

Brianne said, "I thought you'd exonerated Olly after he saved you from Jack on Monday."

"My new motto is to trust no one," said Alene, remembering how her mother used to counsel her against that sort of thinking. "I'm wondering, if Gary used stolen money to do all the renovations in our places of business, are we both culpable? Could the IRS or some other governmental office come after us?"

"Oh Lenie," said Brianne, "We can speculate about where Gary got all that cash, but we'll never know for sure. We can't assume the worst of someone who died."

Alene asked, "So we shouldn't worry about it?"

"There's enough real-life drama to worry about," said Brianne.

Alene agreed. "It's all way too creepy."

The rest of the day passed in a blur. For dinner, Alene sautéed vegetables, added tomato sauce and melted cheese and served it in tortillas with guacamole and black bean sauce. She'd made it so many times she didn't need to think about it, but during dinner she could barely focus on what her children were saying or doing. That night in bed she counted backwards in sevens, starting at seven hundred. She fell asleep sometime around five-hundred and fifty-three.

On Thursday morning, Alene woke at five as usual, and was about to start her exercise routine when the phone rang. It was Jocelyn telling her there was an emergency.

She quickly dressed and got to the café twenty minutes later, at 5:25. She walked around to the alley and used her key to enter through the kitchen door. "Where is everyone?" Alene called out.

Ruthie came back to the kitchen from the café and took Alene's hand, saying, "There's been an accident." She pulled Alene into the café.

Alene looked through the front windows and saw the ambulance and police cars double parked on the street in front of the café. Technicians and police officers were moving quietly and quickly. Grant, Jocelyn and Zuleyka huddled near the pastry counter, despite it not being time for them to come in yet. Alene asked Ruthie, "What happened?"

Ruthie hugged Alene and said, "Someone came in and hit Edith over the head with our industrial blender. She was behind the drinks bar. That's why I called the others in early."

"Oh, shit." Alene felt sick. "But she's alive, right? How did it happen?"

Suddenly Jocelyn was at her side. "I unlocked the door and started setting up," said Jocelyn, pulling her over to where Edith lay on a gurney. "Edith was right behind me. She went in front while I was in the kitchen pulling things out of the fridge and lighting the ovens. I never heard anyone come in after us."

Edith's black socks and pink rubber sandals reminded Alene of the wicked witch's feet, but then she thought about Gary lying face down on Brianne's ugly yellow rug. She avoided looking at Edith's head. The blender's base looked unharmed.

Olly crouched next to Edith. "I'm holding her hand until they take her to the hospital," he said. "I'd want someone to do that for me."

Alene sat down abruptly at one of the tables and turned to Jocelyn, "So you unlocked the back door as usual and the two of you came in the way you always do?"

Jocelyn, pale and sweaty said, "Yes, just like I told you. Edith went straight to the drinks counter while I was still in the kitchen. I ran out when I heard her scream. I saw a kid in a hoodie run back out, but I was worried about Edith so I didn't see his face." She looked at Alene. "He wasn't as tall as Olly."

"Obviously, as if I'd ever hurt anyone," said Olly. "Jocelyn called me and I got here just before you, Alene."

Just a few minutes had passed since Alene had walked in the door. She held her head in her hands. What if Edith had said something to the murderer? Had the murderer tried to shut her up just like he'd tried to shut Joan up?

At least Kacey was no longer a suspect and should be freed immediately. Alene wondered if she'd have to replace the expensive blender.

Chapter 15

Frank and his partner arrived, just moments later. Edith had opened her eyes as the paramedics moved her into the ambulance, but she'd passed out again by the time they tried to question her. Frank gave the paramedics a sign to leave and turned to Alene and Ruthie, who were hovering nearby with the other employees.

He said, "I wish I could have been here to stop this from happening. Do you have any idea who did it? Did anyone get a glimpse?"

"Jocelyn said she saw a short guy run out and she's sure it wasn't Olly," said Alene. "At least Edith's still alive." She joined Jocelyn behind the counter and watched the ambulance pull away.

Alene heard everyone murmuring in agreement. "Well, it looks as if she was pretty badly clobbered," said Frank, still standing. "Did any of you notice anything out of the ordinary?"

Jocelyn said, "I was bending over Edith."

"I didn't see the guy running out," said Olly.

Ruthie said, "This doesn't have anything to do with Edith, but I forgot to tell you that Bill Vanza came in with his girlfriend sometime yesterday afternoon, Alene. He didn't acknowledge me the first time I waved, but then his girlfriend nudged him and they both waved back. The two of them don't come in here very often."

"How did I miss seeing them?" Alene asked.

Ruthie answered, "It was when you and Brianne were talking to Frank."

Frank said, "We were planning to chat with those two again anyway."

"I think you should also check Isobel Vanza," said Alene. "She's playing the role of the disgruntled ex-wife and she hated all three of the people, who were clobbered, in some way."

Lee looked at her with disdain while Frank wore a surprised expression. She added, "Just a thought." Alene turned away from the detective to wave at Grant, Rashid, and LaTonya, who were all peeking from the kitchen. Nothing to see here, folks, she thought to herself.

Olly asked "Can we open up on time now that Edith's en route to the hospital? That is, if you don't mind," he said to Frank. "We all need to keep busy right now. We need to see smiling faces."

Frank said, "That's up to Alene." It was six-forty, and regular customers would soon start standing outside, waiting for the doors to open. "I know you're about to get busy, but I'd like to speak with all the employees who are already here, one at a time. May we use that table in the corner?"

Alene nodded and asked Zuleyka to start the music and take over the drinks counter for Edith. As she was about to unlock the front door, which would have been a pleasant surprise for the customers who were used to waiting outside until exactly seven on the dot, Ruthie said, "Wait a minute."

Everyone looked at her, expectantly. "It doesn't smell like a coffee shop yet. Let's get something in the ovens."

They scattered, and less than ten minutes later, Alene opened the door and stepped back to the dessert counter as the first few customers entered. She greeted a bald woman who always ordered decaf with a poppy-seed muffin. A sweaty-looking man in his fifties rushed in and expressed indignation that his drink wasn't already prepared – Edith always had his espresso ready when the café opened. He asked after Edith and Alene told him that she'd been taken ill.

An hour passed, and Alene was packing a box with six single-serve egg-less vegetable omelets for a man in a wheelchair when Neal showed up. She had to close her eyes and count, ringing up the order and smiling warmly at the customer before turning to scowl at Neal. "What are you doing here, Neal? Can't you get coffee somewhere else?"

"Shouldn't you be grateful that I'm supporting your place of business?" Neal asked, running his fingers through his thinning hair and adjusting his waistband around the tummy he'd recently acquired. "And don't you think it's in my best interest for you to succeed?"

Alene wondered if he'd use one of the metal bowls to bash her in the head now that the police had taken her good industrial blender. "I don't think you care about anyone besides yourself. And you could have easily broken in early this morning to break my blender."

He laughed. "Why would I want to break your blender?"

Alene pointed at him. "I think you could have tried to get rid of everyone who knows that your father helped embezzle money; and I think you could have murdered Gary." This time she had solid evidence to back up her accusation, but why did she know so many people who could be murderers?

Neal winced as if she'd punched him. He said, "Why would I murder anyone, Alene? I run a respected Honda dealership, in case you forget where your child-support comes from." Alene wondered why he had to spit her name out as if it were a swear word.

"Your father could have used stolen money to buy it, Neal," she responded, giving his name two syllables. At least they were surrounded by people and he couldn't hurt her, not even emotionally. "I've thought a lot about it and I've realized that your dad could have been the one who performed all that accounting magic to make all the cash disappear from Hector-Schaf."

"That's ridiculous, Alene," said Neal with a forced chuckle. "May I please have an Americano," he asked Zuleyka at the drinks counter, "with room for cream? I can't believe you really think I could murder someone, Alene." The other customers were either highly amused, or thought they were practicing lines for a play. But Alene couldn't help herself.

She nearly spat at Neal. "Maybe you were hoping to get more out of Gary and Joan because you frittered away whatever you got from your father. You had both the motive and opportunity to kill Gary, push Joan, and bash Edith over the head with my blender. Are you hoping to go after me next, or were you planning to off your mother first?"

Neal's face flushed red and Alene got some pleasure out of watching him struggle with anger as he tried to come up with a reply. Frank, whom Alene had nearly forgotten about, as soon as Neal had started up with her, rose from his table and spoke in a cold, detached voice before Neal could respond. "I'd like to have a word with you, Alene," he said, "Now. In your office."

Alene stared at Frank, finally speechless. Neal preened as if he had been the one to pop her balloon, but Frank said, "Neal, please take a seat and give your statement to my partner, Lee. If you don't cooperate, Officer Batista will cuff you and bring you down to the station. Do you understand?"

"But, I didn't do anything," Neal whined. He sat across from Lee, who didn't respond, as usual.

Alene felt idiotic. She'd lost her temper in front of her customers and employees. She should have forbidden Neal from ever coming in. He drove her batty. As they sat in her office, Frank said, "I understand that this is a stressful time for you, but I hope you realize that I do have experience with murder investigations, and I don't think it's helpful for you to go around accusing people of murder."

Alene bit her lip and looked down at her desk. "He's not a person, he's my ex-husband."

He continued. "Do you have any real evidence that Joan Stone and Patrick Dunn embezzled money or that Neal Dunn was involved somehow? I'm not asking about what you heard someone say - I'm asking for solid evidence, Alene."

Alene blushed, feeling disgusted with herself, and she shook her head. "It was a long time ago, but I remember hearing about it. If it helps, I really think Neal is capable of doing whatever he needs to do in order to get what he thinks he deserves."

"That's not evidence, Alene," Frank told her gently.

"It's anecdotal evidence," said Alene.

He waited. How could she explain the hardest year of her life? Should she mention how learning of Neal's infidelity had caused her milk to dry up so she had to stop nursing three-month-old Noah? Should she tell him how she'd been inattentive to her girls, terse with everyone at work, and distraught that she'd married someone like Neal?

She hadn't said anything to Neal for several weeks after Brianne and Dennis had told her about Joan and him, but her children had felt the tension. Quinn and Sierra had started bickering more often, crying more easily, and needing more time-outs than ever before. They regressed to sucking their thumbs and sleeping together in the same twin bed. Alene backslid to some of her earlier nervous habits such as chewing the ends of her hair and twirling it.

She remembered feeling stifled in the townhouse with Neal still there. Most afternoons she took the children to Ruthie's backyard, which gave them all a little respite from the summer heat. The Rosins had a swing set and a little pool. Ruthie and Benjie would sit with Alene to help her strategize. Benjie thought she needed to confront Neal about the gambling and the affair, but only with a therapist or lawyer in the room. He thought someone who could carry on such a huge deception had no right to be trusted as a husband and father. Ruthie thought that saving the marriage was worth any cost. She argued for Alene to give Neal another chance.

One evening before she could stop herself, Alene strode into the living room and blocked Neal's view of the television, saying, "This is not a marriage." His eyes shifted as if there was something interesting behind her, an irritating habit she'd always hated. "I deserve better than this," she said as firmly as she could.

He glanced at her impatiently and murmured, "I can't deal with your paranoia right now, Alene," before storming from the living room and out of the door without another word. He left his beer and snacks for her to clean up.

Alene took the next day off of work and began packing the children's clothes. That evening Neal came home long after dinner was over and the children were in bed. He said, "Your bitchy attitude is killing our marriage, Alene." He yammered on about how he wouldn't have put the money he used to gamble in the bank, anyway. About how she'd made him feel unloved, so he'd had to find it elsewhere. He said she shouldn't be so irked by what he did to relax, such as going to a casino in Rosemont or to one of the river boats, once in a while. "And why is it a crime to have a little fun on the weekend when all we do at home is deal with the children?"

Alene had said, "Do you mean <u>our</u> children, whom <u>we</u> brought into the world? How pathetic that they're such a chore for you," she had to stop and take a deep breath. "If anyone's still awake, they're going to hear us. I'm not talking about it now." Baby Noah had started crying as if on cue.

Neal retorted, "Why does everything always have to be convenient for you?" She heard him prattle in his nasal, whiny voice, as if through a screen. He'd known Joan for years because she'd worked with his dad, and they were just old friends. Alene wanted to stick her fingers in her ears and sing nonsense syllables like the girls did, but she was still trying, unsuccessfully, to nurse the baby. At some point she stopped listening.

The next day she and the children moved to her father's condo, even though Joan Stone still lived across the hall. After that, Alene and Neal spoke mostly through their lawyers. Her sister had never liked Neal and relished the opportunity to give him a hard time with the divorce. Lydia decided early on that she was going to have fun and started off by nit-picking and arguing about every detail.

Alene took a few sentences to explain all of that to Frank and she also told him how she hadn't wanted to talk much to anyone except Ruthie, who called every night to check up on her even after they'd worked together all day. Ruthie would ask, "How are you doing, Six?" If Alene answered, "Luzon," Ruthie would recall the battle in which Japanese kamikaze pilots rained on the American navy in the Philippines and know that Alene felt overwhelmed.

If one of them felt deceived or cheated, the answer would be, "Versailles," because Hitler had broken the Treaty of Versailles. "Monte Cassino" meant that one of them felt as if she was being bombarded – after the fourteen-hundred-year-old Italian monastery that was bombed by the Americans in their quest to re-take Rome. "Battle of the Bulge" meant that someone was trying to pit them against each other as Germany had tried to split up the Allied forces.

Frank interrupted by clearing his throat. "What about Pearl Harbor?"

"Too obvious," said Alene, "Everyone remembers December 7."

Frank looked amused. He asked, "What would have been the worst battle you could reference?"

Alene answered, "I'd probably say D-day, you know, because it was the climactic battle of the war. We only use the dates of the atomic bombs as nick-names, not as codes."

"Hope you passed the class," said Frank. "But right now, your ex-husband is sitting in the café waiting for me, and I have several crimes to solve."

"We both got A's," she said before rising to take a blackberry-mango crisp cup from the plate Olly was holding just outside her office. "This is a peace offering for you, Frank." She asked Olly to offer them on the house to Neal and Frank's partner. "I'm sorry, really sorry that I lost my temper and my sanity. It won't happen again."

Frank took a bite and gave her a thumbs-up. "You were right about one thing, at least. We know that someone discovered Joan's involvement in the collapse of Hector-Schaf Electronics."

Alene wondered why he'd let her babble on about her divorce and about how she and Ruthie had passed their History of WWII class in college. "Then why did you ask if I had any evidence?"

"You were the one who told me about Hector-Schaf Electronics in the first place," said Frank, chewing the crisp slowly and smiling the same way she did when she was eating something extraordinary, "but you neglected to say anything about Joan being blackmailed."

"I'm sorry," said Alene. "It was a long time ago."

"Do you know if anyone else received a demand for money?" Frank asked. "Like your ex-mother-in-law?"

"Mitzi never mentioned it," said Alene. "She is an honest person and she wouldn't have tolerated illegally-obtained money. I told Gary that she'd probably have tossed Patrick out of her bed and her life if she knew he'd done something illegal such as helping Joan embezzle money."

Alene's jaw had nearly dropped to the floor when Gary had asked if she thought Mitzi had tossed Patrick overboard on their cruise. Gary had also been on board when it happened. "She'd have called the police no matter what the blackmailer threatened her with," Alene told Frank. "I once heard her rail against Neal when he couldn't tell her what charities he supports."

"What about Neal's father?"

Alene said, "Well, you know that he died after falling off a cruise ship, right?"

"That was very unusual and suspicious," said Frank.

"Yeah, it was weird, but the entire cruise industry changed their rules because of it," said Alene. "Gary wanted me to ask Neal if he knew about his father's accounting tricks, but he'd died and it was long after the divorce and I didn't want to ask."

"Are you sorry you didn't ask?"

"I should have been a better friend. I didn't come through for Brianne after someone plowed into Dennis on the bike path. He died on the way to the hospital that day – the same day you drove me to the hospital, when I went into labor with Noah. I just haven't been there for my friends and I feel terrible about it."

Frank leaned over and gently stroked her arm, giving her the chills and pulling her out of her funk. "Why didn't Gary and Joan go to the police when they got the blackmail letter?" He asked. "We have experience in dealing with blackmailers."

"We all asked him the same thing, back then, and I remember him being afraid that Joan would go to prison. He said he was going to pay the blackmailer, thinking it was because of Joan's gambling. Sometimes she was flush with cash and sometimes she didn't have enough to buy coffee. Whenever she was flush, she was careless, and he started hiding away whatever cash he found."

"Where did he find cash?" Frank asked.

"She used to leave it lying around all the time," said Alene. "Gary used some for renovations to the café, bar, and the building's community room."

Frank asked, "Did you know where all the money for these renovations came from?"

Alene answered, "We used to joke about it, but I never knew anything for sure. I mean, I was worried after I found out, because what if the government came in and took the café? What if I need to sell it someday, but I can't prove how all the work was done?"

Alene opened her arms as if to say she'd said everything she had to say. When Frank spoke again, it was hardly above a whisper. "Did the blackmailing ever come up again?"

"No," said Alene.

Frank's lips were a tight line. "Do you know where Gary hid all that money?"

"No," she said. Maybe if she'd persuaded Gary to go to the police when he and Joan were being blackmailed, back then, they'd have gone to jail, but Gary would still be alive and Joan wouldn't be in a coma. "I'd have told you if I knew something like that. Isn't it obvious that someone out there wants it?"

Just then, Jack Stone barged into Alene's little office and sputtered, "I didn't mean to grab your arm, Alene."

Instead of feeling angry or irritated, Alene was shocked. Jack had gotten a haircut, shaved his beard off, and he was wearing khakis with a tucked-in light-blue shirt, brown leather shoes and a matching belt. For the first time since she'd met him, Jack looked like a man instead of a sort-of-bum. She couldn't help asking, "What happened to you?"

Jack said, "Tinley took me shopping and then she shaved my beard and cut my hair. She thought it would make my mother happy to see me like this. We were going to visit her this morning, but the nurses wouldn't let us in."

Alene wanted to ask if Tinley had also taught him how behave like a man, but it seemed too snarky, considering Jack's polite answer. Frank had started fiddling with his phone, obviously checking and responding to text messages. Alene said, "It's nice that you're worried about your mother."

"She's my only mother," said Jack.

She noticed that he had a slightly weak chin now that the beard was gone. He reminded her of someone, but she couldn't place it. Frank must have noticed, because he was looking at her with a questioning look. She stared at Jack, her mind a blank.

Battered: A Whipped and Sipped Mystery

Chapter 16

"Why are you staring at me like that?" Jack asked Alene.

Looking away, Alene said, "Sorry, you remind me of someone."

"Probably my mother," said Jack. "I don't know why they wouldn't let me and Tinley see her."

Alene looked at Frank across the table. Whatever epiphany she'd been about to have went up in smoke. "Yeah, Officer Shaw says they're not letting anyone in until she talks to the police," she told him. "And Kacey's locked up on the hospital's addict ward with no access to visitors."

Frank said, "Kacey's in a safe place."

Alene harrumphed, "Then why are you preventing anyone from seeing her?"

"She's getting the help she needs right now, Alene," he answered. "I'll let you know when she's allowed to see visitors."

Alene's face fell. She hadn't really believed that Kacey was using again so soon after her latest recovery. She thought about apologizing to Frank but decided to just try to look contrite.

Frank turned away from Alene and said to Jack, "Your mother might have seen her assailant, Jack. I'm sure you understand that she's at risk." He looked at his watch. "If you want to visit now, I could bring you over. We can chat on the way to the hospital."

"If it's in your cruiser," said Jack, "I'll only go if I can sit in front."

Frank nodded at Jack and looked at Alene. She felt stunned that Kacey was back in rehab and ashamed that she'd been so impatient with Frank, who said, "There's a crazy person on the loose and I think all of you need to be cautious right now. Can you make sure your staff is on the alert for anything unusual and try not to be alone? Also, could you do me a personal favor and check your phone more often? You do have me on speed dial, right?"

She nodded as Frank and Jack left. He didn't have to speak to her as if she were a child, she thought glumly. She turned away, instead of admiring Frank's muscular back and confident stride. She sat down and added him to her speed dial after her father, Ruthie, Lydia, and Brianne. Grabbing an apple from the counter, she headed to her office. It was the end of the month and she had to finish ordering and to work on payroll.

She holed up in her office for a few hours, drank more decaf espresso with almond milk, and ate a raw kale salad with tart cherries and almonds for lunch. As soon as Ruthie finished her baking and left for the day, Alene pulled out her old blender and made an edamame-avocado dip followed by a kale and parsley dip for the next morning. She grumbled to herself because the dips weren't as smooth and fluffy as those made with the blender whose base was in police custody.

By the time four o'clock closing rolled around and the rest of the staff had left, Alene was starting to get a headache from a sudden afternoon front. It had made the barometer plunge and had turned the sunny day into a blustering, gray early evening. She locked up the café, grabbed the umbrella she kept for emergencies, and ran home. It was only after she stood in front of her building, shaking out her dripping umbrella, she remembered Frank's suggesting that she not be alone. Oh well, she thought, she couldn't live her life as if she were about to be hit by a bus.

In the apartment, Blanca was preparing to leave, Sierra was watching a rerun of some teen show, Quinn was reading in bed, Cal was having a snack at the kitchen table, and Noah was sitting next to his grandfather playing with a piece of string. Noah looked up hopefully as Alene entered the room. "Mommy, will you play with me?"

Alene looked at her father, who said, "So sad this boy has no toys and nothing to do."

"I have toys," said Noah, "but I want to watch the lightning and Sierra won't let me turn off all the lights. It's better when you watch from a dark place – remember all that stuff I learned about light, Mom?"

Alene answered, "I certainly do, Noah. How about we go upstairs to the community room? If no one else is there, we can turn off all the lights. If someone is up there, we can watch from one of our bedrooms."

"The bedrooms aren't as good," said Noah, "because we can only see from one side. We can see in all four directions upstairs. We should bring flashlights too."

Noah ran off while Alene searched the front hall closet and utility drawer and found the flashlight she used to take when she and Ruthie went camping. Benjie and Ruthie had continued to camp even after having children, but Neal hated the mosquitos and inconvenience, so Alene's flashlight hadn't been used in years. It worked fine, after she put in new batteries while Noah waited impatiently by the door.

Alene couldn't bring herself to use the stairs after Joan's assault, so they went up in the elevator. The minute Noah pushed open the doors to the darkened community room he began flashing light up and down until Alene told him it was making her headache return.

"Okay, sorry, Mommy," he said turning it off again. She hoped he would stay cuddly and adorable for a few more years and admired his wiry little body as he ran on the benches that lined the room. Alene couldn't look at those benches without remembering a time when Joan had farted at one of the building parties. Alene had started a wave of laughter for which Joan had never forgiven her.

"Noah," she called out, "can you stop running around and settle down for a bit? Didn't we want to watch the lightning?"

Noah replied, "I am watching the lightning. I'm pretending it can't catch me because I'm Superman." Alene sat down in one of the comfortable chairs in the sitting area of the room and looked around the room. The condo board had used a special assessment to pay for some of the updates, which caused a lot of buzz in the building. Alene had been on the committee to choose new carpet, chairs and tables. Then, because he offered to pay for it, Gary had gotten unanimous support from the association to design and install the built-in benches on which Noah was running.

The kids had long ago noticed that they could run along the benches, which lined three-and-a-half walls, but they had to jump to the floor where the double door opened from the hallway. They could jump up onto the bench again on the other side of the door. Once when they'd all been celebrating something up in the community room, Alene had said that she worried that her children would break one of the benches with their running. Gary had told her he'd made sure those benches could survive even a two-hundred-forty-pound guy like himself.

The community room was the size of two full apartments, so it was a great place to take children when it was too cold or hot to play outside. Noah was already on his fourth trip around the room. She let him watch one more crack of lightning and make one more run around the room before announcing that it was time to go back home to prepare dinner.

An hour later, the smell of tomato pesto soup and fresh bread filled the apartment as Quinn set the table, Noah poured the water, and Sierra placed the butter plate and a bowl of zucchini-dill dip on the table. They all sat down, and Alene was happy to get through dinner without a single argument. The kids finished quickly as usual, and Alene stayed at the table to keep her father company. It took him a long time to eat his meal.

"Dad," said Alene, "do you remember hearing anything about Gary hiding money that Joan embezzled from her company?"

"No," Cal said, "but Gary was always very...handy with the hammer and nails. He could have jury-rigged a kind of box under a bedframe. He could have... hand-built the cabinets in his apartment if he wanted to, and he could have... put safes all over the place. I wish I was that talented. I always called him when it was time to clean the air conditioner filters or put in... a new light fixture. He could do anything. And he had that kid... with the curly hair helping him with the woodworking."

"You mean Olly?"

"Who remembers?"

"But did Gary ever talk about building a place to store stolen money?" Alene asked.

"Why would he talk about something like that? Do pirates go around telling everyone where they buried their treasures? Even if Gary wanted to tell me, everyone in the building knows I can't keep a secret. Remember when

Gloriadine's older son told me they were making her a surprise eightieth birthday party a few years back and I went and spilled the beans that very day? Not on purpose though. I just didn't remember what I wasn't supposed to say. Anyway, what was it that you were asking about?"

Alene got up to finish clearing the table. "Gary hiding money," she said.

Cal said, "You should set your mind to finding the hidden money, since you've always been so good at that sort of thing. If you found a treasure chest, maybe you'd stop working so hard at the cafe."

They heard a knock on the door and the sound of Noah's running to answer it. "Mom," he yelled after opening the door, "it's the Vanzas." Alene wiped her hands on a dish cloth and hurried out of the kitchen, just as Tinley stepped in front of Bill and Jack at the doorstep.

"I sent Bill to the store for ice cream and he bought so much we thought we would see if you guys wanted any. What do you think?" she asked.

Alene didn't think it was a great idea for Noah to have ice cream right before bedtime because the sugar made him get up again and again to go to the bathroom. But it was too late to object after she saw that the choices were cookies and cream, peppermint, mint-chocolate chip, and dark-chocolate-cherry. "Thanks, guys," said Alene, wistfully remembering all the times Gary had brought over treats just before bedtime. She used to get mad at him about it, but who could stay mad at someone like Gary?

"Quinn, please bring spoons for everyone and put away all that stuff on the table, including your paint samples," she said. "Noah, please bring enough napkins and serving spoons and get your toys off the floor. Does anyone want water? Sierra, please bring a pitcher of cold water and a bunch of plastic cups."

Alene loved how well-behaved the children could be when ice cream was involved. All three ran to do their assigned tasks as their guests sat down in the living room. Even Cal joined them although he didn't love sweets — he had a little crush on Tinley. Alene looked at her sitting there, between Bill and Jack, charming them both with her flashy hair and her infectious smile. Alene was glad to see them relaxing after what had happened. Even Jack looked less stressed than when she'd seen him earlier that day.

"Was your mother awake yet, Jack?" Alene asked him.

Jack said, "No, but Officer Shaw talked to the nurse, and she said there were signs that she was getting ready to wake up."

Alene noted again how much better Jack looked. Even with his receding chin and large ears, he looked almost attractive when he was cleaned up. Tinley's chin was also a little weak, but she held her head high, and the cute cut and striking magenta color of her hair drew the eye away. Tinley noticed her looking at them and smiled warmly.

"You two look like you could be related," said Alene.

Bill said, "I hope you don't mean Tinley and me. That would be repugnant."

Jack laughed, "When they get married, we'll be sort of related."

"No, we won't, you dickhead," said Bill, smacking Jack hard on his shoulder. "I'm not even sure you're still my stepbrother now that my dad is dead, and we're definitely not related."

Tinley jabbed Bill with her elbow and smiled to lessen the blow. "Don't be so mean, Billy. Jack's like a little brother to me." She turned her back on Bill and hugged Jack. He looked like a puppy who'd just had his tummy rubbed.

Sierra and Quinn finished dessert and headed to the kitchen with their empty bowls, and from there to get ready for bed. Noah sat in front of his empty bowl constructing something with magnets he'd left under the coffee table. Tinley offered to accompany Mr. Baron back to his room. "Call me Cal," he said, grinning like a schoolboy.

Alene was about to tell Tinley that her kind gesture was unnecessary, since her father had a walker, when Cal started up a one-sided conversation. "I always walk better when I have company, and this way I can show you my pictures. Did you know I used to sail? We had a little Tanzer sailboat, and I could look at it out the front window during the week when I couldn't get out on the lake. I used to work long hours back then. Didn't you tell me you cut hair, Honey? Are you working every day, or do you have some free time to enjoy summer in the city?"

Alene hoped Tinley wouldn't let him bore her unconscious as she heard Tinley respond, "I've been working my tail off for years, Mr. Baron, but I just finally quit. I think I deserve some rest and relaxation."

Alene hoped he'd wait until he was out of her hearing before launching into his tried and true stories about how hard he'd worked and how he knew everything there was to know about tax-advantaged savings vehicles and diversified mutual funds. As much as she loved her father, he was starting to repeat stories. Maybe that happened to everyone when they stopped being able to have new experiences – they had to keep reliving the old ones. She should ask Mitzi to arrange an afternoon, and maybe take her dad to see a play.

Bill and Jack were still sniping at each other and Tinley was still with her father back in his bedroom, when Alene finished cleaning up. Just as she was about to rescue Tinley from her father's monologue, Tinley reappeared and hustled Bill and Jack out the door. As they left, Tinley said, "Now that I've left my job, I hope to stop at your café for a latte now and then – maybe even tomorrow."

"Great," said Alene, knowing that hair stylists often moved from one shop to another. "Edith Vanza is still recuperating from a blow to her head so I'll be there to open at five in the morning."

"Well, maybe not quite that early," replied Tinley as she walked out.

Alene locked the door and called out to her father on the way back to her bedroom. "Need anything, Dad?"

"No, Sweetheart, I'm fine," Cal answered. "She could do better than Bill Vanza."

"I agree," said Alene. "But there is no accounting for taste. Love you, good night."

Battered: A Whipped and Sipped Mystery

Chapter 17

Alene wondered if the same person who'd bashed Edith in the head the previous day was lurking behind a garbage can or in a doorway. It was just before the sun was about to rise and the silvery darkness was lit by flickering streetlamps. She hurried up the alley, relieved to see Jocelyn bolting her bicycle to the iron railing around Whipped and Sipped's bins. They both checked and rechecked the sides of the alley before Alene unlocked the door and turned off the alarm. All they saw were the vitamin store's garbage bags scattered about, as usual. Never in the bins where they belonged. Without speaking, they hustled into the kitchen and re-locked the door. "Guess this is the new protocol until things calm down," said Jocelyn.

"We'll have to let the rest of the staff in one at a time," said Alene.

Jocelyn said, "I thought the doors have to be open during business hours."

"That's not until seven," Alene responded. She felt jittery as she turned on the lights. She started a 70's music track that began with Van Morrison's *Brown Eyed Girl*. "You okay?" she asked Jocelyn.

Jocelyn gave her a thumbs-up and they both got to work. Alene opened one refrigerator and took out trays of yeasted dough that required more rising. Jocelyn turned on the ovens and set coffee cakes, breakfast rolls and muffin trays from the other refrigerator onto the counters so everything could come to room temperature before baking. Alene began punching down dough and dividing it into various shapes for the different breads. When the ovens were ready, she sprinkled on toppings and began baking the first few muffin trays.

Jocelyn unlocked the door and quickly closed it behind each Whipped and Sipped employee. Each one inhaled the heady mix of cinnamon and yeast and headed towards their assigned tasks. There was less chatting than usual, so Alene sang along to Joni Mitchell's *A Case of You*. Jocelyn cut up fruit and filled the bins used in making smoothies. Alene thought about how Edith made solid, consistently good smoothies.

Olly chopped and began the long process of caramelizing a forty-pound bag of onions while watching over the simmering cauldrons of brown rice and black beans he'd prepared the day before. Grant washed mounds of vegetables at the designated sink where grit and dirt flowed down the drain. Sally prepared the day's soup and drained pots of lentils and garbanzos that had soaked all night.

After unlocking the door at seven, Alene stayed in front and watched as customers started to file in. The espresso guy asked about Edith again, hurrying past the middle-aged lady showing way too much cleavage who was seated at her usual table, front and center. A woman who always ordered a mini-quiche with her latte got a scone instead. Most of the regulars were young, well-dressed workers heading either to the El station or to their offices in the neighborhood. Many just ordered coffee, unless they were tempted by the pastries or the trays of fluffy muffins. As usual, most took their food to go. At eight, Ruthie showed up to help Jocelyn replenish the trays and begin preparing new batters and bread doughs.

Alene had just rung up a cappuccino with a citrus-poppy seed muffin for a customer, whose dreadlocks she'd watched grow long and gray over the past ten years, when Neal strutted in as if he owned the place. Bill Vanza followed behind looking as if he was casing the joint. They were both stupid enough to think they could get away with murder. It would have been typical of Neal to plan it all out while Bill did the dirty work. She would like to see them both arrested. Alene checked her watch. Didn't Neal's service department open by seven-thirty and shouldn't they both already be at work?

Neal and Bill saw her, before she had time to sneak back into the kitchen. "Hi Alene," said Bill, "I was just telling Neal how nice it was to hang out last night with your family."

Alene wondered if Bill was trying to frighten her. Everything he said or did seemed menacing now.

"What can I get for you today," she asked, trying to maintain a neutral expression. Neal was supposed to pick up the kids after camp and she hoped he knew that his own mother would kill him if he failed to keep her grandchildren safe. She said, "I meant to remind you, Neal, that if you get to the condo before Blanca leaves at four-thirty, she'll help with the kids' overnight things. They're looking forward to dinner out and hoping for another sleepover at your mom's."

Neal made a long-suffering face solely for Bill's benefit, but Alene was quite sure he wasn't going to "waste" his whole evening with the children. He probably had a date and planned to leave right after dinner. Oh well, she thought, his plans weren't her problem. Bill ordered the vegetarian "huevos rancheros" and Neal asked for a vegetarian stuffed burrito. Both dishes were made with real eggs and cheese, which Ruthie wouldn't touch, but which many customers requested instead of the vegan version. Alene enjoyed a secret hope that the beans in their dishes would cause them some uncomfortable moments later that morning, even though Whipped and Sipped staff soaked the beans and added seaweed and digestive spices to prevent such moments.

It looked as if Bill was assessing the geode collection on the wall above the windows. "The best ones are at Brianne's," said Alene, "but we've got the largest ones here." Remembering how they'd been scattered on the floor near Gary's body, she scrutinized Bill's face for any sign of guilt. What if he'd tried to get Edith's help in searching for Gary's treasure somewhere in the café? Maybe he clobbered her with the blender because she had no idea what he was talking about. What was he looking for, though?

The geode collection was handsome, but hardly worth the time to climb up on a table and pry from the strong industrial glue that kept it in place. Had Bill tried, and had Neal served as his lookout? It seemed that ever since she'd known him, Neal had liked nothing better than to get something for nothing. Alene only breathed freely after they had left, pleasantly surprised that they'd both tossed their garbage and recycling into the proper receptacles.

After that the day went smoothly. She walked home slowly after closing, suspicious of everyone who passed by and hardly noticing the bright sunshine. Blanca had left by the time she walked in the door at five, but the children were parked in front of the television, still waiting to be picked up. Alene called Neal, who told her that he was with a client and couldn't leave work for a while. He asked her to bring the children to his mother's, and she seethed for a bit, wondering if he'd planned on her driving them all along.

She told her father that dinner would be late and cajoled the children into getting out the door. Then she battled

232

Friday rush hour traffic to chauffeur them to Mitzi's apartment just three miles away. By the time she pulled her car back into her own garage it was after six and Alene felt as if she was ready to put on her pajamas and go straight to bed. But Cal loved their Friday nights alone together, usually watching a movie that they couldn't see while the children were at home. She'd already set out the ingredients for fish tacos—which Cal loved. She just needed to whip up the guacamole and cut up veggies while the whitefish fillets sautéed in a pan.

As she unlocked the door to their condo, Alene heard her father explaining myasthenia gravis, the disease that now permeated their lives and required constant vigilance. "It's why I need a walker. I was the picture of well-being until this fluctuating muscle weakness started a few years ago. It causes me to slur my words a little, not sure if you can tell."

Cal was smiling at Tinley, who was sitting with excellent posture on the couch next to Cal's chair, her hair now an electric blue. Hadn't it been magenta just the previous night when they were all eating ice cream? Alene wasn't sure where her father thought all his flirting was going.

"Hi Tinley," said Alene. "I'm sorry if my dad is boring you with his medical saga. Do you want to join us for fish tacos? I've got plenty." She went into the kitchen and put a pan on the stove while she took the fillets out of the fridge and set them in the pan with bubbling butter and olive oil. "I'm serving them with roasted vegetables and guacamole." It was nice to see Tinley without her awful boyfriend, but did that mean Bill had gone over to Mitzi's with Neal and the children? The last thing her kids needed was to spend the evening watching Neal and Bill act like teenagers.

"I'm not boring you, am I, honey?" asked Cal.

"No, Cal," said Tinley, "I just wish I had a father to tell me stories about his health problems, and I'd pat his knee and tell him he looked great for his age. I wish I had a mother to put her arm around me and tell me she's proud of me." She wiped her eyes with the back of her hand. "Sorry, I'm just kind of a mess right now." Alene had thought she seemed a little agitated.

Cal patted Tinley on the knee. "You look beautiful, Sweetheart. Ask Alene what a mess looks like. When she was going through her divorce, she stopped washing her hair and taking care of herself. You wouldn't believe how she looked." Alene was only half-listening while carefully lifting the fish fillets out of the hot pan and setting them on paper towels to drain.

"Dad," Alene said, "do you really need to tell that story?" She knew he was still traumatized from the divorce, even though it had been nearly eight years ago. "I'm sorry, Tinley," she continued, "I know what it's like to long for your mother." Alene added sliced onions and peppers to the pan and gave them a stir.

Tinley's lip trembled. "At least she'd be glad that I'm done with Bill."

About time, thought Alene, taking a moment to roll her eyes before turning back towards the living room. "I know break-ups are hard, but I'm glad to hear you booted him out. He was just not in your league, Tinley."

"I agree, Sweetheart," said Cal. "A girl like you needs someone special." He wheezed and leaned back into his comfy chair.

"You shouldn't lower your expectations," said Alene, mincing scallion and cilantro for the guacamole. "Self-absorbed guys like Bill are a dime a dozen." Wasn't she suddenly quite the scholar of relationships? Ruthie should hear her speaking with such conviction. What if Bill was upset about the break-up, and came across the hall searching for Tinley? What if he was angry and violent? Cal was useless, and how could she and Tinley protect themselves against someone who'd already hurt three people?

Tinley said, "Yeah, I know."

Alene added fresh lime and salt to the avocado and stirred it before setting it aside. She glanced at Tinley. Looking at her profile, and maybe because of her very short wig, Alene noticed that her chin reminded her of... "You know what," said Alene, "you and Jack Stone have a similar chin. That's who you remind me of." She started preparing a vegetable tray. Even if it was just for her father and herself, she liked the presentation to be colorful and appetizing.

"We're related," said Tinley, who was now on her feet and pacing behind Cal.

"No way," said Alene, "How about that, Dad? Tinley's related to Jack Stone!" Cal had dozed off and didn't respond. "How are you related?" she asked Tinley, who was walking back and forth now, in front of the dark wood bookshelves. She seemed a little fragile, but she'd probably know how to calm Bill down if he started banging on the door. Alene looked over at the door to make sure it was locked.

"We have the same father," Tinley said.

"Oh," said Alene, feeling as if she'd been given a piece of some unknown puzzle. Why hasn't anyone mentioned it before? I don't think Joan ever told any of us who Jack's father was."

"His name was Henry Willis and he was the chief executive officer at Hector-Schaf Electronics. Joan Stone was his secretary, and she had an affair with him that basically ruined my life."

Alene stopped to think, her knife paused in mid-air as she recalled meeting that guy with the big ears and hairy arms. She remembered giggling with Neal at the sight of the old guy flirting with his date. But hadn't Alene always been grossed out at people her parents' age acting that way? She remembered that Brianne had been incensed because the guy was married to someone else. "Oh my," said Alene, setting the knife on the counter and moving the cut-up jicama and carrots to a small tray. "Would you like something to drink, Tinley, like iced tea or something stronger?"

Tinley nodded and sat back down on the couch. "Do you have any scotch, please?" she said in a small voice. "Joan was a manipulative bitch who destroyed my father."

"Oh Tinley," said Alene, coming around the counter to the cabinet that held her liquors and wine rack. "I never liked her but I had no idea."

"She started the affair with my father when I was just a baby, and Jack was born two years after me." As Tinley rubbed her eyes, Alene noticed that her hands were shaky. "When my mother found out about it a couple years later, she fell into a tailspin."

Alene poured a small amount of scotch into a glass and placed it with the bottle on the coffee table in front of Tinley, quickly sweeping off the kids' things – a tape measure, Quinn's book, and that roll of paint colors she'd toss after having the girls' room painted.

"I'm so sorry, Tinley," said Alene. She returned to the kitchen and started cutting up red, yellow and orange peppers for the vegetable tray. "Did your mother come out of it all right?"

"No, she started drinking. When I was nine, my dad's company went bankrupt and we lost our house." Tinley downed her drink and poured herself more. "But she wasn't in her right mind. I came home from school one day and they were sitting in the car with the engine going, in the garage. They were both dead. She left a letter for me on the kitchen counter explaining everything. Can you imagine reading a letter like that from your mother?"

Alene was surprised that Tinley could tell such a story without a hint of emotion. She wiped her hands and approached Tinley with arms wide open, ready to give her a big hug. "Oh, my God, how awful," said Alene.

"Somehow neither one of them remembered that I needed parents," Tinley looked away at the wall and Alene felt like the hugging moment had passed.

"I had no idea you'd suffered so much. It's amazing that you pulled yourself out of such a difficult life," said Alene, back behind the kitchen counter. "How did you turn out to be so well-adjusted?"

"I'm not all that well-adjusted," said Tinley, rising from the couch and facing Alene, who saw that Tinley's face had turned red and she seemed to be shivering although the temperature was in the seventies. The corners of her mouth slanted down. "My father was a spineless idiot who couldn't see that Joan Stone and Patrick Dunn were destroying his business."

Alene took a sip of her tea and tried to soothe Tinley, who spoke over her in a jagged voice, "They created a dummy company." She spat out the words. "They siphoned millions of dollars out of my father's business." Her tone was angrier and louder, and her lip was curled up in disgust. "I got nothing when my parents died."

"You sound justifiably bitter," said Alene, looking at Tinley across the kitchen counter and thinking that she was starting to look a little creepy. Her usually pretty smile was distorted with anger and her face had turned blotchier as she spat out her story.

Tinley glanced briefly at Alene. "Bitter? What's the next thing after bitter? I got kicked out or ran away from three foster homes. I got framed and spent a year in jail, where at least I learned how to cut hair. I got married and my husband tried to mow me down. Then, about ten years ago I found out that Joan Stone was married to Gary Vanza."

"I remember their wedding," said Alene, trying to calm and distract Tinley. "Both Jack and Bill got drunk. Sandy, as you can imagine, just stood in the corner and rocked on his heels."

Tinley kept speaking as if Alene hadn't interrupted. "I was having a tough time after my divorce and started googling everything to do with Joan Stone. I went after Bill to get closer to Jack, you know, my half-brother. Then I saw how Bill pushed Jack around and treated him like a half-wit," said Tinley. "I actually hate Bill. I'm going to make sure he pays for everything he did."

Alene couldn't have agreed more. She said, "I hope so, Tinley. It's hard to imagine how he could have hurt so many people." Frank would be amazed when Alene told him how she'd learned the truth about who was responsible for the three attacks. Maybe Bill had also been the biker who'd knocked down Dennis Flynn. She'd ask Tinley later. Alene said, "Believe me, I understand how it feels to realize that you've been in a relationship with a completely repulsive human being who doesn't care about anyone else. Don't kick yourself, Tinley. We all make stupid mistakes. You can be sure that Bill Vanza will pay for his crimes. Tell me how I can help you? Do you want that detective's number?"

Tinley rose from the couch, picking up her purse and adjusting the cute little summer dress she was wearing. Alene thought she looked much better now that she wasn't bright red with her eyes popping out. What she'd gone through was just heartbreaking.

Alene added, "You can join my dad and me for dinner if you want, Sweetie. The fish tacos are almost ready. I'm cutting up strawberries for dessert. I only need to clear off the table and wake up my dad."

"Put down the knife, Alene," said Tinley, who suddenly looked very serious. "You're not getting it. Joan and Gary hid my money somewhere. It belongs to me." She reached into her purse and pulled out a pair of sharp-looking scissors, which she then unsheathed.

Alene shook the cobwebs from her head and brought her hand to her mouth. Had she just invited a murderer to dinner? She glanced at her father, who was still sleeping. Before Alene could respond to Tinley, her cell phone rang. It was probably Ruthie, who always called on Friday afternoons before the sun went down. Ruthie then turned off her phone for the next twenty-four hours, and Alene couldn't reach her between Friday and Saturday night, even if there was an emergency.

Tinley said, "Sit down, Alene, and don't even think about answering that call."

Of course, thought Alene, Tinley had worked at a salon, so she probably carried scissors with her all the time. She could have used them to stab Gary Vanza. That's why they couldn't find the murder weapon. But couldn't it still have been Bill who stabbed Gary? Could it really have been Tinley?

Alene asked, "What's going on?"

"I think you know what's going on, Alene. It's my money," said Tinley as the phone stopped ringing and then started up again. "You're going to help me find it or you'll pay the same price Gary paid."

"It's just Ruthie," Alene said as calmly as she could, her mind reeling. Would Tinley hurt her father? As she held up the phone to show Ruthie's picture, her eyes lit on the wheel of paint colors that she'd just set to the side of the counter. Sierra had been badgering Alene to paint her half of the bedroom a different color from Quinn's half.

"She'll just call back on the house phone," said Alene, still standing in the kitchen with the counter between her and Tinley, "and then on my dad's cell and again on my phone until I answer. Once when I didn't answer, she called Brianne, who rushed over to check on us." Alene was thinking fast. "I just need to tell Ruthie—what color paint I've decided on for the café's art wall." She held up the roll of colors she'd just set on the side of the counter. "Ruthie's been hounding me for days about it. Would that be all right?" She hoped the story sounded plausible.

Her cell stopped ringing and the house phone started. As Alene stepped cautiously into the living room, where the phone sat next to her father's chair, Tinley advanced with the scissors until they were just an arm's length from Alene's neck. "Be careful about what you say," Tinley warned with an impatient expression.

Alene wondered how her father could continue to sleep. She gingerly reached across the table and picked up the phone. "Hi, Ruthie? I've decided on 'Normandy', the grayish-blue color. Remember that one? Normandy." She shakily scrolled through the wheel of paint colors until she found it. She held it up for Tinley to see, hoping she didn't look as scared as she felt. "Have a good Sabbath, Ruthie. I love you." She gently placed the receiver back down and looked up at Tinley, who was still holding her scissors and sneering. Alene was glad she'd managed to say "I love you" to Ruthie.

"What do you want from me, Tinley?" asked Alene, her throat dry and constricted.

"You have no idea what Joan and Gary did to my family," said Tinley. "I want my money and you're going to find it for me. Now."

Ruthie had to have understood Alene's message. She couldn't have said Operation Overlord or D-day – that would have been too obvious; and Normandy really was a color. "You must have been really hurt, Tinley," she said, trying to sound sympathetic and buying time. "But why did you kill Gary? Joan was the one who stole all of that money."

"I would have killed her," said Tinley, "but that wasted drug whore showed up."

Alene had been so sure that Kacey was clean! Even though she was scared to death, she thought about the

240

apology she owed to Frank Shaw. She prayed that Ruthie would contact him immediately.

Tinley started pacing. "Some of the money was wired directly into their accounts," she said, "but Gary hid the cash Joan took from my father. He tried to fake me out. I jabbed him with the scissors so he would hurry, but he was a clumsy idiot."

"That means you didn't intend to kill him. If you turn yourself in, you'd be charged with manslaughter instead of murder." Alene was listening with one ear, hoping to hear the police at the door. "It's a shorter sentence. I'd help you, Tinley, but I don't know where Gary hid that money."

"Your father says you do," said Tinley.

What had Cal told her? How many minutes had passed since Ruthie's phone call? "What do you want me to do, Tinley? I have no idea where to start."

Tinley said, "I have the scissors, Alene. You better figure it out, and fast."

"You could be holding a bomb and I still wouldn't know where to look for hidden money," said Alene, eyeing the shelves Gary had built. "I can't even find the toys my son drops in the couch cushions."

She noticed that the shelves were the same design as Gary had used for Brianne's and also for the ones in the café that housed Dennis's gem collection. Gary had also designed and built the diagonal railings that held the freshly baked muffin trays on the wall behind the pastry counter. He'd also built shelves to hold the bottles of alcohol behind the bar at Tipped. Those weren't as thick as the others.

The shelves he'd built for her dad were thick and solid. They looked as if they could hold hundreds of pounds. The wood was at least three inches thicker than the bookshelves she'd put together in the girls' bedroom a few years before. Why had Gary used such thick pieces of wood? What if it was an illusion? Maybe he'd attached two quarter inch shelves on either side of the joist, leaving space in between? He could have glued or nailed a three-inch board all along the edge, then stained the whole thing so that it looked like a unified piece. Nobody could tell that there might be space between the two horizontal boards – space perhaps filled with rolls of cash.

"I'll need my screwdriver set," said Alene, "and a hammer." What if Gary had used a nailset to pound in nails, filled the holes with putty, and then dyed everything that dark brown? Cal had built shelves like that in her sister's room years before, and Alene had been his assistant. She remembered how they'd glued the front edge on and wondered if she could pry this one off, unless Gary had wanted access and had used screws instead.

Tinley pointed her scissors at Alene and said, "I'm not afraid to use these so don't try anything." Alene led her to the closet where she kept the household tools. Cal was still sleeping when they returned to the living room. Alene felt grateful that he wouldn't be traumatized by what was happening. She was also beyond grateful that the children were away.

Alene felt all along the edges of the shelves to figure out how Gary had connected the wood. She found screws every foot or so under the shelf, which meant that Gary had also twisted into the uncomfortable position she was in, bent over and looking up as he installed the shelves. Alene moved too quickly, causing her to bang her head against the wood. She had to rest for a moment.

"Don't stop," ordered Tinley with a new harshness in her voice.

Alene, held her head, hoping the dizziness would fade. She said, "I'm going as fast as I can, but Gary probably used a drill to install the screws, and I only have a little screwdriver." He must have known that there was a faster way to get the money to Tinley and he had deliberately chosen to buy time with the screwdriver, but that had been a miscalculation on his part. What if Alene literally screwed up?

She found and removed five of the screws, but the shelf still held solid. Suddenly there was a loud rap on the door. Still holding her scissors menacingly, Tinley gave her a sign to be silent. A moment later the doorbell rang, and whoever stood there pounded again. Alene heard Frank's voice calling out, "Answer the door, Alene."

Tinley ordered Alene not to move and they both looked at the door, when suddenly without warning, Alene's father rose from his chair behind where Tinley was standing and pointing her scissors at Alene. He managed to lift his walker and he smashed it onto Tinley, who fell off balance and inadvertently stabbed herself in the hand. At the same time, the door was opened with a key (Alene wondered how Frank had gotten one at such short notice) and he and his partner charged in, their guns pointed at Tinley. Two other officers followed the detectives into the apartment and stood with their guns drawn as well.

The scissors had slid under the couch and Tinley lay on the floor in front of Cal, clutching her hand and groaning. Cal lowered himself back into his chair with a self-satisfied smile. "That'll teach you to underestimate an old guy with a walker," he said to Tinley, who glared back at him. "And you can forget about having any of Alene's fish tacos."

Alene sank to the couch and burst into tears. "Thank you," she said, thinking that she really had to remind the children to always carry scissors facing downward.

"As I told this young lady one before, 'It's not the size of the dog in the fight, it's the size of the fight in the dog'," said Cal, leaning back into his chair and looking proud of himself. "Right, Frank?"

Frank's partner cuffed Tinley, who was in too much pain to resist, and one of the officers gave her paper towels for her hand and then read her Miranda Rights. Alene would have liked to have said something snappy but couldn't come up with anything worthwhile. Tinley was in pain, but her expression was still defiant. Alene would have also liked to jump up and smack her, but Frank was standing there.

As Tinley was marched out of the apartment, Cal got in one last comment. "Confucius said that to know what is right and not do it is the worst cowardice. You should be ashamed of yourself, young lady." Then, completely worn out, he closed his eyes.

Chapter 18

Alene was so relieved and in need of a release that she burst out laughing. "Exactly what I was thinking, Dad. I couldn't have said it better myself."

"Your friend Ruthie," said Frank, his hand resting gently on Alene's arm, "called to tell me your message. She made sure I knew what she meant about the paint."

Alene said, "That's my Ruthie."

"Is there really a color called Normandy?" Frank asked, raising an eyebrow. He'd stayed in the apartment with them.

"Show him, Alene," said Cal, slowly rising to his feet and righting his walker. "You're in luck, sir, because Alene just made her delicious fish tacos and there's plenty to go around."

Alene leaned back into the couch and covered her face so Frank wouldn't see how blotchy she got when she cried.

She stayed up past midnight watching the dismantling of her bookshelves. They counted and bagged the bricks of money, wrapped in plastic and carted them away. Finally, she tossed in her bed until a small pill eased her way into sleep. She woke early Saturday morning feeling a little drugged but didn't want to drag someone else out of bed to open the café.

She left a note for Blanca in case Cal was achy after his heroics, walked briskly to the café in the brightening early morning light, and was already unlocking the kitchen door as Jocelyn bicycled up the alley. Once everyone had arrived, Alene briefly updated her employees about what had happened. There were questions, sighs of relief, and much texting to absent staff members and other friends or family. After the morning rush quieted down, Alene sent Olly to deliver baskets of baked goods to Joan, who in addition to the concussion, had suffered several broken bones from her fall, and to Edith, who was still recuperating from being clobbered on the head. Alene included a note to each of them in which she conveyed her regret for the pain they'd undergone and relief that the bizarre terror was over. She would have liked to text Kacey but knew that cell phones weren't allowed on the drug rehab floor of the hospital. At least they knew that Kacey was getting clean. Maybe Frank would be willing to convey a message.

After all the baking was underway and the next day's doughs had been started, Alene immersed herself in experimenting with variations on the vegetable dips she'd begun creating and selling. The afternoon flew by, and then it was time to close up and get her children from Mitzi's building in the Gold Coast neighborhood. She wanted to tell them about what had happened, but Noah and Quinn chattered about their day from the moment they got in the car until Alene interrupted to tell them that she'd decided to stop by the Rosins' before heading home. "Maybe we'll even stay through dinner," she told the kids. "We'll see."

Alene knew that Ruthie and Benjie and their children were nearly always at home on Saturday afternoons. After

Tinley had been carted away, Alene had gone into her bedroom and left a message telling Ruthie what had happened and thanking her for being the best friend anyone could ever hope for. Alene parked near the Rosins' house and turned to remind her children of the rules.

"No television or computer, because today is their day of rest," she told them. "Don't make them feel bad by asking to do anything they're not allowed to do. Understand?" Alene looked first at Quinn and Noah removing their seatbelts in the back seat before focusing on Sierra sitting next to her in front. "They can't use pens or markers either, and for sure no phones."

"So, what the heck do they do all day?" With a big melodramatic sigh, Sierra unlocked her seatbelt. "Anyway, I'm like the last one in my grade who doesn't even have a cellphone." Alene knew that was not at all true.

"They probably read. They play games, they have people over or go to friends' houses for lunch, and they take naps. It sounds wonderful to me," said Alene. "Even if the kids aren't home right now, they're probably playing on the block, so it shouldn't be hard to find them."

"I suppose you think I'm going to run down the street calling out for Shaily until I find her?" Sierra asked with a toss of her hair.

"I'll help you, honey," said Alene.

Noah asked, "If Avi isn't home, can I ask Benjie to help me find him?"

"Sure, you can. And you too, Quinnie," said Alene. "He'll help both of you."

Ruthie and Benjie both grabbed Alene and hugged her the moment they opened the door. "I am so relieved...so grateful you survived, Six," said Ruthie, tears in her eyes. "Benjie cannot believe you managed to say the word 'Normandy' with a knife at your throat." Ruthie wiped her eyes. "These are tears of happiness that you and your dad are okay," she said, hugging Alene again and led everyone into the kitchen.

Alene still hadn't told the children what had happened. "What's Normandy?" Quinn asked with wide eyes. "Who held a knife at your throat, Mom?"

"Duh, a bad guy," said Noah. "How'd you stop him, Mom?"

Sierra asked, "Was it the person who killed Gary?"

"You didn't tell us bad guys killed Gary." Noah furrowed his brow.

"Grandpa told me he was murdered," said Sierra, beaming because she'd kept the secret from her younger siblings.

Alene would really have to talk to Cal again about what not to tell the children. "Grandpa was actually a hero. He lifted his walker and brought it down on the bad person's arm which distracted her so that she dropped her weapon." Alene reenacted Cal's heroic effort. "Then Ruthie called the police, and they came and arrested her. She's going to jail, and everything can go back to normal."

"Thank God," said Benjie. "If you hadn't called us back after Frank got there, Ruthie would have cancelled dinner and we'd have walked all the way over to find out if you were okay." All three adults shuddered at the enormity of what might have happened to Alene and her father.

"Did everything happen in our living room?" Sierra asked, sounding momentarily like a child bubbling with curiosity.

"Were there guns?" asked Noah.

Quinn was bouncing with excitement. "What happened after Grandpa hit the bad guy with his walker? How did that distract her? How did they arrest her? How can a bad 'guy' be a *her*?"

"Who got arrested?" Noah asked. "Did they use cufflinks?"

"You mean handcuffs, stupid." Sierra noted with authority. "I can't wait to tell everyone at camp tomorrow."

"Me too," said Noah. "I'll be the only one in my group whose mom got attacked."

Quinn pulled on her shirt, "Who was it, Mom? Did grandpa kill the bad person with his walker?"

"Whoa," said Alene, "nobody got killed and we're all fine."

"But who got arrested?" Noah asked again.

Alene had rehearsed how she was going to tell them. "It was Tinley Rico, you know, Bill's girlfriend. We all thought she was a nice girl, but it turned out she never learned that money is something you earn for yourself and not something you expect someone to give you."

"It couldn't have been Tinley," said Sierra. "She seemed so normal."

"Tinley turned out to be a very unhappy young woman," said Alene. "Maybe something didn't work right in her brain, but she hurt a lot of people, and that's not right."

"I liked her," said Quinn, in a small voice. "Her hair was always so pretty."

Sierra glanced briefly at Alene before giving her sister a weary look. "Guess you're just not a good judge of character." "You liked her too, right?" Quinn asked, looking troubled. "Lots of people liked Tinley, right, Mom? I am too a good judge of character."

"Never mind, Quinnie," said Alene, looking at her elder daughter sternly. "Listen guys, Grandpa is a hero for hitting Tinley with his walker, but Ruthie's a hero for remembering our secret code. She knew what I meant and immediately called the police." Alene pivoted to Ruthie, saying, "I'm sorry we're interrupting your Sabbath, but I wanted to see you as soon as possible. You saved our lives."

Ruthie had led them back to the front porch with a platter of cookies and brownies. Now that their insistent questions had been answered, the kids hovered above the platter choosing what to take. Benjie held out a hand to Noah and they went in search of Avi Rosin with Sierra following behind to look for Shaily. Quinn set her lemonade down and ran to join Ruthie's middle daughter, Eden, and her friends playing in the backyard. Ruthie and Alene sat on the porch swing with their lemonades. "How are you feeling?" Ruthie asked Alene.

"Like I've survived a tornado," said Alene. "After they took Tinley away, my dad invited Frank to stay for dinner."

Ruthie raised one eyebrow and asked, "Did he stay as a sort of cop-wanting-to-interview-you- more-but-you-offered-food-so-he-took-it? Or did he stay because he has a little crush on you and wanted to get to know you better now that he might not have a reason to pop into the café all the time?"

Alene stopped swinging on the bench. "Hmm, I'm not completely sure, but when they were cuffing Tinley, I started shaking. It was sort of like the feeling you get when a bus speeds past just as you've stepped back onto the curb. He put his hand on my arm and I felt like he'd sort of rescued me."

"That's not always healthy, Alene," said Ruthie. "You don't want to be in a relationship just because he rescued you. On the other hand, your crush could have started when you gripped his hand for ten hours of labor, eight years ago."

Just then Quinn came running through the house towards the front porch, closely followed by Ruthie's ten-year-old daughter. "Mom," said Quinn, "Eden and I want to know what code you and Ruthie used so we can have a secret code too."

Alene looked at their angelic little faces and hoped they'd never be in the kind of danger she'd just escaped. She took a deep breath and said, "Well, first of all, be born on the anniversary of a major nuclear explosion."

"Although hopefully there won't be any more of those," said Ruthie.

"Then, when you get to college, make sure to get a really wonderful roommate."

Ruthie smiled, "Take some classes together."

"Memorize the battles of whatever war you're learning about," said Alene.

"And learn all the names of those battles, especially those that lead to the liberation of Western Europe from Nazi control," added Ruthie.

Quinn and Eden looked at each other, neither understanding where the conversation had veered. "But what was the code word that meant Ruthie had to call the police?" Quinn asked.

Alene shuffled in her seat. "Remember that roll of paint colors that I kept asking you to put away?"

Quinn nodded, "I thought I did put it away."

"You also helped save my life, Sweetie."

"Way to go, Quinnie," said Eden, hugging her with both arms.

Alene continued, "I was looking through the paint colors and I happened to see one named Normandy." Alene said, stroking Quinn's soft light-brown braids. "That was the name of the beach our troops landed on, during the Second World War. You can make up your own code if you want. Maybe choose a word to mean 'danger.' It has to be something you wouldn't normally say, so you can't choose a word like donut, right? Maybe you can look through the paint colors and figure out meanings for the different colors."

Satisfied and excited about their new project, the two girls started yelling words to each other as they flew down the stairs into the back yard. "Zucchini," Quinn called out. "No," said Eden. "Your mom makes stuff with zucchini all the time."

Ruthie and Alene poured themselves glasses of iced tea and walked out to the front porch to sit on the swinging bench together. Benjie returned and announced that Avi's friends had been delighted to have a fourth player for their game of tag. He joined them on the porch, squishing in next to Ruthie. He was a bit winded from rushing back to the house after dropping off Noah. The three adults sat quietly for a few moments breathing in the sticky, sweet July air. "I have one more question," Ruthie asked.

"What's that?" asked Alene.

"Was there a hidden treasure?"

Alene smiled. "Although he turned out to be a complicated, flawed human being, Gary was an excellent carpenter. Those four-inch shelves were actually two thinner pieces of wood with space in between."

"Unbelievable." Ruthie shook her head.

"The cops dismantled the shelves in my apartment last night and every shelf was packed with cash. Frank said they're getting a court order to sift through the Vanzas' apartment and then the café. I told him they were welcome to come in to Whipped and Sipped anytime but Frank said they had to follow protocol." Alene paused to take a sip of her drink. "They're also looking for safety deposit boxes and other bank accounts. Frank told me that if they found evidence of money wired to accounts in other states or countries, they'd have to bring in the FBI or the CIA."

"FBI and CIA are code words for 'I want to spend more time with you'," said Benjie.

Alene shrugged with a little smile on her face. Ruthie flicked Benjie with the back of her hand and asked Alene, "Did they make a mess taking apart all those bookshelves in your living room?"

"Yeah, but they said they'll send workers to fix everything this week."

"Will they repaint the walls?" said Ruthie.

Benjie smiled, "I can suggest the perfect color."

Ruthie elbowed him. Benjie mimed a microphone. "Thanks, ladies and gentlemen, I'm here all week."

Recipes used in this story

Chapter 1

Recipe #1: Vegan Sweet Potato or Pumpkin Muffins

1 cup unsweetened almond or coconut milk
1/3 cup EVOO, canola or coconut oil
15oz of cooked, mashed sweet potato or one 15oz canned pumpkin
1 cup packed dark brown sugar
1 TBSP apple cider vinegar
2 cups all-purpose flour (or 1 ½ cups all-purpose and ½ cup whole
    wheat flour)
½ tsp salt
2 tsp pumpkin pie spice
1 tsp cinnamon
2 tsp baking soda

Combine first 5 ingredients in blender or processor – pulse until blended. Sift last 5 ingredients into the blender and pulse 3-4 times only until blended. Pour into greased cupcake liners or greased muffin tin (about half full). Bake about 20 minutes at 350 degrees (convention oven) until golden brown. Serve with maple syrup, berries, whipped coconut milk, or jam

Chapter 2

Recipe #2 Oven-Baked Sweet Potato-Black Bean Empanadas (makes 20+)

2 cups all-purpose flour (still being tested)
1 tsp baking soda
1 ½ tsp kosher salt
1/2 cup olive oil
1 tablespoon cider vinegar

1/2 cup ice cold water
1 cooked medium sweet potato
1 cup rinsed and drained black beans
Liquid from the can of black beans
1 red pepper (or poblano if you want heat) roast, remove seeds and
  membrane, chop
1 teaspoon cumin seeds (toss in heated pan until fragrant, or use
  powdered cumin)
1/3 cup chopped scallions
2 or more tablespoons chopped cilantro (use parsley if someone
  hates cilantro)
½ to 1 teaspoon chili powder (depending on how much heat you
  want)
1/2 teaspoon salt

Gently mix first flour, baking soda and salt with oil until
combined. Stir together egg, vinegar and water, then combine and
use hands to form a ball. Wrap in plastic and let it rest about an
hour in the fridge. Meanwhile, mash the sweet potato with the rest
of the ingredients. Divide and shape the dough into 10 equal balls.
Roll each ball of dough into about a 5" circle on a lightly floured
surface. Spoon about 3 tablespoons of sweet potato mixture onto
each circle. Moisten edges with water and fold dough over filling.
Seal edges with a fork. Place empanadas on a large greased baking
sheet (or parchment paper/silicone) Cut diagonal slits across each
empanada. Bake at 400° 15 minutes until golden. Great for
appetizers. (Or, serve 2-3 per adult with salad, guacamole and
salsa for dinner)

Chapter 3
Recipe #3 Gluten-free peanut or almond-butter Chocolate Chip Cookies

1 cup smooth or chunky peanut or almond butter
½ to 1 cup packed dark brown sugar (optional, really)
1 egg (or flax egg, or whip up half a can the liquid from a can of
  garbanzo beans and fold it in)
1/2 tsp vanilla

1/2 tsp baking soda
1/4 tsp salt
1/2 package semisweet vegan chocolate chips

Line two baking pans lined with silicone baking mats or parchment paper. Preheat oven to 350 degrees. Stir first five ingredients together with a spoon until smooth, then stir in chocolate chips. Drop unformed globs of it about 2 inches apart on the baking sheets. Bake about 12 minutes until they are slightly browned and puffy. Cool on pan and then transfer to a rack. They store well. Delicious cold from the fridge.

Recipe # 4 Easy Homemade Tomato Sauce w/ vegetables

1 onion (cut in pieces)
3 cloves garlic (cut in pieces)
2 TBSP olive oil
1 can tomato paste (or tomato sauce if that's what you have, but it makes a thinner sauce)
1 zucchini (peel skin for brighter red color and cut in pieces)
1 handful parsley (you can always add more)
1 tsp oregano
1 tsp basil (of course a handful of fresh basil will make it even better, but who always has it on hand?)
1 tsp thyme
1 tsp salt
½ tsp pepper
1 TBSP cider vinegar (to add at the end)

Sauté onion and garlic until soft for about 5-10 minutes (microwave them if you're rushed but this is best). Place everything in a blender or processor with a cup of water (add more as needed). Blend until smooth. Transfer to a pot and simmer 10-15 minutes until flavors blend or let it sit and then zap it in the microwave. Add cider vinegar to brighten the color and taste. Pour over pasta, roasted spaghetti squash, or use as pizza sauce. It'll last at least a week.

Chapter 4

Recipe #5 Creamy citrus-cannellini dip

1 can white beans (rinsed and drained)
1 cup of chopped fresh parsley including stems
Juice and pulp of ½ a lemon or a small peeled orange/tangerine
(about ½ cup)
1 tsp cider vinegar
¼ cup olive oil (any kind, but I use EVOO)
½ tsp kosher or sea salt
1 or 2 tsp sage (start with 1 and add according to your taste)
1 tsp dried mint

Mix in blender or processor until smooth. Season to taste, add more juice and sage if necessary. If you want to turn this into a soup, add 1-2 cups of water.

Recipe #6 Kale and Parsley Dip

4 cups of loosely chopped kale (or about half a package of any dark
greens like arugula)
About 1 cup fresh loosely chopped parsley
1 whole small-medium peeled orange or tangerine
1 tsp apple cider vinegar
¼ cup olive oil (EVOO is best)
½ tsp kosher or sea salt
¼ tsp pepper
¼ cup golden raisins (or any honey or agave)

Mix in blender or processor until smooth. (might need to be sweeter or saltier depending on your taste). Serve with vegetables/pita/chips or over chicken/fish/meat/rice/pasta etc.

Recipe #7 Roasted Red Pepper Mushroom Dip

2 large red peppers, cut up and broiled about 10 -15 minutes until
   starting to blacken
1 cup chopped up mushrooms
Juice of ½ small lemon or a small whole peeled orange or
   tangerine
Handful of cut up fresh parsley
1 tsp apple cider vinegar
¼ cup olive oil (EVOO is best)
½ tsp kosher or sea salt
½ tsp pepper

Mix in blender or processor until smooth. (Season to taste – might
need more salt)

Recipe #8 Alene's White Gazpacho

3 cloves garlic
1 sweet onion (small to medium)
1 peeled cucumber (medium to large)
1 peeled zucchini (small to medium)
White part of a fennel bulb (optional, adds licorice taste)
1 cup green grapes and/or 1 small peeled, seeded apple
½ tsp lemon zest
¼ to ½ cup skinless almonds
1 slice of bread (optional but it adds gravitas)
2 or 3 stalks celery (less if you are not celery lovers – blend in or
   use a stalk to stir)
2 cups water, unsweetened almond milk or coconut water
1 tsp salt
½ tsp white pepper
1 tsp cider vinegar

Sauté garlic and onion. Add to blender with other ingredients and
zap until smooth. Season to taste. Pour into a glass or a bowl and
serve. Makes about 4 large, 6 small servings

Chapter 5

Recipe #9 Lemon-Leek Chicken

About a pound of skinless, boneless chicken breasts or thighs
2 leeks (cut in about 1/2/ inch pieces)
2 TBSP olive oil
4 cups low-sodium vegetable or chicken broth (box or homemade)
1 cup rice, faro, or orzo
½ tsp dried dill
½ cup fresh parsley
½ tsp lemon zest
Juice of ¼ lemon (or more to taste)
1 tsp apple cider vinegar
½ cup fresh chopped dill
½ tsp kosher or sea salt
½ tsp pepper

Sauté leek in olive oil (I use EVOO but any will work). Pour in stock/broth. Add chicken and simmer about 15 minutes. Remove chicken and let cool. Add ingredients through lemon zest to pot, including whatever grain you choose. Simmer covered until grain is cooked, about 15 minutes. Continue simmering 5-10 minutes if you want a thicker (less soup-like) sauce. Return chicken to pot, squeeze in lemon juice and season w/salt and pepper. Serve in soup bowls with a generous amount of chopped dill over each serving

Chapter 6

Recipe #10 Spiced Nuts

1/2 tsp kosher salt
1/2 tsp ground coriander (or cumin)
1/2 tsp paprika or chili powder (or both if you like spice)

½ tsp allspice
1/2 tsp. garlic powder
1/4 tsp. ground cinnamon
1 TBSP olive oil (I use EVOO)
2 cups raw almonds, cashews, pecans and/or walnuts

Preheat oven 325 degrees and line or grease a baking pan. In a big bowl, stir spices together then mix with the oil. Stir in the nuts until evenly coated. Spread onto pan Bake 5 minutes. Stir. Bake another 2-3 minutes. Remove from oven and stir again. Cool at least an hour. Store in airtight container. Lasts longer if you keep in fridge but they'll get scarfed up quickly. Alene's father and kids eat them while they're cooling

Chapter 7

Recipe #11 Fudgy gluten-free Blackies

1 can chickpeas, rinsed and drained into a separate bowl
Drained liquid from the can (about ¾ cup)
1/4 cup unsweetened cocoa powder
1/3 cup olive oil (EVOO is best)
1 cup packed dark brown sugar
1/2 teaspoon cinnamon
2 teaspoons pure vanilla extract
1/4 teaspoon salt
1 teaspoon baking soda
1 teaspoon instant decaf or coffee crystals
1 1/4 cups chocolate chips

Blend: beans, cocoa powder, brown sugar, olive oil. Add in cinnamon, vanilla, salt, baking powder, instant decaf. Mix the liquid from beans until frothy and peaks form (up to 15 minutes). Fold it into mixture from blender, or add to blender and pulse just a few times until blended. Fold in chocolate chips. Smooth onto 9x13 (covered with parchment and greased). Bake at 350 for about 25 minutes until toothpick comes out clean. Cool, cut into sections

Chapter 8

Recipe #12 Vegan Chocolate Apple Cake

2 large cut-up Granny Smith apples (no seeds)
½ cup water
½ cup olive or canola oil
1 TBSP apple cider vinegar
1 cup packed brown sugar (or 1 cup honey)
1 tsp pure vanilla extract
3 cups all-purpose flour
½ cup unsweetened cocoa powder
2 TBSP instant decaf or coffee crystals
2 tsp baking soda
1/2 tsp salt
2 tsp ground cinnamon
1 cup semi-sweet, vegan chocolate chips

Heat oven to 400 degrees. Blend apples with water, oil, vinegar and brown sugar until texture is like applesauce. Scrape down, add vanilla and pulse once or twice. Add dry ingredients and pulse just until blended – scrape sides with a spatula. Gently stir in chocolate chips. Pour into one 9x13 or two 9" greased and sugared round pans (or use parchment paper). Bake 10 minutes at 400, then reduce temp to 350. Bake additional 30 until a toothpick comes out clean. Serve as is (or frost with #13)

Recipe #13 Chocolate Sauce (or Frosting) with fruit

½ cup cocoa powder
1 seedless sweet apple, pear, or peeled orange
Handful of cashews (optional – but they'll make it thicken into
    fudge)
¼ cup brown sugar (or ¼ cup raisins or ¼ cup liquor like Triple
    Sec or Sabra)

½ cup water
1 tsp apple cider vinegar
2 tsp pure vanilla extract
1 tsp chocolate extract (optional)
1 TBSP instant decaf or coffee crystals
½ tsp ground cinnamon
Pinch salt

Blend in processor until completely smooth (sweeten to taste)

Chapter 9

Recipe #14 Dijon Pistachio Baked Fish

2 or 3 large salmon/steelhead fillets (like what they sell at Costco)
2 TBSP horseradish
2 TBSP Dijon mustard
2 TBSP capers
1 TBSP chopped pistachio nuts
1 TBSP apple cider vinegar
1 TBSP any brown sugar or honey (optional)
1 TBSP olive oil (I use EVOO)
1 TBSP chopped parsley (dried or fresh)
1 TBSP chopped dill (dried or fresh)

Place fish on a foil lined tray, preheat oven to 350 degrees. Use a big spoon or fork to mix all ingredients together. Spread mixture evenly over the fillets. Bake about 20 minutes uncovered. Serve with rice or salad for a main course or plate smaller portions onto romaine or red leaf lettuce as a first course

Chapter 10

Recipe #15 Vegetarian Eggplant Parmesan with Home-made sauce

1 large eggplant with skin, cut into ¼ inch slices
2 TBSP EVOO
1 onion, chopped
3 or 4 cloves garlic, minced
1 zucchini, chopped
1 carrot, chopped
Bunch of fresh basil, chopped (or 2 TBSP dried)
¼ cup fresh parsley + ¼ cup for sprinkling on top
1 28 oz can diced or chopped tomatoes
2 tsp oregano
1 plus ½ tsp salt
½ plus ½ tsp pepper
1 tsp apple cider vinegar
16 oz. container of part-skim ricotta cheese (or cottage cheese)
1 egg
Spinach (either 2 cups fresh, chopped, or 10 oz frozen/drained)
8 oz grated pizza cheese (or combine 2 other grated hard cheeses)

Sprinkle ½ tsp salt and ½ tsp pepper over eggplant slices, let rest 10 minutes. Bake on a greased lasagna pan or 9 x 13 inch pan for about 30 minutes at 375, cool. While eggplant is in the oven, sauté onions, garlic, zucchini, and carrots until soft. Stir in the tomatoes and herbs. Simmer until ready to combine everything. Add vinegar. Mix spinach with ricotta/cottage, ½ tsp salt, ½ tsp pepper, egg. Pour about 1 cup of the tomato mixture on the bottom of lasagna pan (easier cleanup if you line pan with foil). Place one layer of eggplant slices on top of the sauce. Smooth half of the ricotta/spinach mixture over the eggplant layer. Sprinkle with first 4 ounces of grated cheese. Layer the rest of the eggplant and cover with half of the remaining sauce. Smooth second half of ricotta/spinach mixture on top. Pour the rest of the sauce over everything and sprinkle with the rest of the grated cheese. Cover and either freeze, refrigerate, or bake covered at 375 for 35 minutes. Remove foil for additional 10-15 minutes until golden and bubbly. It has a lot of ingredients, but this pan feeds a lot of people (about 8-10)

Recipe # 16 Carrot Top or Fennel Dip

Tops of one bunch of washed carrot greens OR a whole fennel bulb
    with greens - cut into large pieces
About 2 cups fresh parsley (or more – that's half the amount of
    what they sell at the grocery store)
1 small orange or about 1 TBSP fresh lemon juice
1 tsp apple cider vinegar
¼ cup EVOO
½ tsp kosher or sea salt
¼ tsp pepper
¼ cup golden raisins (or agave – just don't use dark raisins)

Mix in blender or processor until smooth. (Season to taste, sometimes needs either a little more agave or lemon).

Chapter 11

Recipe #17 Gluten-free Vegan Cookies

Drained liquid from one can of chick peas (aka garbanzo beans),
    chilled
1 cup packed brown sugar
2/3 cup olive or coconut oil
1 TBSP apple cider vinegar
2 tsp pure vanilla extract
2 cups all-purpose flour
1 tsp baking soda
1 tsp baking powder
1 tsp cinnamon
½ tsp salt
Variation 1: add ½ cup unsweetened cocoa powder and ½ cup
    semi-sweet chocolate chips

Variation 2: add 2 TBSP decaf or coffee crystals, ¼ cup hot water, and 1 TBSP molasses

Variation 3: add 1/2 cup coconut, 1/2 cup whole oats, ½ cup nut milk, ½ cup softened raisins

Use only one variation at a time!

In blender, mix sugar, oil, vinegar, vanilla and ingredients for variations 2, 3 or 4. In separate bowl mix flour, soda, powder, cinnamon, salt (plus ingredients for variation 1). In mix-master, whip chick pea liquid at least 12 minutes until soft peaks form. Slowly add the liquid ingredients, then the dry ingredients until just mixed. Drop overflowing teaspoon of batter onto greased parchment or silicon. Bake at 375 for 7-9 minutes until lightly browned and then cool before removing. Keeps well in a cookie tin or covered with foil.

Recipe #18 Healthy Fruit Crisp

4 -5 cups washed mixed berries, or berries with cut up apple/pear
½ tsp pure vanilla extract or ¼ cup liquor like Triple Sec
Juice of 1/2 lemon (if using apple) or 1 orange (optional)
1 TBSP agave, maple syrup or brown sugar
2 cups quick or old-fashioned oats
½ cup ground or slivered almonds (optional)
½ cup ground or shopped walnuts (optional)
¼ cup coconut, canola or mild olive oil
2 tsp pure vanilla extract
1 tsp cinnamon
1/3 cup agave, maple syrup, or brown sugar
2 Pinches of salt

Preheat oven to 350 degrees. Mix fruit with vanilla, 1 TBSP sweetener of choice, optional lemon/orange, first pinch of salt. Mound fruit into a sprayed pie or tart pan, place on foil or baking sheet in case of spills. Mix dry ingredients with oil and 1/3 cup sweetener of choice. Pat oat mixture to cover entire mound of fruit. (OPTION: spread 1/3 of the oat mixture on the bottom of the pan to form a crust, use remainder on top). Bake covered for first 45 minutes, then uncover and bake an additional 15 minutes until top is golden. Serves 8-10 or more. Great for breakfast with vanilla yogurt.

Recipe #19 Chocolate-Bear Cake with frosting

2 cups all-purpose flour
1 cup packed light brown sugar
¼ cup sugar
½ cup unsweetened cocoa powder
2 tsp instant decaf or coffee crystals
2 tsp baking soda
¼ tsp salt
¼ cup extra virgin olive oil
1 tsp pure vanilla extract
1 cup coffee/mocha stout (room temp) or any dark beer

Frosting:
¼ cup brown sugar
¼ cup cashews
1 TBSP apple cider vinegar
¼ cup unsweetened almond or coconut milk

Preheat oven to 350. Grease and sugar an 8" springform. Combine dry ingredients in food processor. Add wet ingredients except beer, pulse a few times. Add beer and mix enough to blend well. Pour batter into greased and sugared prepared pan. Bake 50-55 minutes until cake springs under pressure. Cool before removing from springform pan. While cake is baking, blend the rest of the beer bottle and frosting ingredients. Put frosting in fridge to firm up while cake is baking – stir it a few times as it thickens. Spread frosting only after cake is completely cooled and frosting is firm.

Chapter 13

Recipe #20 Chocolate Cashew Pie

1 ripe banana or ½ cup pitted dates
1 cup unsalted cashews
½ cup cocoa powder
½ cup chocolate chips
¼ cup agave or maple syrup
Juice of one lemon
1/3 cup coconut or olive oil
1 tsp instant decaf or coffee crystals
1 tsp pure vanilla extract
1/8 tsp salt

Blend everything until smooth (in a high-tech blender or a food processor). Pour into greased pie pan. Freeze at least 4 hours, decorate with mint leaves or powdered sugar

Chapter 14

Recipe #21 Overnight Oatmeal

Each serving goes in a separate jar (with lid)
½ cup rolled oats
1 cup unsweetened milk of some kind
1 TBSP mixed chia, hemp and flaxseed
1 TBSP shredded coconut
½ tsp pure vanilla extract
1 TBSP maple syrup, honey, brown sugar or agave
Handful of golden raisins, chopped almonds, cranberries, or berries (mixed)
One small grated apple or cut up banana is also yummy
Pinch of salt

Cover the jar tightly and shake to blend. Store in frig until morning. Some eat as is but Alene's kids like it heated up in the microwave.

Recipe #22 Butternut Squash Tuna a la King

2 TBSP olive oil
1 leek or small onion (any kind!), chopped fine
1 cup chopped mushrooms
1 cup mixed chopped carrots, celery, zucchini, red pepper (all or just a few)
1 cup butternut squash soup
1 tsp Tajin clasico seasoning
1 tsp basil (dry) or a handful of fresh, chopped
½ tsp granulated or powdered garlic
Salt and pepper to taste

In a sauce pan, sauté onion in olive oil until soft (about 10 minutes, stir often). Add mushrooms and mixed vegetables. Sauté another 10 or so minutes until soft. Gently stir in butternut squash soup. Stir in flaked tuna and herbs/spices. Take pot off the stove. Season to taste. Serve over toast or pasta (also good with a little cottage cheese or in a pita with melted cheese)

Chapter 15:

Recipe #23 Single Serve Egg-less Vegetable Omelets

1 cup chickpea flour
1 onion, chopped small
½ red pepper, chopped small
1 cup mushrooms, chopped small
1 medium tomato, chopped small
1 clove garlic, minced
½ tsp each: cumin, coriander, turmeric, salt, pepper

¼ tsp ginger or grated fresh ginger
1-1 ½ cups water

Stir all ingredients to together and add enough water to make it into a batter. Heat a non-stick pan and spray with olive oil. Ladle about ½ cup into the center of the pan and spread to about 4-5 inches. Cook about 3-5 minutes on each side until golden. Keep finished omelets warm and covered with foil until serving. Serve with a salad, salsa, chutney, or one of Alene's vegetable dips

Chapter 16

Recipe #24 Edamame-Avocado Dip

12 oz frozen bag raw edamame (Trader Joe has them)
1 avocado
½ cup lemon juice
About 2 tsp mixed herbs (basil, parsley, oregano - whatever you
    have)
½ tsp dry garlic or a fresh clove
½ tsp salt
½ tsp pepper

Cook edamame and garlic in the microwave about 1 -2 minutes, cool. Toss everything into food processor or professional blender. Taste for seasonings and add more salt, pepper or lemon as needed

Recipe #25 Tomato-Pesto Soup

About 4 - 5 large or 6 -8 medium tomatoes (quartered)
1 large yellow onion (quartered)
2 large carrots (cut into pieces)
3 cloves garlic
¼ cup olive oil

1 TBSP balsamic or apple cider vinegar
1 cup water or soup stock
generous handful of fresh basil – two handfuls if you love basil
generous handful of fresh parsley
handful of pine nuts for serving
salt and pepper to taste

Line a pan with foil and spray w/olive oil. Spread out tomatoes, onions, carrots, garlic. Roast in pre-heated 400-degree oven about 20-30 min until soft. Cool vegetables until touchable. Throw into processor with herbs, vinegar, liquid and seasoning. Pulse until smooth. Taste to correct seasoning. Serve dribbled with jarred pesto or extra olive oil (optional)*

*basil, pesto and garlic = pesto, so the flavors are already in the soup – dribbling is for presentation

Recipe #26 Zucchini Dip/Sauce

1 small or medium zucchini, cut into pieces w/skin
2 or 3 cloves garlic
Olive oil spray for the pan
Juice of ½ small lemon (about 2 TBSPs)
¼ cup water (if you want to use this as salad dressing, use EVOO instead)
1/3 cup golden raisins (you can use honey, agave, or brown sugar – don't use dark raisins)
2 TBSP tahini (or use 1 TBSP sesame seeds + ¼ cup water)
¼ tsp each: salt, pepper
½ tsp each: cumin, coriander, turmeric
1 tsp dried basil
1/2 oz (about a handful) of fresh mint

Saute zucchini and garlic in hot, sprayed pan until lightly browned (5-7 minutes). Add everything to blender and process until smooth. Season to taste (add more salt or if you like it sweeter, add a tspn of any honey or agave. Makes about 1 ½ cups (serve with fish, chicken, meat, vegetables...).

Chapter 17

Recipe #27 Orange Poppy Seed Muffins or Loaf

1 medium thin-skinned orange (cut into 8 sections, with peel but no seeds)
2 eggs
¾ cup extra-virgin olive oil or canola oil
1 cup sugar
2 cups all-purpose flour
2 tsp baking powder
½ tsp salt
1 TBSP poppy seeds

Glaze:
¼ cup orange juice
¼ cup lemon juice
¼ cup sugar

Put orange pieces and ½ cup sugar in processor and pulse until mixed. Whisk eggs and other ½ cup sugar, add to processor and blend until well-mixed, about a minute. Add in oil, flour, baking powder, salt and poppy seeds, pulse until combined. Spread into an oiled silicone loaf pan (spread with sugar) or lined with wax paper or use paper muffin cups. Bake at 350 for 50-60 minutes until toothpick comes out clean (40-50 for muffins). While baking: Simmer glaze ingredients for about 3 minutes in microwave or until thickened, then strain

For Cake: After removing from oven, use knife to separate sides of the pan. Poke holes over the top of the cake, then pour glaze over it and let it soak in until cake has cooled. Turn upside down onto serving plate and carefully remove pan.

For Muffins: out of the oven, just poke a few holes and put 1 TBSP of the glaze on each one. Serve plain or sprinkled with powdered sugar, or with chocolate sauce (in recipe #12)

Recipe #28 Vegetarian 'Huevos' Rancheros

15 oz. extra firm tofu
½ cup rice or nut milk
1 tsp apple cider vinegar
1 onion, chopped
1 clove garlic, minced
1 tsp basil
1 tsp turmeric
1 tsp smoked paprika
1 tsp salt
1 tsp pepper
8 corn tortillas
Olive oil
1 can black beans (frijoles)
1 avocado
¼ cup chopped cilantro or parsley
¼ cup any kind of salsa
Juice of about 1/2 lime
Salt to taste

Blend all huevos ingredients until smooth. Heat pan, spray w/oil, sauté onions and garlic until lightly browned, set aside in a bowl. Spray pan again and add mixture in 3 installments to same pan. Stir until it looks like scrambled eggs. Add to onions and garlic but wait until all scrambled before stirring gently. While cooking tofu mixture, combine avocado with lime juice, cilantro and salsa. Smash drained black beans in pan with salt and pepper, stir until warmed about 5 min. Toast tortillas in a 350 oven or broil for a few minutes on each side, until bubbled. On separate plates, place each crispy tortilla, top with smashed black beans, then the tofu/onions, then guacamole. Squeeze a little extra lime juice on top or serve with a fresh sliver of lime.

Recipe #29 Vegetarian stuffed burritos

6-8 wheat or whole grain tortillas
1 large onion, chopped
2 TBSP olive oil
½ tsp each ground cumin, chili powder, coriander, and salt
1 large red pepper, chopped, about a cup
1 cup corn kernels, fresh or thawed
1 carrot, grated
1 small chopped up zucchini (Optional – I forgot it once and the burritos were still good)
1 TBSP apple cider vinegar
1 15 oz. black beans, drained and smashed
1 15 oz. can chopped or stewed tomato or chop 2 large fresh tomatoes
1 medium jalapeno, seeded and minced (Optional, but some people love the extra kick)
1 cup grated jack or cheddar cheese
Season to taste before rolling the mixture into the tortillas
Sour cream, chopped cilantro, guacamole or sliced avocado for serving (optional)

Sauté onion in oiled pan, then add pepper, zucchini, carrot, and corn until they're all softened. Stir in spices, cider vinegar and tomatoes. Spread all tortillas with smashed black beans. Spread generous amount of veggie/tomatoes over beans on each tortilla. Add chopped jalapeno and cheese to some or all the burritos. Roll each burrito and wrap tightly in foil. Place into a baking dish/pan and warm at 200 until ready to serve. Serve with sour cream, cilantro, extra grated cheese, and salad for a full meal.

Recipe #30 Alene's Fish Taco Dinner

2 ripe avocados
Either 3 TBSP jarred red salsa OR make your own:
        2 TBSP chopped tomato
        1 tsp Tajain Clasico Seasoning
        1 TBSP chopped onion/scallion
2 lbs. of any white fish fillets (tilapia, cod, etc.) – serves 4 -6 as part of a meal
½ tsp each: onion powder, garlic powder, cumin, chili powder, paprika or smoked paprika
Juice of 1 lime
Olive oil spray
Eggplant, peppers, zucchini, onions, sweet potatoes (and other veggies on hand), sliced about ¼ thick
Chopped red cabbage, white cabbage, carrot, scallions or red onions, parsley or cilantro (any combination works, but try to use at least 3 different colors)
½ cup olive oil
¼ cup apple cider vinegar
TBSP agave or sugar (optional but yummy)
Salt and pepper to taste (start with 1/2 tsp each in salad and on fish)
Optional garnishes:
1 cup sour cream
½ cup chopped scallions
1 cup shredded yellow cheese

Easy guacamole: mash together Avocado + about half of the lime juice + 3 TBSP salsa. Spray a foil lined baking pan. Spray fish with olive oil. Make spice rub, salt and pepper to taste, rub over fish fillets, place on foil-lined baking pan, let rest for 20 minutes or so while you prepare the veggies and salad. Spray another foil lined baking pan, place vegetables. Sprinkle with salt and pepper. Bake in 400-degree oven until slightly browned, about 25-30 minutes. Wrap corn or wheat tortillas tightly in foil and leave in the oven until just before serving. In a separate bowl add chopped cabbages, carrot, and scallions, mix with olive oil, vinegar, juice of half lime, agave or sugar, salt and pepper (toss together and chill). Either bake the fish in the oven for 15 minutes, or pan sauté about 3-4 minutes each side. Serve veggies and fish tacos with salad and guacamole. Set out bowls of sour cream, scallions, shredded cheese for garnish

A Sneak Peek at *Smothered*

The next Whipped and Sipped Mystery

Alene Baron slammed a packet of frozen peaches, mangos and strawberries onto the counter. Jocelyn DeVale, standing next to Alene, snapped her hand away just in the nick of time. "Whoa, take it easy," said the barista.

"Just look out the front window," said Alene, as she unwrapped the frozen fruit and added it to the blender. All morning she'd been thinking about a cold, creamy smoothie and had forced herself to study her spreadsheets and finish the payroll before leaving her desk. After the smoothie, she'd be ready to do something about the disturbing owner of the vitamin and sports nutrition shop next door to her café.

The Whipped and Sipped Café was known for its excellent coffees, healthful, mostly vegan baked goods, and nutritious, meal-replacing smoothies. Alene had worked for months to perfect recipes that combined protein, vitamins and minerals, without sacrificing creamy, delicious flavor. Seven days a week they had customers lining up from seven in the morning (eight on weekends) until they closed at four in the afternoon. Even in winter, customers came in on their way to work to get coffee or even a smoothie.

Then six months before, Stanley Huff had opened Healthy Belle Vitamins and Supplements, which sold a host of medical-sounding, and in Alene's mind, possibly dangerous weight-reducing and body-building services. In addition to unending rows of vitamins, minerals, and weird products containing collagen made from animal parts but promising health benefits, the store sold cheaper, commercially made smoothies in plastic bottles. She'd just studied those spreadsheets – her smoothie sales were down.

And he was a dreadful neighbor. He let his employees put up sidewalk signs that crossed onto Alene's property and blocked part of her window. He let them toss bags of garbage into their shared alley instead of using the bins. He set up a speaker so that every time a customer opened the café door, Alene could hear the booming, repetitive music they played in the kind of gyms she hated, where everyone strutted around wearing spandex, showing off already picture-perfect bodies. Alene was so frustrated, her hand trembled as she scooped hemp, chia and flax seeds on top of the fruit.

Jocelyn, the barista, sighed and said, "Stanley was smoking a cigarette when I went to vape in the alley, and he pretended he didn't see me. I really hate him." She folded her arms and looked dejected.

Alene, thinking that Jocelyn hadn't endured enough to hate the guy, said, "I agree, but he's the kind of guy who deserves only scorn. Hate requires too much skin in the game." Stanley Huff, owner of the vitamin shop, looked like he had tried every single one of his own products, so that even though he was nearly sixty, he was still muscled and erect. Was it the connective tissues of animals that kept his teeth bleached and his hair thick and silvery, or did he just pay for those in a salon?

277

He wore expensive slacks and shirts, loafers without socks, and had probably been over-spraying Jovan Musk for Men since the previous century. He and his wife owned a condo in the same building where Alene and her children lived with her father. Alene suspected they kept a cat, despite the building's no-pet rule, because her two younger children, both allergic, would sneeze and rub their eyes whenever one of the Huffs got on the elevator.

Sylvie Huff was oversized in every way and wore her hair dyed the color of a tropical fruit. Why didn't Stanley add an occasional weight-reducing pill to her oatmeal? Alene hadn't seen much of Sylvie lately, but Stanley seemed to be always standing in the lobby of their building arguing loudly on his cell phone. He'd start opening packages on his way to the elevators, leaving a trail of trash for the building staff to pick up. And regardless of signs limiting the use of machines in the workout room, he'd stay on the good treadmill for an hour. Then he'd leave without wiping off his sweat.

"I'd be happy to push him into traffic," said Jocelyn, the barista, as she added a scoop of seeds and a handful of baby kale to the blender. In the six months since Jocelyn had worked at Whipped and Sipped, Alene had learned that she meant what she said. Before she'd transitioned, Jocelyn had worked on code for the US Navy. She'd dropped out of SEAL training when she broke an ankle, but that was after forty-eight straight hours of running with a sixty-pound backpack. Back in Chicago after a stint in Afghanistan, she'd moved in with her old high school pal, Olly Burns.

Olly had been at Whipped and Sipped for years and had helped Jocelyn get the job. He'd been Alene's first "chance employee." Alene had decided, when she bought the café, to hire people who didn't necessarily have all the earmarks of stellar employees. That meant inexperienced students, ex-offenders, and those like Olly, a skilled woodworker who'd never held onto a real job and made money fabricating wooden puzzles and toys to sell at street fairs. Three or four of his best pieces were on one of the shelves he'd helped build for Alene, and occasionally someone asked if they were for sale.

After Olly's first few months, she knew she'd made the right decision—he told her that he was happier with woodwork as a hobby and loved working in the cafe. She'd owned Whipped and Sipped for nearly eight years already and Olly functioned as sort of an assistant manager, but lately she'd been thinking she should make it official.

"Stanley's got it coming," Jocelyn added. "You have no idea how much he's got it coming."

With high cheekbones, a wide forehead, huge brown eyes and clear, unblemished skin, Jocelyn was a tall, beautiful woman who drew stares, even from other women. Alene wished her own ponytail was as lustrous and that she wasn't just another pale, lackluster late-thirty-something mother of three with bags under her eyes.

Jack Stone, another one of Alene's "chance" employees who'd lasted nearly six weeks, sauntered out of the kitchen holding a mop. He tossed back his long golden ponytail and said, "I've definitely had more experience than Jocelyn at pushing people into traffic." Jocelyn raised a highly plucked eyebrow.

"No, thanks, Jack," said Alene, thinking he was too well-known to the police to stray even a step off the straight and narrow. He was 34 and still lived with his mother, Joan Stone, who was still recovering for a terrible fall, across the hall from Alene. Their building was the kind of place where everyone knew everyone, and each resident had at least one neighbor with whom he or she wasn't speaking. Jack had begged Alene for the job, and although he'd been a drug-dealing bully who'd both scared and hassled her, Alene had hired him earlier that summer. She hadn't thought he'd last more than a week, but much to everyone's surprise, he'd been mostly on time, mostly civil, and mostly got along with her other employees.

"You don't even know who we're talking about, Jack," Alene added when the blender stopped. She really should visit his mother at the rehab facility where she'd lived ever since she got out of the hospital. She'd suffered broken bones and a brain injury after being pushed down a flight of stairs in their building.

"Again, you're underestimating me," said Jack. "I could hear you from the kitchen."

"I don't want trouble," said Alene, wondering if talk of pushing Stanley into traffic had offended any of her customers. The café was busy that morning. Alene waved to an attractive woman with long, wavy auburn hair and a gap between her two front teeth who came in promptly at ten every morning and sat at a table by the window sipping coffee and working on her computer. Alene didn't know her name, but she knew the woman's order and remembered that she worked on branding for a marketing company. "But Stanley Huff is insufferable."

Alene kept a mental record of every time Stanley hit on one of her young employees, offering a cigarette and casually brushing against them, or grabbing their hands and effusively complimenting their lovely hair or smooth skin. LaTonya James and Zuleyka Martinez had been amused, but he'd frightened Kacey Vanza, who worked the grill and assisted the pastry chef. The previous week, Kacey had gone into Stanley's store with her boyfriend, Kofi Lloyd, an artist who was seeking a day job. Kacey told Alene that while Kofi was talking to the manager in the office, Kacey had been nibbling on a spinach hand-pie from the café. Stanley sidled over and somehow backed her into a corner. She screamed, and Stanley sidled away as Kofi ran out to see what happened.

Kacey had been shaken. Both Kofi and Alene wanted to call the police, but Kacey didn't want to ruin Kofi's chance of being hired. Back in the café, Kofi had hugged her protectively, and said, "As if I'm gonna work for someone who'd do that?"

"I agree," said Alene. "Stanley assaulted you, Kacey."

"Agreed, said Jocelyn, who always managed to hear whatever was going on in the café. "Don't you ever let anyone get away with that."

Alene thought about calling Frank. She'd first met Officer Frank Shaw when he drove her to the hospital and helped her deliver her son. Neal, her soon-to-be ex-husband, hadn't managed to make it to the hospital in time. Over the years, she'd forgotten all about Frank, who worked homicide for the Chicago P.D., until earlier in the summer when he'd popped back into her life. He'd been stopping at the café nearly every day, often with his partner. Outside of the café, they'd met twice for drinks and they'd taken two long walks along the lake. His first kiss had made her weak in the knees, but was she more interested in him than he was in her? She hadn't felt her heart beat that fast in years, and sometimes kissed her own arm, imagining how it would feel when it was really Frank's mouth.

Kacey had brushed Alene off. "Nothing really happened," she'd said. "Kofi and the manager came out of their meeting and Mr. Huff switched gears like nothing happened. He started yelling at me for bringing food into his store."

"He has some nerve," said Alene. There was probably nothing resembling real food in his entire store.

Jocelyn said, "All women need to stand up against men like him."

"Kofi said he'd bash Stanley's head in if he ever tried to touch me again," said Kacey, absent-mindedly cleaning the espresso machine. "But you can't believe how many guys try stuff like that." As if Alene hadn't once been cute and young? She wished Kacey had let her tell Frank – he would have done something about it.

"Nobody likes that vitamin dude," said Jack, who was adjusting his ponytail after precariously leaning his mop against the wall. "Also, Alene, I'm begging you to change the soundtrack to something less menstrual."

"You know I love folk music, Jack," said Alene. "As do most of our customers, you know, the ones who love watching a clean-looking man holding a mop." Jack's mop fell to the ground as Alene handed a box of pastries to a tall, imposing woman wearing a long, flowery dress. The woman chuckled. Alene had demanded that Jack wear clean clothes, trim his beard and do something about his shaggy ponytail before starting work at the café. "You can switch it to the Leonard Cohen mix."

"Leonard Cohen," said Jack, picking up the fallen mop and blushing as the woman looked him up and down as if he were for sale. "I guess anything's better than this."

"Can we get back to the Stanley problem?" Alene asked. "It's just that he's a bully and I hate bullies." She wondered if Jack remembered bullying her younger sister when they were in middle school even before his mother married Alene's across-the-hall neighbor over twenty years ago. Did he understand that he'd been an abysmal neighbor all those years until his mother's accident? He'd somehow morphed into a nicer, non-frightening person since then, but who knew how long that would last?

"We're apparently still talking about that silver-fox jackass from next door," Jack said to Jocelyn, who'd come out of the kitchen with a fresh tray of carrot and zucchini muffins. "He lives in our building."

Jocelyn narrowed her eyes. "Oh, I definitely know who you're talking about. His wife, Sylvie, always orders the smothered tofu quiche and a muffin with a mocha latte."

Alene liked when her employees remembered the orders of regular customers, but Jocelyn then added under her breath, "She should probably skip the muffin and the latte."

Alene gave her a disapproving look and Jocelyn playfully slapped one of her hands with the other as if washing off the problem.

A woman wearing a low-cut dress, who often sat reading at the large table closest to the counter, held up a finger and announced in a booming voice that she wanted a tofu-broccoli quiche smothered in onions. "Please tell the chef that I like my onions extremely well done," she added. She was probably in her late forties and had long dyed-blond hair. She usually spent enough so that Alene felt uncomfortable saying anything, but it would have been nice if she sat at one of the smaller tables.

Alene gave a thumbs-up and gestured to Jack to convey the message about the onions to Kacey. "Stanley Huff is just an obnoxious bully," she said.

"I know all about him and I'm well aware of the man's failings," said Jocelyn with a disdainful look. "And we've all served his super-sized wife."

"Her name is Sylvie," said Alene, hoping none of the waiting customers had heard. Why, in describing people, did everyone go immediately to their weight? Alene aspired to be more like Ruthie, her pastry chef and best friend, who was never, ever judgmental. Oops, Alene needed Ruthie to submit her order for supplies. She'd meant to ask for it first thing that morning. If she was going to forget what she had to do every time Stanley irritated her, Alene wondered how long the café could last.

Now Stanley had sent an underling outside to set up the stupid sidewalk sign, and the guy was setting it up in a way that nearly blocked the café's door. Alene threw up her arms and was about to head outside, but Jocelyn rushed ahead to the sidewalk, picked up the sign, and tossed it into the street. She stood and slapped her hands against each other as if to say, "So much for that pesky problem." Then stepped back into the café, waving regally to all the customers as if in a beauty pageant. Café patrons often stared at Jocelyn, confused by the contrast between her massive height and a complex melding of feminine and masculine traits. In other words, after noticing her cleavage, they stared at her Adam's apple. She was saving up money for gender confirmation surgery, the first part of which was having that offensive body part removed.

Alene took a deep breath and righted the table Jocelyn had pushed over in her rush to the sidewalk. Gesturing to the customers that everything was fine, she still felt unsettled. Alene watched as Stanley Huff charged into the street to retrieve his sign. Before veering back into his store, he came so close to the café's window that Alene could see what looked like a black eye. "He probably deserved it," Alene muttered. "And he probably sells expired vitamins and finds loopholes to avoid taxes."

At that moment, Olly emerged from the kitchen carrying a tray of mushroom, onion, and jalapeno muffins. Passing Alene, he shook his orange curls and said, "As much as I might agree, you have no evidence that he actually sells expired vitamins, and unless you've suddenly transformed into a sophisticated hacker, ain't nothing you can do about it."

Alene lightly cuffed him on the arm and said, "You don't know anything about my hacking skills, Olly Burns."

"I'm quite sure you don't have any, my dear Alene," said Olly, giving her an air-kiss as he inserted the tray into one of the glass cases behind the counter.

"I can't change the music," Jack shouted, disturbing several customers, who looked up from their mugs, displeased at being interrupted yet again. "I can't stand this stuff, but the system is tied to your cellphone, Alene."

What was it with her employees these days? "It'd be good if you just asked quietly next time, okay, Jack?" said Alene, walking back to her office to change the music. Why did so many people lack common sense? Like Stanley Huff. Most of what they sold and promoted at Healthy Belle was probably nonsense – it was one thing to tell people that they'd feel better if they ate healthfully made desserts and smoothies, like those served at the café. At Whipped and Sipped, only fruit-and-root-derived powders and pure, legitimate vegan supplements were added to smoothies and baked goods. It was quite another thing to tell buyers that their illnesses would be cured, their skin would clear up overnight, and longer life would be guaranteed if only they bought such and such from who knows where. How could a place like that be successful? And she'd heard that Stanley already had an online business and was planning to open a chain of the shops so that gullible people everywhere could spend money on unproven and sometimes dangerous treatments.

Also, Stanley had had so much turnover that it was hard to keep up with his staff. She wasn't sure if the guy who'd just tried to set up the sidewalk sign was the same manager who'd interviewed Kacey's boyfriend. But this guy, with his turned-up nose and sandy hair had probably been the one who tossed the current garbage bags into the alley just outside the Whipped and Sipped Café kitchen door. Why couldn't they use the bins? They probably didn't even separate their garbage from their recycling.

Healthy Belle was definitely having an economic effect on Alene's bottom line. They sold sweetened fruit bars, gluten-free but chemical-laden packaged desserts, and bottled smoothies that all cost less than anything offered at Whipped and Sipped. Customers would come into the café, order a coffee, and sit at one of Alene's tables munching surreptitiously on something from a Healthy Belle bag. Didn't they notice the sign on the door clearly stating, 'NO OUTSIDE FOOD'? And Stanley had the nerve to yell at Kacey for bringing a hand-pie into his store.

Alene stood with her hand on the door leading into the kitchen. "Does anyone know the name of the new Healthy Belle manager?"

Jocelyn, who kept an eye on everything as though she were still in the navy said, "That's Myles. Myles Taylor."

"How do you know that, Jocelyn," asked Jack. "Did he ask you out already?"

Jocelyn shot him a withering look. "If I'm interested, I do the asking out, Jack." She turned to Alene and said, "Don't let it get to you. It is not worth getting worked up over Stanley Huff and his little followers."

"In my recollection, Jocelyn" said Olly, who'd known her since high school, "you used to beat the crap out of people who annoyed you."

Jocelyn opened and closed her mouth, looked down and said, "As you know, Olly, some battles are just not worth fighting." It was rare for Jocelyn to swallow a thought, but Alene didn't have time to ask because now there were several people waiting at the counter. First in line was Phyllie Evans, the daughter-in-law of Sylvie Huff, about whom they'd just been talking.

About the Author

G.P. Gottlieb holds undergraduate and graduate degrees in piano and voice. During her career as a cantor, a high school music teacher, and the administrator of the law center at DePaul University College of Law, she has also written stories, songs, and several unwieldy manuscripts. She is a graduate of the French Pastry School's Bread Boot Camp. Furthermore, she is the host of New Books in Literature, a podcast of the New Books Network and partner of LitHub. After recovering from breast cancer, she turned to writing in earnest, melding her two loves, nourishment for mind and body in recipe-laced murder mysteries.

"Reviews are really important for indie authors to get the word out about their books. If you enjoyed reading Battered: A Whipped and Sipped Mystery, would you please take a moment to add a brief review on Amazon, Barnes and Noble, or Goodreads? Also, please visit me on my website (gpgottlieb.com) for must-read mystery book reviews, more of my recipes-to-die-for, or to listen to some of my New Book Network podcast interviews. Thanks!" – G. P. Gottlieb

Other Exquisite Speculative Fiction from D. X. Varos, Ltd.

Immortal Betrayal
Immortal Duplicity
Immortal Revelation
Prophecy of the Awakening
Daniel A. Willis

The Inquisitor's Niece
Erika Rummel

The heiress of Egypt
Samuel Ebeid

We Have Met the Enemy
Where the Allegheny Meets the Monongahela
Felicia Watson

A Storm Before the War
Phillip O. Otts
(coming Sep. 2019)